Lily Alone

Jacqueline Wilson

Lily Alone

ILLUSTRATED BY NICK SHARRATT

DOUBLEDAY

LILY ALONE
A DOUBLEDAY BOOK
HARDBACK: 978 0 385 61864 9
TRADE PAPERBACK: 978 0 857 53050 9

Published in Great Britain by Doubleday,
an imprint of Random House Children's Books
A Random House Group company

This edition published 2011

3 5 7 9 10 8 6 4 2

Set in 13/17pt Century Schoolbook by
Falcon Oast Graphic Art Ltd.

RANDOM HOUSE CHILDREN'S BOOKS
61–63 Uxbridge Road, London W5 5SA

www.kidsatrandomhouse.co.uk
www.rbooks.co.uk

Addresses for companies within The Random House Group Limited
can be found at www.randomhouse.co.uk/offices.htm

THE RANDOM HOUSE GROUP Limited Reg. No. 954009

A CIP catalogue for this book is available from the British Library.

Printed and bound by
Clays Limited, Bungay, Suffolk

To Milan, Macey-Grace,
Tom, Scarlett and Isaac

It was my fault. We were all sitting squashed up on the sofa on Friday night watching *Coronation Street*, the second episode of the evening. Well, none of us were actually *watching*. Pixie was squatting on the arm of the sofa rubbing tomato sauce round her mouth, telling us over and over again that she was wearing lipstick like Mummy. My littlest sister, Pixie, could win the world record for repetition. She's three and talks all the time, though most of what she says is nonsense.

My other sister, Bliss, is six, but she hardly talks

1

at all. She was lying on her back on the sofa twiddling her long pale hair and snuffling into her old teddy. She had her favourite fairy-tale book tucked beside her. Her twin brother Baxter was driving a matchbox up and down her legs, pretending it was a car, making silly whining racing noises.

I was flipping through the pages of one of Mum's magazines, wondering what it would be like to be rich and famous and trying to choose which lady I wanted to be. It was hard taking them seriously because they all had bushy moustaches. Baxter had clearly been busy with his blue biro at some earlier stage.

Mum was the only one of us sitting up properly and watching the screen but I knew she wasn't following all the *Corrie* people. She didn't change position when the adverts came on. She just sat staring, her chin on her hand, her eyes big and blank.

'Mum?' I reached out and gave her a little poke. 'Mum, are you OK?'

'Yeah.'

'You don't look OK.'

'Oh, shut up, Lily,' Mum said wearily.

She was always acting tired now, since Paul died. She was too tired to get up in the mornings, too tired to go to bed at night. She was too tired to go to work and then when she lost her job in the canteen, she was too tired to get another one. She just stayed at home smoking and staring into space.

I made her go to the doctor because I was dead worried about her. He gave her tablets for depression. He said it was natural to grieve for a while when you'd lost your husband. I didn't get that. Mum didn't like Paul much when he was around. None of us liked him, not even Pixie, and he was her father. He'd either be yelling and slapping at us, even Mum, or he'd be zoned out on the sofa, looking stupid in his vest and pants and socks. We weren't allowed to sit on our own sofa when Paul was around. Mum muttered that he was a waste of space and a big mistake. She said she'd always had lousy taste when it came to men. That's what I couldn't understand. Whenever she didn't have a man she turned into Zombie Woman, acting like it was the end of the world.

I couldn't bear to see her like that, especially looking so ordinary in her old baggy T-shirt and trackie bottoms. Mum could look fantastic when she wanted, better than any of the ladies in the magazines. When she got all dressed up to go out she could make my heart stop she looked so gorgeous. So that's why I said it.

'Mum, why don't you go out?'

'What?'

'Go on, go down the Fox, see some of your old mates.'

The Fox and Hounds is the pub over the road from our estate. It's got a garden so in summertime the kids and I used to hang out there with Mum and Paul – and before that with Mikey, Baxter and Bliss's father. Mum says she used to take me there when it was just the two of us. She'd wheel me there in my buggy and I'd sit crunching crisps, happy as Larry. I was always an easy baby, Mum said. She didn't half get a shock when she fell for Baxter and Bliss. And Pixie's a nightmare, *she* won't sit in her buggy for two minutes at a time. She arches her back and screams when you try to get her in it.

'Don't be daft, Lily. I can't go down the Fox, not with you lot.'

'I'm not being daft. I meant to go on your own. The kids will be all right. I'll babysit.'

Mum looked at me, chewing one of her fingernails.

'Really?'

'Yeah, of course.'

Mum went on chewing, her hair in her eyes. I could tell she was considering. She'd left me in charge of the kids heaps of times, when she had to go to the post office or the newsagent or the off-licence (though it was *my* job to run down to the chippy).

'I shouldn't leave you lot on your own in the evening,' Mum said.

'You used to, when you first started going out with Paul,' I reminded her.

'Yeah, but I shouldn't have. And that was when you were all tucked up in bed and asleep.'

'I'll put the kids to bed. I do it half the time anyway.'

'I know. You're a good kid.' Mum reached out past Baxter and Bliss and stroked my cheek with her finger. 'I forget you *are* a little kid sometimes.'

'I'm not little! I'm eleven. And I'm old for my age.'

'Yeah, you act like a little old woman a lot of the time. I love you, Lily.'

'I love you too, Mum. Go on, go and get dressed up. I'll be *fine*.'

'Well, maybe just for one drink, to cheer myself up a bit?'

'Go *on* then.'

Mum smiled, looking just like Pixie when you buy her an ice cream, and rushed off to her bedroom. Pixie toddled after her. She loved watching when Mum dressed up.

'So Mum's going out then?' said Baxter, driving his 'car' across my face.

'Leave it out,' I say, swotting at him. 'And give me that matchbox – you know it's dangerous to play with matches.'

'I'm not playing with the matches. I'm playing with the *box*. So can we stay up, yeah? We'll watch a DVD, right?'

'Not a scary one,' said Bliss, hunching up into a little ball.

'*Not* a scary one,' I promised, though that was going to be a challenge. Bliss can't even watch *Up* without shaking. I think it's the dogs. Her dad Mikey had an Alsatian, Rex. It wasn't a truly scary dog like a Rottweiler or a pit bull but it could be a little savage at times, even when it was a puppy. It looked all cuddly and cute so Bliss treated it like one of her teddies and once tried to dress it up. Rexy got fed up and bit her. It was only a little nip but it made her hand bleed. She was always terrified of dogs after that.

'You're no fun, Bliss. I want to watch a really, really, really scary DVD,' said Baxter. 'Let's watch a vampire film and then we can all turn into vampires and *bite*.' He pretended to take a chunk out of Bliss's neck. She screamed as if she was literally pouring blood.

6

'What's up?' said Mum, putting her head rou. the door. She'd got one eye shadowed and outlined, but hadn't done the other one yet, so she looked lop-sided. 'They don't want me to go, do they?'

'They're fine, Mum, they're just being silly. Shut up, you two,' I said, bashing at Baxter and Bliss with a cushion. 'You want Mum to go out and have a lovely time, don't you? *Don't you?*' I said, digging at them with my feet.

'Yes, Lily,' said Bliss, her hands round her neck, staunching her imaginary wound.

I dug Baxter, harder this time, and put my hand on his matchbox car.

'Yes, go out, Mum,' he said, snatching his car back.

'Well then, I will,' said Mum. 'You can keep them in better order than I can, Lily. You'll make a lovely little mum one day.'

No I won't. I'm not ever going to be a mother. I'm not going to live with any man and have a load of kids yelling round me all the time. I can't stick men, apart from Mr Abbott, my teacher. I wouldn't mind marrying Mr Abbott but Mum says he's not the marrying kind. If I can't have Mr Abbott I won't have anybody. I'll make lots and lots of money and live in a lovely big house all by myself. No one will throw their toys on the floor or spill juice on the carpet or bash the television so it goes on the blink. My house will stay as pristine as a palace. It will get featured in all the magazines and little girls will cut out photos of it and stick them in their scrapbooks because my house will be so beautiful. I'll design it myself. That's how I'll make all my money. I'll be a famous interior designer with my own television programme.

I went to find some paper to draw on, deciding to make a start straight away. Baxter and Bliss wanted to draw too, but there was only one clean page left in the old drawing pad.

'It's *my* drawing pad,' said Bliss, which was strictly true. It was one of her presents last Christmas, along with some fat wax crayons.

'Yeah, and *you* can crayon on the cardboard back, that's the best bit,' I lied.

'What about *me*?' said Baxter, trying to snatch the drawing pad for himself.

'I thought you liked drawing in magazines?' I said. 'Why don't you give all the ladies beards as well as moustaches?'

So Baxter scribbled determinedly, giving every celebrity a bushy beard, adding a distressing amount of body hair while he was at it. Bliss crayoned a big pink cube with little wires sticking out, and then added four little wiry cubes. She said it was our family portrait but we had to take her word for it. I sat up cross-legged, resting my precious piece of paper lengthwise on a tray, and started designing my dream house. I drew it sliced open so I could show all the rooms inside. I didn't just stick at living room and kitchen and bedrooms. I had a studio with a proper artist's easel and a potter's wheel, a music room with a piano and a drum kit, a library stuffed to the ceiling with books, a conservatory with butterflies flying about the flowers, and a swimming pool the entire length of the basement.

Pixie stayed watching Mum, which was wonderful. She was usually a royal pain when we drew. She hated it that she wasn't old enough to draw properly herself so she'd snatch at our pens and crayons and then scribble rubbish all over our pages.

She came skipping in at last, going, 'Look at Mum, look at Mum, isn't she pretty?'

Mum looked lovely, her long hair piled up with the front bit crimped into little curls. She had matching Cleopatra eyes now and a big shiny scarlet mouth. She wore a tight pink top that showed a bit of her red bra and a little black skirt, black tights and her best red high heels. Pixie and Bliss and I love to shuffle along in Mum's high heels, pretending we're grown-up ladies out on the town.

'You look totally knock-out, Mum,' I said, and Baxter whooped in agreement.

'You really think I look all right?' Mum said anxiously. 'I think I've got a bit baggy and saggy since Pixie was born.'

'You have *not*. You look fantastic,' I said.

Mum peered down critically at her chest.

'I couldn't half do with a boob job,' she said. 'There's hardly anything there.'

'Stick a couple of oranges on your chest, Mum,' said Baxter, cackling with laughter.

'You shut up, you cheeky little whatsit,' said Mum.

She seemed so different now she'd put on her make-up and fancy clothes. I was pleased my suggestion had perked her up no end.

'You go and have a great time, Mum,' I said.

'Well, I'm not even sure if any of the old crowd will be there. I'll maybe just have a couple of drinks and come home. But even if I'm having a right laugh I promise I'll be back home by midnight. Don't want to turn into a pumpkin, do I?'

'It was Cinderella's *coach* that turned into a pumpkin,' said Bliss.

Cinderella's her favourite fairy tale. I had to

10

read it to her every night from our big fairy-story book. She took it all very seriously.

Mum kissed Bliss on her pale cheek, gently pinched Baxter's nose (he hates being kissed) and picked Pixie up and twirled her round and round till she squealed. Then Mum gave me a quick hug.

'Thanks, babe,' she said, and darted off in her high heels.

For a few seconds we were all silent after she'd slammed the front door. The flat seemed suddenly still. Then the *Corrie* theme started up and it sounded weirdly melancholy. Baxter leaped up and started running round the room, yelling at the top of his voice, pretending to be a police car, siren blaring.

'Stop that row, Baxter,' I said.

'I'm going to catch you and arrest you and beat you up in my cells,' said Baxter, driving himself straight at me.

'No, I'm the boss of a really mean gang of criminals and I'm going to have you wiped out,' I said. I grabbed hold of him and wrestled him to the floor. We were only mock-fighting but Bliss started begging us not to hurt each other.

'Stop it, Baxter. OK, you win. March me off to the cells in handcuffs,' I said, offering him my wrists. 'It's OK, Bliss, we're just mucking about. Hey, where's Pixie?'

She'd gone wandering off to Mum's bedroom. I found her sitting in the middle of the bed rubbing lipstick all over her face.

'Pixie! You are *naughty*,' I said, though I had to struggle not to laugh because she looked so funny.

'*Not* naughty! I want real lipstick like Mum,' she said. 'I want to be a pretty lady.'

'Mum will be mad if she finds out – that's her best lipstick. Here, what do you look like?' I picked her up and stood her at the dressing table. Pixie laughed at her war-paint.

'Come on, let's wash it all off.'

'No, no, I like it!'

'Well, you're going to have to wash it off before bedtime. It *is* your bedtime, Pixie. Come on.'

Pixie wasn't going anywhere. She jumped up and started careering about the flat, waving her arms like windmills. I chased her round for ages.

'I'm not tired yet, I'm not tired yet!' she gabbled.

'Look, *I'm* getting tired running after you. Maybe *I'll* go to bed now,' I said, and I threw myself down on Mum's bed and lay still as stone, my eyes shut.

Pixie giggled uncertainly. She ran a few more steps and then stopped.

'Lily?' she said.

I didn't move. I heard the little slurpy sound of

her putting her thumb in her mouth. She snuffled and sucked for a minute. Then, *'Lily!'*

I sat up and grabbed her and pulled her onto the bed with me for a cuddle. She squealed and wriggled and thumped me with her little fists.

'You frightened me, you meanie,' she said.

'Ah, I'm sorry, Pixie. I forgot you're so little. Like a little, little baby. Here, let's turn you into a real baby.' I pulled Mum's soft blanket off her bed and wrapped it around Pixie and picked her up in my arms.

'There now,' I said, carrying her into the living room. Baxter was sorting through our pile of DVDs, chucking the ones he didn't fancy over his shoulder. Bliss had found my crumpled page of dream house and was carefully walking her fingers into every room.

'Look at my new little baby, Baxter and Bliss. Isn't she lovely?' I said. 'Say hello, little baby.'

'Coo coo, coo coo, coo coo,' said Pixie, trying hard to play the game and do baby talk.

'What's she saying? *Poo poo?*' said Baxter, sniggering. 'The baby's done a big poo poo!'

'I *haven't*!' said Pixie, struggling to get out of her blanket.

'Poo poo!' Baxter repeated maddeningly, holding his nose.

'Stop teasing her, Baxter, it's mean. And quit chucking those DVDs around. *I'll* choose,' I said, tucking Pixie up on the sofa beside Bliss. 'There, you'll look after my baby properly, won't you, Bliss?'

'Can she be my baby too?' said Bliss. 'Can I feed her?'

'Want my bottle!' said Pixie. She wasn't playing now. She still had a real bottle at night. It didn't have to be full of proper milk. It could be weak tea or Ribena, anything. She just liked lying on her back and sleepily sucking.

'OK, OK, I'll fetch you your bottle in just a second. We're all going to watch . . . *Peter Pan*.'

'That's boring. It's just for babies,' said Baxter.

'No, it isn't. There are pirates in it, remember?'

'The pirates are scary,' said Bliss.

'Not really – and remember, there's little Tinker Bell in *Peter Pan*, you like fairies, and mermaids too, and you like Wendy's house,' I said.

I still liked all these things myself, babyish or not – and I especially loved the flying part. I would give anything to be able to soar straight up into the sky. I've dreamed about flying but I can't do it properly even in my dreams. I just skim the surface of things and I have to move my arms and legs jerkily, as if I'm swimming. It's not really flying properly, more mid-air gymnastics.

I want to fly up and away, effortlessly, like a bird.

I suppose what I really need is a good pair of wings. When I was little I used to feel my back and wonder if my sharp shoulder blades might be wings just starting to grow. I still imagined them sometimes, great white feathers tucked up tight like a fan, neat against my back. I'd pretend I could spread them any time I wanted and fly away. Sometimes I wouldn't walk straight home from school to our first-floor flat. I'd puff my way up all the steps to the top balcony and stand there clutching the rusty rail, peering out, pretending I could just let go and soar over the treetops of the huge park.

Peter Pan and Wendy and John and Michael flew without benefit of wings as far as I could remember. I wanted to check out their flying technique, so I was firm with Baxter and Bliss about my choice of DVD. Pixie was a pushover. She had inherited Bliss's old Tinker Bell costume and loved wearing it. She ran off to get changed. It took quite a while as she wasn't very good at dressing herself, usually ending up with a leg in a sleeve or arms through the neck hole. The costume was pretty sticky because she'd spilled juice all down it the last time she'd worn it, but she didn't seem to care. I fixed her a fresh bottle to keep her quiet

15

while she was watching, and I filled a big bowl with cornflakes.

'This is our popcorn, like we're really at the cinema,' I said, switching the DVD on.

I settled myself in the middle of the sofa with Baxter in the corner on one side of me, where he couldn't torment the girls. I let him hold the corn-flake bowl to make him feel special. I settled Bliss and her teddy in the other corner and squeezed Pixie in beside her, cuddling her close. They all fidgeted and argued and spilled cornflakes for the first ten minutes but then they quietened down and watched properly. It was as if the sofa itself had spread little leathery wings and flown us straight to Neverland.

We didn't budge until the cast list started rolling.

'Again!' Pixie begged. 'Put it on again.'

'Don't be daft, it's *way* past your bedtime.' I looked at the clock. 'Quick, it's gone closing time at the Fox. Mum will be back in a minute and if she finds us all up she'll be really mad. Come on, who can get into bed first?'

Pixie toddled off to her little cot all by herself. It was much too small for her now but she screamed if we tried to make her sleep on the mattress with us. She scrambled over the bars and snuggled up, falling asleep as soon as her head hit her pillow. She was still wearing her Tinker Bell costume, with lipstick scribble all over her face, but I couldn't be bothered to wash and change her.

Baxter was much more of a challenge.

'Come on, Baxter, get into bed!'

He squared up to me, hands on his hips.

'Who's telling me to get into bed? *You* can't boss me around. You're not my mum,' he shouted.

He was only clowning around. I always tell him what to do, far more than Mum, but he just wanted to be difficult. I had to tip him over and pull his jeans off his waving legs and then stuff him inside his duvet. He immediately got up again, duvet pulled right over his head.

'Baxter! Lie down!'

'I'm not Baxter. I'm the Duvet Monster and I'm going to smother you,' Baxter growled, staggering about the bedroom.

'*Don't* be the monster, I hate that,' Bliss said.

She seemed the easiest of the lot. She got into her nightie and lay down on our mattress cuddled up – but long after Baxter was sound asleep she was still awake, snuffling into a teddy tummy. I reached out and put my arm round her.

'Bliss? Go to sleep,' I whispered.

'I can't. Not till Mum comes back.'

'She'll be back any minute,' I said. I wasn't sure where she could have got to. It was definitely past closing time at the Fox. She'd said she'd only have a couple of drinks. I hadn't necessarily believed that – but she'd promised to be back before midnight.

I lay with my arm round Bliss, my legs twined round Baxter's twitchy little feet, listening. I heard guys yelling and messing about down on the forecourt and then a series of thumps as they chucked beer cans about. They sounded like young lads. Mum wouldn't be with them. Then I heard a couple having a screaming row and I tensed up, but the woman's voice was too low and hoarse to be Mum's. I listened to them swearing at each other and then the sound of a blow. Bliss tensed up.

'Shh, it's all right. They'll go home now,' I said.

'Mum?'

'She'll be back soon. I bet she's gone back to one of her friends' flats for another drink. But don't worry, she'll be fine.'

'Back by midnight?' Bliss mumbled.

'Yes, definitely,' I said, though I was pretty sure it was gone midnight already.

When Bliss went to sleep at last I wriggled cautiously off the mattress and padded into the kitchen. I flicked the light on. The clock showed it was ten to one. I shivered, wrapping my arms round

18

myself. She'd promised to be back by midnight.

A horrible series of images flickered in my head. I saw Mum screaming in a car, a man hurting her; Mum weeping and bleeding in a gutter; Mum lying horribly still, her eyes open, her face blank. I smacked my forehead, trying to make the images go away.

I poured myself a glass of water and sipped it slowly, but I'd started to shiver and the glass clinked uncomfortably against my teeth.

'Come *home*, Mum,' I whispered.

I sat down at the kitchen table and picked at the edge until my nail was sore. My feet were numb with cold so I got up and walked round and round the table. It was nearly summer – Mum had gone out without a jacket – yet I felt deathly cold. I wanted to go back to bed and warm myself up, but I didn't want to wake Bliss or Baxter. I wished I wasn't the oldest. I wanted to be the littlest, like Pixie, with people telling me what to do. That was the scary thing. I didn't know what to do if Mum didn't ever come back.

I smacked my head again, trying hard not to think it. I wondered if I should put on some clothes and go out looking for Mum – but if the kids woke up and I wasn't there either, they'd be terrified. And *I* was terrified at the thought of setting out round the estate in the middle of the night. It wasn't just the thought of all the drunks and smackheads and bad lads. It was the dark itself. The thought of starting out along the dark balcony and feeling my way down the pitch-black stairwell made me shiver even more.

I went into the living room and lay on the sofa, my head on Mum's cushion. I could very faintly smell her musky perfume. I nuzzled into the cushion like Bliss with her teddy. The hard edges of the fairy-tale book were digging into my chest. I fingered the pages, thinking of all the weird people trapped inside: Cinderella with her pink and blue and white ball-gowns folded flat; Snow White crushed inside her glass coffin; the Three Bears flattened into floor rugs.

I remembered when I was little and there was just Mum and me. She read me those stories then, over and over. She showed me the label inside the front cover.

To Lily Green, First Prize for Reading, Writing and Spelling.

I couldn't read myself then, let alone write or spell, but I knew the shape of an L, the dot of an i, the curly tail of a y.

'It says Lily. That's my name! Is it my book, Mum?' I asked.

'It was my nan's book. I loved my nan, much more than my mum, *your* nan. She used to read me stories from this book when I went to visit her.

20

This is her school prize, see. She was ever so bright, my nan. I named you after her, Lily, and you're going to be ever so bright too.'

I wasn't that bright. I couldn't figure out how this Lily could be young enough to go to school and old enough to be a nan, but I liked the sound of her and I loved her story book. I wanted to go and visit her, but Mum shook her head sadly and said she was dead. And now *my* nan was dead too. She got ill just after the twins were born.

'So we're all on our ownio now,' Mum said.

We must actually have a set of *other* nans, the mothers of our dads, but we'd never met them either. Mum was right, we were on our own . . . so what would we do if anything happened to Mum?

I was the oldest and bravest. What was I doing, weeping into Mum's cushion? I turned it over, wiped my eyes with the hem of my nightie and burrowed down again. At some stage I must have gone to sleep.

I woke with a start. I heard scuffling and then foot-steps creeping slowly towards me.

I leaped up, first clenched.

'Hey, hey, it's *me*, babe. It's only me!'

'Oh *Mum*!'

I wound my arms round her and hugged her hard. She sat down on the sofa and I climbed onto her lap as if I was little like Pixie.

'What you doing sleeping on the sofa, Lily? Did Baxter start kicking you?'

'No, no, I just couldn't sleep in with the kids. I

was worried. Where *were* you? You said you'd come back before midnight.'

'Hey, don't go on at me! And shush, you'll wake the others.'

'What time is it?'

'I don't know. Five, maybe? Later – or earlier, whichever,' Mum giggled.

'Are you drunk, Mum?' I couldn't see her face properly in the dark, but her voice sounded softer than usual, and a little slurred.

'Drunk with love,' said Mum, and she giggled some more.

I slid off Mum's lap.

'Not again,' I said.

'Oh, come on, Lil, don't be like that. Oh darling, I'm so happy. I can't believe it. I just went down the Fox for one drink, like I said – and then I met the man of my dreams.'

'In the *Fox*?' I said.

The men who drank there were all from our estate, old guys with red faces and beer bellies, and young lads with tattoos who always seemed angry.

'Not in the Fox, sweetheart. I went on clubbing afterwards, didn't I?'

'By yourself?'

'No, I met up with Jenny and Jan, they worked in the canteen too, remember? Well, they were having a girlie night out, cheering Jan up because her bloke's just walked out on her. They said they were going on to Chancers and asked me to go along too. I didn't really want to, truly. I haven't been to Chancers for donkey's years and it's all really young kids there. I was all set to come home, I swear I was, but Jenny was very persuasive and I felt I couldn't let them down under the circumstances, so I went. I so nearly *didn't* – and then I'd never have met Gordon.'

'Gordon?' I tried the name out. 'He sounds posh.'

'Well, he *is*, kind of. He talks posh anyway, but he tried not to. He's so *sweet*. And you should just see him, Lily. He's drop-dead gorgeous, I swear he is.'

'Like?' I said, unimpressed. I didn't know what my own dad looked like but the twins' dad Mikey was this big fat ugly guy, and Pixie's dad Paul was thin and pinched and weedy, yet Mum had thought *them* drop-dead gorgeous in their time.

'He's like a film star, truly. The moment I saw him my heart practically stopped. Think blond hair, blue eyes, tall, with a really washboard stomach, and so *tanned*. Well, he would be tanned, he lives in Spain.'

'He's Spanish?'

'No, no, he's just hanging out there for a bit, helping out in his uncle's nightclub. He's having a – what do they call it when posh kids muck around for a year before going off to uni?'

'A gap year. Mum, he's a kid. How old is he, *eighteen*?'

'He's nineteen, and he certainly doesn't act like a kid, I promise you.'

'Mum!'

'There's not that much age difference. Seven years. Anyway, I didn't tell him how old I am.'

'Did you tell him you've got four kids?'

'Well, I didn't want to overwhelm him with information, not straight away, like. I *will* tell him, obviously.'

'So you're seeing him again?'

'You bet. Tonight. We're going to the Palace up in town. He's doing a recce of all the big clubs, because this uncle of his wants to expand his own clubs in Spain.'

'So, is he coming here?'

'No, do you think I'm mad? I don't want him seeing this dump, it might put him right off. I'm meeting him up in town, OK?'

'And you think he'll actually turn up?'

'Hey! What sort of remark is that! *Yes*, he'll be there. We had the greatest time ever, Lily. I'm not going into details, but believe me – it was great. It was like all the love songs, all the romantic films. We just looked into each other's eyes and it was like we were on a rollercoaster up to heaven.'

'Oh Mum! You haven't half got it bad,' I said, yawning.

'You wait till you grow up, Lily. You'll know what it's like then.'

'I don't ever want to grow up. I'll be like that boy Peter Pan. I'll stay young for ever, and I'll fly – out of the window, up in the air, all the way to Neverland.'

'What are you on about, you daft banana? Come on, let's get you to bed. You come in with me, babe.'

So I went and cuddled up in Mum's bed. It was so warm and soft and cosy just with Mum. Her sheets smelled of her perfume. There were no squirmy little bodies and sharp elbows and kicking feet. I stretched out luxuriously and fell fast asleep.

I didn't wake up till eleven, and that was only because Pixie was bouncing on my head. I tried to slide her under the covers to have a cuddle but she was too fidgety – and I could hear Baxter thumping and yelling in the kitchen, sounding as if he was throwing saucepans about.

'Kids!' Mum mumbled, putting her head under the pillow.

She didn't get up till lunchtime, and I worried that she might be in a bad mood. It sounded as if she'd been drinking an awful lot last night. But when she got up at last she gave us all a kiss, even Baxter, and then she had a bath and put on her jeans and T-shirt and flip-flops, and said, 'Come on, kids, let's go down the shops.'

We hadn't been out to the proper shops for months. Mum would go to Lidl and Londis every few days, but that was her limit. But now she got us all rounded up, wiped a damp flannel over Baxter and Bliss, gave Pixie a harder scrub, discovering she had lipstick and tomato sauce even in her *ears*, and then we set off for the bus. I wheeled Pixie in her buggy, while Mum held Bliss's hand. Baxter won't ever hold on to anyone. He charged ahead of us and then circled back, leaping about crazily.

'You behave now, or I'll tell your dad,' said Mum.

Mikey's the only one Baxter will listen to. Baxter insists on having his hair cut really short, just like Mikey, and he tries to walk like him too, swaggering along with his hands stuck in his pockets. Baxter swears like Mikey too. He swore now at Mum, and she gave him a push and told him to button his lip or she'd take him home right that minute. Baxter hunched up and looked sulky, but then the bus came, and there was no one sitting on top up the front, so he could charge up there with Bliss and play at driving the bus. Mum and Pixie and I sat behind. Mum counted out just how much money she'd got. I looked in her wallet worriedly.

'You haven't forgotten I need a tenner for my

gallery trip, Mum? Everyone else has paid now.'

'For God's sake, that school, they're always on at me for money,' said Mum. 'What are they doing, forever taking you kids on all these trips to places. Why don't they keep you in the classroom and learn you stuff? You don't want to waste your time and my money going to some gloomy old gallery, do you?'

I swallowed. Mr Abbott was taking all our class on the school trip – and I so loved Mr Abbott. He wasn't shouty or sarcastic like the other teachers. He didn't ever tell me off because my socks were dirty or my hair needed brushing. He didn't act like he thought I was thick. He treated me like a real person, asking me questions and acting like he really wanted to know the answers. I especially wanted to go to the gallery with him, because he said I'd love the paintings. I really liked doing my own paintings at school. I'd painted an angel with huge wings all different colours of the rainbow and Mr Abbott liked it so much he pinned it up on the wall.

'It's treat money for the kids,' said Mum.

I sighed.

'OK, OK.'

'And you're included too, darling. In fact you can have more than your fair share, because you've been such a good kid. What would you like, babe? New earrings? Hair slides? Bracelet?'

'Me! I want earrings!' Pixie said.

'Me too,' Bliss whispered.

'What about you, son? Are you after earrings too?' said Mum, leaning over and ruffling Baxter's stubby crew cut. 'Long dangly earrings with sparkly bits.'

'Leave it out, Mum,' said Baxter, swatting at her. 'I'm driving the bus. Whoops, now you've made me run over two old ladies. Never mind, they're just boring. I'll get those young ones too – squish, squash, squeal.'

'My son, the homicidal maniac,' said Mum.

'Your *son*?' said a fat bloke across the aisle from us. 'They're not all *your* kids, are they? I thought you were their big sister!'

'No, I'm their mum,' said Mum.

'Go on! You don't look old enough.'

'I was a child bride,' said Mum, smiling.

She was only fifteen when she had me. When I was little we got mistaken for sisters all the time. Sometimes we even *played* we were sisters. I liked it best when I acted the big sister and Mum was the little one and had to do what I said. We used to play all these lovely games together until Mum lumbered herself with Mikey and the twins. He cleared off and Mum said good riddance. But then she got off with druggy Paul and started Pixie. She is hopeless with men, my mum. She was even tossing her hair about and acting all smiley-smiley with this silly fat man on the bus.

'Where are you off to, then?' he asked.

'The shops, the shops!' said Pixie.

'And McDonald's,' said Baxter. 'I'm going to drive the bus right up to the entrance. No, I'm going to drive it *into* McDonald's, right up to the counter!'

'Cheers, mate – then I can buy myself a Big Mac too,' said the fat man. 'Then you drive round to my place and you kids can all play in my nice garden while your mum and I have a little cosy get-together indoors.'

'No! Don't go, Mum,' Bliss whispered, taking him seriously.

'Us "cosy together"?' said Mum, laughing. 'As if, Mister!'

'Why not, eh?' he said. 'Your old fella still around, is that it?'

'I've got myself a *new* fella,' said Mum. She breathed in deeply, her eyes sparkling. 'A lovely new fella, so sorry, mate. I'm taken.'

'Then he's a *lucky* fella,' said the fat man, which was quite nice of him.

He wasn't the only guy looking at Mum on the bus. She looked so different today. Since Paul died she mostly just scraped her hair back in a limp pony-tail and didn't bother with make-up and wore washed-out old T-shirts and trackie bottoms and no one looked at her twice. But now, with her hair curled and her make-up and her tight top and good jeans, she looked wonderful. My heart thumped with pride when I looked at her.

It was a struggle getting us all downstairs when we got to the shopping centre. Baxter wanted to stay driving the bus till the last possible second. I had to prise his hands off the rail. Bliss threw a wobbly going downstairs, clutching me tight, scared she was going to fall. Pixie wriggled so much in Mum's arms she very nearly *did* fall. Then we got the buggy caught up with some old lady's shopping trolley, and this young lad leaped up and helped Mum. It was as if she had put a spell on every man in the town.

'Come on, kiddies, shopping, shopping, shopping!' said Mum, running along, even though she was wearing high heels, Pixie squealing with delight in her racing buggy.

We went to the Flowerfields shopping centre first because Pixie loved the singing dancing teddy bears in the main entrance hallway. Baxter loved them too. He lumbered about growling, pretending he was a bear. Poor silly Bliss was still a bit frightened of the giant bears and nuzzled her head against Mum, not looking.

'They're lovely bears, just like the Three Bears in

our fairy-story book,' I said, trying to encourage her.

'They're not lovely, they eat you all up,' said Bliss indistinctly, because she was sucking her fingers.

'You're getting your fairy stories mixed up. That was the wolf in Little Red Riding Hood,' I said.

'I'm a bear-wolf and I'm going to *eat you up*, Bliss,' Baxter growled, waving his arms around and thrusting his face against hers.

Bliss squealed and Mum shook both of them.

'Stop being so daft, you two. Pixie's got far more sense and she's half your age. Stop messing about or you won't get a treat, do you understand?'

But she wasn't really cross at all. She was loving the bears too, singing along to all the silly songs and doing little dance steps round the buggy.

We watched the whole bear routine three times and then went off shopping. We spent way more than ten pounds but I didn't comment. But I couldn't keep my lip buttoned when Mum flashed a new credit card. She said her friend Jenny had 'sold' it to her. I felt sick as soon as I saw it. Mum wasn't supposed to have any credit cards at all. She'd got into a lot of debt when she first met Paul and she'd tried to buy stuff using a stolen credit card and she'd ended up in the magistrates' court. I was so scared then in case they sent Mum to prison, but she played dumb and they let her off with a fine, thank goodness. I was sure they wouldn't let her off again if she tried anything dodgy.

'*Mum!*' I hissed, as she flashed her card in Claire's, buying bangles and a sparkly hairslide for Bliss and a little pink handbag and a lipstick set for Pixie.

'Stop fussing, Lily,' Mum said firmly.

'But you're not meant to.'

'Shut *up*,' Mum said. She raised her eyebrows at the shop assistant. 'Kids! She's just sulking because I won't let her have the necklace she wants.'

This was so mean I nearly cried. I just stood there, red-faced, trembling that the credit card would be rejected – but amazingly Mum knew the right pin number and the transaction went through. Baxter was barging about the shop, pointing at everything, going, 'Yuck, too pink, yuck, too girlie,' over and over again.

When we got outside the shop Mum prodded him in the stomach and went, 'Yuck, nasty smelly bad boy!' Then she looked at me. 'Don't give me that look! I could knock your block off, making all that fuss in there. You were acting like I'd nicked that card.'

'Well, didn't you?'

'I *told* you, I got it off Jenny.'

'And where did she get it from?'

'Just stop it, Lily. Who do you think you are,

someone from *The Bill*? OK, don't feel you *have* to accept a present off my dodgy card.'

'I don't want one, thanks,' I said, and I marched off further up the mall.

I felt tears pricking my eyelids and blinked furiously. I wasn't a crybaby. I certainly wasn't going to start blubbing in public. I forced myself to stride out, swinging my arms as if I didn't have a care in the world. I couldn't hear the clatter of the buggy or the chatter of the kids. Weren't they following me? My heart started banging in my chest. No, maybe I really didn't care. I was really cheesed off with Mum and fed up with my brother and sisters. I was better off on my own.

'I am Lily and I walk alone,' I muttered. I stepped onto the escalator to the next floor. I looked down as I rose upwards. 'I am Lily and I *fly* alone,' I said, spreading my arms. I imagined stepping off the escalator, swooping out into the atrium, circling round and round the glass roof, while all the crowds of shoppers pointed and marvelled down below.

My arms rose of their own accord and I leaned sideways over the moving handrail.

'Lily! What the hell are you doing? Watch out, you'll topple over!' Mum was yelling up at me, dragging Pixie in the buggy onto the escalator and yanking at Baxter and Bliss. I waited at the top for them, acting nonchalant.

'You mad girl, what were you *playing* at?' Mum said, giving me a good shake. Then she hugged me hard. 'I thought you were trying to top yourself.'

'Oh, Mum, don't be crazy. I was just playing I could fly.'

'Fly? You're the crazy one. Stop playing silly flying beggars.'

But later, as we wandered around the toy shop, Mum seized a little sparkly pair of fairy wings.

'Here you are, Lily. This is what you need,' she said, snorting with laughter.

'Oh, ha ha,' I said, flicking the toy wings contemptuously, though if I'd been as little as Pixie, or even Bliss, I'd have clamoured for them.

'What do you want for a present, babe, seriously?' said Mum, as she bought Baxter a toy fork-lift truck.

'Nothing.'

'Oh, come on, stop sulking,' said Mum. 'Look at the face on you! Hey, cheer up, cootchy-cootchy-coo.' She tickled me under the chin as if I was a baby.

'Leave it out! Mum, stop it!' I doubled up, spluttering. I'm hopelessly ticklish and it's a horrible disadvantage. You find yourself shrieking with laughter even when you're furious.

'That's my girl!' Mum said, digging her thumb and

finger in my cheeks. 'My Little Miss Smiley's come back. Come on, pet, I'm in the mood for treating you. What do you want?'

'Well . . . can I have a big drawing pad just for me?'

'Of course you can, silly.'

Mum didn't get any old drawing pad with rough paper from one of the pound shops. She took us to a special art shop and bought me a giant pad of smooth white cartridge paper, and a new big set of felt-tip pens, all different subtle shades, so I could draw real-looking people, not girls with bright red skin and canary yellow hair. She spent more than the tenner I wanted for the school trip but she was having such fun it seemed mean to point this out. She bought us all sweets and chocolates too, and a couple of celebrity mags for herself and comics for the kids. She wanted to buy me a magazine too, so I chose *My Gorgeous Home* so I could get ideas for my own gorgeous home in the future.

'You want *this* one?' said Mum, wrinkling her nose. 'You're the weirdest kid ever, Lily. Look, it's twice the price of all the others!' But she bought it all the same.

'Now it's *my* turn for treats,' said Mum, and she pushed the buggy into a big fashion store.

I got really worried then. Each time she used that credit card I was scared it would be refused – and even if it was genuine, I knew Mum would never have enough money to pay the bill at the end of the month.

'Mind the kids while I just try this top and skirt on, Lily. Oh, and this dress! Do you think I can just about wriggle into it? What is it? You've got that face on again.'

'Mum, it's nearly two hundred pounds!'

'Yeah, well, why should I always have to make do with cheap rubbish from down the market. I'm going up to town tonight, you know I am. I want to look the part.'

'But how will you ever pay it off?'

'You were born middle-aged, you. You've got to have a bit of fun while you can. Live for the moment, Lily, that's my motto. Snatch a bit of happiness when you get the chance.'

Mum tried the clothes on. The top was a bit too low and showed a lot of Mum's bony chest.

'Never mind, I can get one of those push-up bras, that'll do the trick. The skirt's OK, isn't it, Lily?'

I thought the skirt was too tight and too short, but it wasn't very expensive so I said it looked great. I hoped Mum would stick with the top and the skirt, but she tried the dress on too. It really did look lovely. It was pearly grey, very silky and slinky.

'Oh, look, it's dead classy, isn't it! Oh, wait till

Gordon sees me in this. He'll love it, I know he will.'

'Gordon, Gordon, Gordon,' said Pixie, chuckling at the funny name.

'Who's Gordon?' asked Bliss.

'My new boyfriend,' Mum said proudly.

'*I'm* your boyfriend, Mum,' said Baxter. 'Yeah, I'm going to take you out dancing in that pretty dress.'

'It *is* pretty, isn't it, darling? You think I should buy it, don't you?'

'Yes, of course, Mum.'

I sighed. It was hopeless. The kids were just egging her on, because they didn't understand. I was starting to get really worried. It wasn't just the credit card. Mum was getting so worked up about meeting Gordon. I kept wondering if he would even turn up. I'd watched enough romances in the soaps on telly. Young men sometimes fell for older women, but their relationships were never long term. Posh people sometimes hooked up with poor people, but generally it was for a one-night stand. Gordon was young and posh, Mum was older and poor – *and* she had four children.

Perhaps that was why she needed to buy the slinky dress, with the skirt and top as back-up out-fits. She bought them all and kept poking her hand into the carrier bag to stroke them lovingly. She took us to a McDonald's for lunch, buying us all burgers and French fries, but she just nibbled a few chips herself.

'I'm too excited to eat,' she said. 'Besides, I need to keep my tummy as flat as possible – that new dress doesn't half cling.'

'Mum, you've got to eat.'

'I'll probably be having a meal with Gordon. Somewhere fancy, with waiters and soft lights and maybe a violin playing.'

'You're making it all up!'

'Well, why can't I pretend a bit? You do all the time, Lily.'

'Yes, but you're the grown-up. And you're making it up too much.'

Mum bent her head close to mine. 'Don't spoil it for me,' she whispered.

'I just don't want you to get hurt,' I said.

'Is Mum going to get hurt?' Bliss asked anxiously.

'No, of course I'm not, pet. I'm going to go out and have the night of my life,' said Mum.

'With Gordon,' said Pixie, sucking on a chip.

'Is he going to be our new dad?' Bliss asked.

'No, love!' said Mum, laughing.

I breathed a sigh of relief. At least she wasn't crazy enough to believe that.

We went home on the bus and Mum spent hours in the bathroom, soaking herself, slapping on a mud-pack facial, and tweaking her eyebrows. Baxter played out, driving his fork-lift truck along the balconies, while Bliss and Pixie dressed up in their new finery and played a game of grown-up ladies.

I sat at the kitchen table with my new drawing pad and felt tips and my magazine. I had peace, I had privacy, everything I always longed for, but somehow I couldn't use my precious time properly. I flicked through the magazine quickly, noting a velvet sofa here, a painted table there, but not really taking it all in. I started drawing an ideal living room on the first page of my pad, but I drew the sofa far too small, shrunk to the size of a shoe on my vast white carpet. I couldn't get the legs on my table right, so it lurched sideways, its bowl of oranges and apples about to spill.

I tore the page out, crumpled it up and threw it across the room.

'Temper, temper!' said Mum, padding into the kitchen in bare feet.

She was wearing her old faded pink dressing gown but the rest of her was brightly coloured. She'd put a rinse in her hair to bring out the gold, she wore amazing make-up, and her finger- and toenails were blue.

'What do you think?' said Mum, waving her fingers at me.

'You look like you're going mouldy at the edges.'

'Thanks a bunch! It's called Blue Moon. It's the new trendy colour. All the models are wearing it. Don't you like it really, Lily?'

'It looks fine,' I said. She was looking at me so hopefully. '*You* look fine, Mum. Really lovely.'

'How old do you think I look?'

'Young.'

'Yes, but how young?'

'Fifteen?'

'Are you taking the mickey? Actually, I look a lot better now than I did when I *was* fifteen, with my stomach stuck out to here and my face all over spots. God, I looked a sight then. I thought my life was over and I'd never have any fun ever again.'

'Because of me?' I said in a very small voice.

'But I was wrong, wasn't I?' said Mum, putting her arms round me. 'You're the best thing that ever happened to me, Lily. You're not just like a daughter – you and me are best mates, right?'

'Yeah, right,' I said, hugging her back. I rubbed my cheek against hers.

'Careful, don't smudge my make-up! Listen, I've been thinking about tonight. I felt a bit bad leaving you last night. I think I'll get a proper babysitter. I thought of asking Jenny or Jan, but maybe they've got plans to go out themselves, seeing as it's

Saturday night. How about if I ask Old Kath along the balcony to sit with you?'

'Mum, I can't stick Old Kath! And she's barmy, anyway.' She was this old woman who used too much black hair dye and now her hair had mostly fallen out, so her scalp showed through her black wisps. She couldn't see to do her make-up properly any more, so she had blue smeared all over her eyes and her postbox-red lipstick crept into the creases of her face, giving her a clown's mouth. I might have felt sorry for her, but she was mean and shouted at us kids – and she said bad things about Mum behind her back.

'Well, yeah, she is losing it a bit now. I saw her shuffling off to the shops in her dressing gown and slippers the other day. OK then, not Kath. I don't want to ask all them foreigners along the balcony, none of them can speak English. And not that Alice Doo-dah, she's definitely Care in the Community. So maybe I could call Mikey? He's way overdue to see the twins, isn't he?'

'Mum. Please, please, please don't call Mikey.'

He was *much* worse than mean old Kath or any of our other neighbours. He was big, with bulging muscles and scary teeth, just like his dog, Rex. Baxter thought he was great and followed him everywhere, but Bliss was so scared of him she twitched whenever he came near her. He didn't hit her, he hadn't ever hit any of us properly, but I'd seen him hit Mum so I hated him. He didn't like me either. He called me Slyboots Lil and told me to quit staring at him.

'Look, it's about time Mikey did his fair share. He is your dad.'

'No, he isn't!'

'Well, stepdad. He was all set to take you on too. I'm going to give him a ring, see if he can help me out.'

'Oh, Mum, *please* don't,' I begged, but she wouldn't listen. She dialled him on her mobile.

'Hey, is that you, Mikey? It's Kate here, babe. What? No, the twins are fine. But they're missing you, especially Baxter. Yeah, he really misses his dad. So I was wondering, could you come over tonight? Yeah, I know it's Saturday night. You're going out? Look, mate, *I* want to go out too. I bet you're just going down the King Edward with your mates, I know you. What? Look, I don't want you to come round some *other* Saturday, I want you to come round *now*. I've got this real hot date up in town, this really gorgeous young guy—'

She was such a fool. As if Mikey would come now she'd told him that. But she couldn't stop showing off about Gordon. Then Mikey interrupted her.

'*What?*' said Mum. Then she said something bad back to him and rang off.

'The cheek of him,' she said, breathing hard. 'Well, to hell with him.'

'What did he say?'

'Never you mind. I'll show him. He thinks that just because he walked out on me no one else could ever want me. How dare he! Oh, I wish he could see Gordon. He'd be totally gobsmacked, I tell you.'

'I'm glad he's not coming. I can't stick Mikey. Look, we don't *need* a babysitter, Mum. We'll be fine.'

'Yes, but I mightn't be back till late. Really late. Like, all night,' said Mum.

'That's OK,' I said. 'We were fine last night, weren't we?'

'Yes, you were. You're a good little kid, Lily. I'm grateful to you, darling. You understand, don't you? It's not that I *want* to leave you on your own, but I haven't got any option, have I? And guys like Gordon don't often come along. You have to grab them when you can!'

Mum fixed our favourite tea, sausages and baked beans. She changed into her grey dress while we were eating and retouched her make-up. Then she came into the kitchen and gave us a twirl.

'Do I look OK?' she asked.

'You bet,' I said.

'You look lovely, Mum,' said Bliss.

'Lovely, lovely, lovely,' Pixie said, clapping her hands.

Baxter tried to give Mum a wolf whistle, but he couldn't whistle properly because he'd lost his front teeth, so it came out as a funny hissing sound that made us all laugh.

Mum gave us all a kiss goodbye, and she was off.

3

To tell you the truth, I thought she'd be back early. I was pretty sure this Gordon wouldn't turn up. I thought Mum would wait up in town a while, maybe have a drink to cheer herself up, and then come back home once she knew the kids would be in bed. I'd make her a cup of tea and give her a cuddle, and if she cried I'd wipe her eyes and tell her he wasn't worth it. I'd act all grown up, like I really was Mum's mate. I was almost looking forward to it.

But Mum didn't come back. We watched telly and then we played a long, boring game of snap. It got especially tedious because Baxter wanted to change the rules and shout a rude word beginning with S whenever two cards were the same – and then Pixie kept shouting it too, and we couldn't shut her up. It was hard work getting them calmed down and into bed. Pixie was still sleepily mumbling the rude word when I tucked her up in her cot.

I had to chase Baxter all round the flat before I caught him and hurled him on top of the mattress, and then I had to lie on top of him to keep him there before he calmed down at last and went to sleep clutching his new fork-lift truck. Bliss went to bed without making a fuss, but when I looked into our bedroom half an hour later she was still wide awake. I let her get up again and come in the living room with me.

'Come and cuddle up on the sofa, Bliss. I'll tell you a story if you like,' I said.

She nuzzled up to me obediently, tucking her head neatly under my shoulder. She was always lovely to sit with. Baxter was a nightmare, wrestling and kicking all over the place, and Pixie had become a hopeless fidget too, unable to sit still for two seconds.

'You are my absolute favourite, Bliss,' I said, putting my arm round her. 'OK, shall I read a story from our book? *Cinderella*? For the nine hundred and ninety-ninth time.'

'Could you tell me a story out of your head?' Bliss coaxed. 'A fairy story, but without any witches or giants or dragons.'

'OK then, I'll tell you a story about . . .'

'About a little girl called Bliss?'

'And a big girl called Lily,' I said.

'And Baxter? And Pixie?' said Bliss.

'Well, they're *in* our story, but they're fast asleep in an enchanted forest.'

'There won't be any witches, will there?'

'No, absolutely no warty old witches. We're fairies anyway, you and me, Bliss, and our magic is *much* stronger than any old witches.'

'Are Baxter and Pixie fairies too?'

'Of course they are. Baxter wears a special pink sequin fairy dress with matching sparkly pink wings.'

Bliss snorted with laughter, as if I'd told the funniest joke ever.

'And Pixie wears a little white fairy frock, with weeny white wings, only she's hopeless, she's forever crawling around the grass and trying to climb trees in the enchanted forest, so she's always all over grime and grass stains. She's only a baby fairy so she can't fly properly yet. And Baxter doesn't fly properly – he swoops round and round the tree trunks, throwing acorns at squirrels and trying to catch all the birds. But *we* fly wonderfully, Bliss.'

'What colour dresses have we got?'

'Well, you have a *blue* fairy frock.'

'Blue's my favourite colour,' said Bliss happily.

'Yes, it's a very pretty sky-blue colour, and you have the most beautiful rainbow wings. You're the prettiest fairy I've ever seen.'

Bliss pulled the thin wisps of her hair.

'Do I have long golden curls?' she asked.

'Absolutely, way down to your waist, and I brush them every morning and tie rainbow-coloured ribbons in your hair to match your wings.'

'What about you, Lily? Do you have a blue dress too?'

I nibble a little piece of skin on my lip, deliberating.

'I don't mind you having blue, Lily. Tell you what, you could wear blue because we're twins, see, you and me,' Bliss suggested.

'No, no, I'm the big sister fairy. I have to keep you in order.'

'But I'm always good.'

'You're good *here*, but you might be a very naughty little fairy in the enchanted forest. You might pull the heads off all the flowers and chase the rabbits and eat all the wild strawberries instead of sharing them with us.'

'So I'll be like Baxter?'

'*Worse* than Baxter. And when you do something *really* outrageous, like tearing your blue dress and running around in your fairy knickers singing rude songs at the top of your voice, I shall have to catch you and spank you with my fairy wand.'

Bliss was rolling around on the sofa, giggling.

'So what colour *is* your fairy dress?' she spluttered.

'I think it's purple. Yeah, purple like those pansy flowers. I'll have a very fine soft purply bodice and then a sticking-out paler purple skirt, lots and lots of layers, so it swooshes around me as I fly. My wings are pale purple too but they shade to dark at their feathery tips, and I have tiny, tiny purple pansies in my hair.

'Oh, how lovely! Can I have purple too, please, please?'

'No, your blue is *much* prettier, and purple wouldn't go with your rainbow wings. You have to be co-ordinated, Bliss.'

'What does that mean?'

'All your colours have to go together. Baxter is a beautifully co-ordinated fairy – he's got little dark pink underpants that go with his fairy frock and he wears shiny pink lipstick to match.'

Bliss was snorting with laughter now, her own face bright pink too.

'You're so *funny*, Lily!' she said. 'You will always be my sister, won't you? I mean, really. You won't go off anywhere?'

'I'll always be your big sister, Bliss, and I'll always look after you, I promise,' I said.

'Mum is coming back, isn't she?' said Bliss.

'Of course she is. You snuggle down and go to sleep with me on the sofa, and when you wake up again I bet Mum will be here and she'll be telling us off because we're not in bed.'

Bliss snuggled down obediently and went to sleep. We woke with a start at dawn, as Mum crept through the front door. She found us on the sofa and kissed us both.

'What are you funny girls doing in here on the sofa? Have you been watching telly half the night? You're very naughty girls.'

'Oh, Mum, Lily *said* you'd tell us off and you are!' Bliss said delightedly.

'What? You want to be told off, you daft ha'p'orth?' said Mum, tickling her.

'No tickles, no tickles!' Bliss begged.

'Well, you go and get into bed with Baxter and have another little snooze, there's a good girl.'

'I'm not a good girl, I'm a bad fairy,' Bliss said, but she trotted off to the living-room door. Then she turned back. 'Aren't you coming too, Lily?'

'Lily and I are going to have a special big girls' chat together,' said Mum. 'Off you go now – or I'll tickle you till you squeal.'

'I'm going, I'm going,' said Bliss, disappearing.

'Ah!' Mum said, yawning and stretching. 'She's a funny little thing, isn't she? Here, Lily, go and make us a cup of tea. You and me need to talk.'

I went to put the kettle on. Gordon had obviously turned up after all. Mum was in such a good mood. She looked good too, even though her make-up was all gone and her hair tucked back behind her ears. She looked like a girl again, not a mum of four. I felt so happy for her. Well, most of me did. Another deep-down, meaner part of me was jealous. Why couldn't *I* ever make her happy like that? Why weren't the four of us enough to make her happy?

I poured the tea and took two mugs into the living room. Mum was wandering around, doing little dance steps and fluffing out her hair.

'Here you are, Mum,' I said putting the mugs down.

'You're a pal.' Mum came and sat beside me. 'Well? Is he still the man of your dreams?'

'You bet he is,' said Mum. 'Oh, Lily, I can't believe it! He's so wonderful. I'm just so lucky.'

'Yeah, well, you haven't been very lucky in the past, have you? Are you *sure* Gordon's truly OK?'

'One hundred per cent perfect, I tell you. Well, as far as I can tell, at this stage. Obviously, I need to spend more time with him, to make certain sure. That's what I want to talk to you about.' Mum took a sip of her tea. 'Lily, he's asked me to go to Spain with him.'

'What?'

'Don't look like that! Just a little holiday, love. He's flying back tonight and he's asked me to go with him. Isn't that fantastic?'

'But – but what about school?' I said stupidly. 'And we'll have to get passports – and how will we afford the aeroplane tickets?'

'Hey, hey, it's not all of us. Don't be daft, Lily, he's not going to fork out for four kids, now is he? It's just me – and I've got a passport from the time I went on that trip to Magaluf, when the twins were tiny. Mikey looked after them then – and he can look after them now.'

'Not Mikey!'

'Look, I know you don't like him, but you can keep out of his way. He's a good dad to the twins – and he's wanting to see them, he said so – he just wouldn't give up his Saturday night with the lads.'

'Mum, please don't leave us with Mikey.'

'Now stop it. There isn't anybody else. It'll just be for a few days.'

'Don't go!'

'Hey, hey. I can't mess Gordon about, love. He's booked my ticket online, it's all done and dusted. I'm going tonight! It's so romantic, just like those films where they whisk you away to Paris for the weekend.'

'Can't you just go for the weekend?'

'Well, this *is* the weekend, silly. I'm not going for *long*, only a few days. I'll tell Mikey I'll be back before Saturday, just to keep him sweet.'

'Mum—'

'Look, don't sit there giving me that look. I really need a little holiday. I haven't been away anywhere for years and years, and it's really doing my head in, stuck here in this dump. You've no idea what it's been like for me, Lily. I don't see why I can't have a little holiday like anyone else. I've given up nearly everything to keep you kids happy – and now just this once I'm going to put myself first. That's not so bad, is it!'

'Couldn't we all go somewhere, Mum?'

'Look, Gordon doesn't have a clue about you lot. I don't want to put him off. He's a young carefree lad. I'll tell him eventually, of course I will. He'll come round to the idea, and you're all lovely kids – but it's a bit too soon to start playing happy families.'

'But we *are* a family, Mum.'

'Look, just shut it, will you? Here's me on cloud nine, and there's you, trying to spoil everything.' Mum thumped her tea mug down on the table. 'Now, I'm going to get a bit of shut-eye for a couple of hours before the little ones start making a racket. Do you want to come and cuddle up too? Or are you going to sit there in a sulk?'

'I'll sit, thanks,' I said.

'Right. See if I care,' said Mum, and she walked off out of the room, swaying her hips in her new dress.

I sat huddled up, my head on my knees. I decided that I hated Mum. No, of course I didn't really. I hated this Gordon for wanting to take her away, but it was hard hating someone I didn't even know. Well, I knew Mikey and I certainly hated him. I thought of him crashing around our flat, yelling at all of us, and shivered. Even when he was in a good mood he could never get it right. He wrestled with Baxter but he was always a bit too rough, forgetting that Baxter was only a little boy. Baxter would go bright red in the face trying not to cry, and if his tears spilled over, Mikey would jeer at him and call him a wuss. He'd try playing with Bliss, silly card games, but she'd get so nervous and twitchy she'd lose again and again, hanging her head in shame. Mikey was better with Pixie, even though she was much smaller and not his own daughter. She'd fetch her teddy bears and he'd pretend to feed them, and then he'd turn into a big bear himself and growl at Pixie. She'd scream with delight and beg him to growl even louder – but more than once she'd got so excited she'd wet herself.

I certainly didn't play any silly games with Mikey. He didn't try to play them with me. He never had, even when I was little. Once I heard him say to Mum, 'That kid gives me the creeps the way she looks at me.' He gives *me* the creeps.

I cried for a bit and then wiped my eyes with the back of my hand and went to find Mum. She was curled up in her bed. I got in beside her and tried to cuddle up.

'I thought you were sulking,' she murmured, but she put her arms round me. 'Here, babe. Don't put those cold feet on me though, they're like little blocks of ice.'

'Mum, I've been thinking. We truly don't need to get Mikey to come. I can look after the kids, easy-peasy.'

'Don't be daft, Lily.'

'I *can*. I did last night and the night before.'

'Yes, but I can't leave you kids on your own for a whole week.'

'It's not a week, you said just a few days.'

'Well, I'm not quite sure. We got this cheap

one-way ticket. Probably I'll get a flight back Friday. Or Saturday. But whenever, I can't leave you all that time. If anyone found out, I'd get thrown into jail for child neglect. It's against the law, babes. So you'll just have to put up with Mikey. Now, let's get to sleep, eh?'

Mum went to sleep in a few seconds. I lay beside her, clinging onto her with both hands. I just had to hope that she'd change her mind when she woke up. But there was no chance. When Baxter and Bliss and Pixie all came tumbling into the room Mum woke up and told them straight away that Mikey was coming to look after them. Bliss went very quiet but Baxter cheered, and Pixie clapped her hands and said, 'Mikey growly bear, Mikey growly bear,' over and over again. They didn't even seem to be taking it in that Mum was going off on holiday without us.

I couldn't take it in either. She wasn't *really* going to go, was she? Mum often made things up. She once told us she'd got a job as a singer in a nightclub. She went on and on about it, even saying this man had offered her a contract to make an album. I truly believed her, but it turned out she'd just gone to a karaoke bar and sang a few songs there. Another time I heard her telling some of the mums at school that this photographer had stopped her in the street and had been desperate to take glamour photos of her, and she was going to be a Page-Three girl. I'd been there in the street with her and it wasn't a proper photographer at all, it was just a silly lad mucking about with his mobile phone.

Perhaps Gordon had said something casual about his job in Spain, saying Mum should come and see him there some time – and now she was making it up that he'd definitely invited her and she'd booked a ticket. I felt a lot better thinking that, especially as Mum made no attempt to phone Mikey and fix up for him to come over. Maybe she was simply playing pretend games, the way I sometimes went up to the top balcony of our flats and stood on tiptoe and pretended I could stretch out my arms and step into space. I felt that if I could only will it hard enough, wings would sprout from my shoulder blades, open up like umbrellas, and carry me over the rooftops. I would soar up above our tower block, away from everyone, in peace – just Lily alone.

Mum messed around all morning, doing the dusting and vacuuming, letting Bliss faff around with a duster and Pixie ride on the hoover. She put Baxter in charge of sorting the rubbish but he just put a black plastic bag over his head and ran around pretending to be a monster.

'Stop it, Baxter! It's ever so dangerous putting

plastic bags on your head. You could suffocate,' I said, trying to snatch it off him.

'Leave him be, Lil, he's just having a bit of fun,' said Mum, aiming at my feet with the hoover.

'But it *is* dangerous. What if Pixie copied him?'

'*What if Pixie copied him?*' Mum repeated, mimicking me, making me sound horribly prim and silly.

'Pixie copy, Pixie copy, Pixie copy!' Pixie shrieked.

'See!' I said.

'I see a right old grumpy-guts,' said Mum, sticking her tongue out at me.

'Grumpy-guts, grumpy-guts, grumpy-guts,' said Pixie, and Baxter ran at me in the black plastic bag, making moaning monster noises at me.

I stomped off by myself. I lay on the mattress to draw my dream house in my new pad but the lines kept going wonky. I flipped through my magazine instead but the pictures blurred. I put my head in the grubby darkness of my pillow and curled up small, my arms round my knees.

I decided to stay like that all day, but Mum had put a chicken in the oven for Sunday dinner. She didn't usually bother to cook much, but every so often she roasted a chicken for a special treat. I didn't think I was the slightest bit hungry until I smelled it cooking. By the time Mum dished up the chicken with roast potatoes and peas and carrots I was ravenous. She only had to call me once and I came running.

'*There* you are! Were you having a little nap, babe? Maybe you won't be so grouchy now. Come on, sit yourself down and get tucked in.'

We all sat round the kitchen table, eating. Pixie never usually sat still. She'd grab a handful of food off her plate and run round the room with it, but now she sat up straight on the bench, scarcely wriggling. She stuck a roast potato on her fork and licked at it as if it was an ice lolly, making little murmurs of appreciation. Baxter stuffed his food down, chewing with his mouth open. Bliss ate daintily, careful not to let her chicken touch her potatoes, keeping her peas and carrots separate too, eating one tiny mouthful of each in turn. Mum didn't eat much herself, she just nibbled at a little bit of chicken.

'Who's going to pull the wishbone with me?' she said, hooking it out. 'Come on then, Lily – pull.'

I pulled and the little bone snapped.

'Oh, you've got the biggest piece. You get the wish,' said Mum.

I clasped the greasy little bone in my hand, closed my eyes, and wished hard.

Please don't let Mum go on holiday without us!

But after dinner she went to her room and started packing her case. Bliss and I lay on her bed, watching her. Baxter drove his fork-lift truck under her bed, crawling around in the dust. Pixie staggered about in Mum's high heels, getting in the way.

'I wish I had a decent bikini,' said Mum. 'Look, Lil, do you think my posh red bra and pants look a bit like a bikini?'

'No, they look like a bra and pants.'

'Oh well, I'll just have to buy myself a bikini when I'm there. What should I wear for the flight? Should I dress up in the grey dress to look my best – or dress down in jeans and a T-shirt, making out it's no big deal?'

'*I* don't know. Why don't you wear your red bra and pants?' I said.

'Ooh! You've still got the hump, then. Little Miss Camel, that's you,' said Mum. Then she blinked at me earnestly. 'Please don't spoil everything, Lily. Just wait till you get a boyfriend. Then you'll understand.'

'I'm not ever ever ever getting a boyfriend,' I said.

'Well, you can be an old maid then and not have any fun at all,' said Mum.

'It's not fun to go off and leave your kids,' I mumbled.

'I'm *not* leaving you, you nutcase. It's just for a few days, I keep *saying*. And Mikey will be looking after you. Shall I ring him now? No, maybe I'll leave it to the last second, just as I'm going – then he'll *have* to come, no arguing.'

'But, Mum—'

'And no arguing from you either. I've just about had a bellyful. You shut up.'

So that's what I did. I was so stupid. I should have argued like crazy. I should have begged and pleaded and cried. I should have frightened Bliss and made her cry too. I should have thrown my arms round Mum. I could have done so many different things to stop her all that Sunday, but I let her carry on packing and have another cup of tea and then do her make-up. She was ready to go, her denim jacket on, her newly washed hair brushed out, bobbing on her shoulders.

'OK, now I'll tackle Mikey,' she said, dialling.

She listened, then frowned. 'Oh dammit, it's his voicemail. Mikey? Listen, Mikey, it's me, Kate. Hey, you know you were saying you want to see the kids? Well, I've fixed it all up for you. You need to come over to my place as soon as you get this message. I'm going abroad for a few days with my new boyfriend – yeah, truly – so it's your turn to play Daddy for a while. The kids are so excited you'll be coming – aren't you, Baxter, mate?'

Baxter gave a whoop.

'Hear that? OK, Mikey, don't let me down, will you? Them kids mean all the world to me. Cheers.'

She clicked her phone off and looked at us, nibbling her lip.

'I want to talk to Dad,' said Baxter.

'No, love, I was just leaving him a message,' said Mum. She looked at me. 'So, can you be in charge of the kids just till Mikey gets here, Lil? Why does he have to have his phone switched off? Typical! Anyway, you'll be all right, won't you, Lily? He'll come round the minute he gets the message.'

'Mum—'

'You'll be fine, I know you will. And I'll phone you every day, I promise, just to check you're OK. And I'll bring you all a present when I come back. What would you like, Lily? *I* know, one of them Spanish dancer costumes. A red one, all over ruffles.'

'I don't want any present,' I said – though I'd always *loved* Spanish dancer costumes. I could *see* the red one with ruffles and I ached to own it.

'I want a dancer costume – a pink one!' said Pixie.

'Can I have blue?' said Bliss.

'I don't want a soppy costume,' said Baxter, disgusted.

'No, my little man, I'm going to get you a toy bull,

a great big black bull, and you can be the bull-fighter,' said Mum.

'Oh *yes*! A really fierce bull with horns, but I won't be afraid of it, will I?'

'You're not afraid of anything, my Baxie. Now you be a good boy for Mikey, and don't tease your sisters, you hear me? Bliss, you speak up for your-self if you want anything, and Mikey will do his best. Pixie, don't be a little pickle, you be a very, very good girl.' She kissed each of them and then threw her arms round me. 'I'll be back soon, Lily, I swear I will.'

Then she picked up her case and ran for it, out of the door. She didn't even give me a proper kiss. She was just suddenly gone. We heard her heels tap-tapping along the balcony.

Baxter and Bliss and Pixie all looked at me. It was as if they'd only just realized what was happening.

'Mum come back in a minute?' said Pixie.

'No, she's gone for a week now, nearly,' I said.

Pixie's bottom lip quivered. 'No, in a minute,' she said.

'Where's Dad then?' said Baxter, looking around as if he was hiding in a cupboard somewhere.

'He'll come when he gets Mum's message,' I said, my stomach churning.

'He won't bring his dog, will he?' said Bliss.

'I don't know.'

'Mum in a minute!' Pixie shouted at the top of her voice, over and over, as if she could make it come true if she said it enough times.

'Shut *up*, Pixie,' I said, picking her up, but she went on bellowing right in my face.

'Why isn't Dad coming yet?' Baxter asked, kicking the table leg.

'Why did Mum go without us?' Bliss said.

'*I don't know!*' I shouted, startling them all. Even Pixie was shocked into silence.

They all looked near tears, even Baxter. For a moment I hated all three of them. *I* wanted to shout and question and cry. I felt like sinking to my knees and howling like a baby. But I couldn't. I was the eldest. I had to look after them.

'Come on, you sillies. Let's – let's all do drawing. I'll give you each a page of my lovely new drawing pad, OK? Baxter, you can draw a big scary bull. Bliss, you can draw yourself dancing in a blue frilly dress with those clapper things in your hands – castanets. And Pixie, I'll help you draw – you can use my best crayons, OK? And while we're drawing we'll all have a bit of chocolate, Mum's got some in the cupboard.'

I got them all sitting up at the kitchen table drawing, great lumps of chocolate stoppering their mouths. Pixie drooled all down her chin as she scribbled.

I'd done it. I'd got them all happy and distracted for the third evening in a row. I tried to join in, drawing a whole troupe of Spanish dancers, but their legs wouldn't go right, kicking out at odd angles, while the chocolate covered my teeth and tongue in brown slime.

I kept picturing Mum in my head, meeting up with this Gordon, going off with him on the train to the airport, waiting for her flight. If I was thinking of her, why wasn't she thinking of me? Why didn't she suddenly think, *Oh my God, I can't leave Lily and Baxter and Bliss and Pixie – I especially can't leave them with Mikey*. Then surely she'd say to Gordon, *No, I'm sorry, I love you very much* (though she's only known him three days) *but I love my kids more, I have to go back.*

I made chicken sandwiches for our tea, then

found the little piece of wishbone and held it in my fist, wishing all over again. I imagined Mum suddenly rushing to get the train back. I went through every stage of the journey with her. It was so real inside my head that I almost heard her heels tap-tapping back along the balcony.

But she didn't come. And Mikey didn't come either. Baxter got more and more restless. He pretended to be a bull himself, his hands curved at the top of his head as horns, and then he ran round after the little girls, butting them. He wasn't really hurting them, but Bliss started crying, and Pixie fell over and cried too.

'You're all stupid sissy girls, you're no fun at all,' Baxter bellowed. 'You wait till my dad gets here. He'll play with me – us boys together, we'll sort you out.'

'Well, he's not here, is he, your precious dad? I'm glad, see, because we don't need Mikey bossing us around, do we, girls?' I said.

Bliss agreed. Pixie wasn't so certain.

'Growly bear Mikey,' she said, and then she started up her maddening chant.

I shut them all up by going into the kitchen and fetching down a big tin of peaches from the cupboard.

'But we've had our tea,' said Bliss. 'We had chicken sandwiches.'

'Well, we can have *another* tea, *if* you're all good,' I said.

'Can we have whirly cream too?' asked Baxter.

'We can have two squirts each,' I said. 'Though *I'm* doing the squirting, Baxter. And you all have to be sitting down properly at the table, quiet as mice.'

'Squeak, squeak, squeak,' said Baxter, being a very loud mouse.

We ate our peaches and cream. The kids were meant to savour them slowly as a special treat, but they swallowed them down in three or four gulps and then jumped up, on the rampage again. If I could only get them quietened down with food we'd have eaten everything in the cupboard by ten o'clock.

It was half-past eight now. I had to face it, Mum wasn't coming back. She was on her plane, maybe flying over our heads right this minute. And where was Mikey?

At that exact moment the phone rang. I ran to it, praying that it was Mum after all, coming back from the airport. No. It was Mikey.

'Lily? Look, hand me over to your mum. I've been trying to get her on her mobile but she's got it switched off. What's all this rubbish about a boyfriend?'

'She's gone on holiday with him.'

'No, she's not. You tell her to cancel all her daft plans, pronto. *I* can't take a week off and look after all you kids. Who does she think I am, Mary blooming Poppins? It just so happens I'm on the coach up to Glasgow at the moment. I'm going to be helping a mate with a building job for a couple of weeks. So tell her to get her skinny butt back home to look after my kids, OK?'

'But Mikey—'

'What?'

All I had to say was 'She's already gone.' That would have been enough. I couldn't stand Mikey and he couldn't stand me, but I knew he cared about Baxter and Bliss. He had a very soft spot for Pixie too. If I'd said we were all alone Mikey would doubtless curse and swear but he'd call his mate and get off the coach and come all the way back to look after us. But I didn't want him to come. When he was in a bad mood he frightened us all, even Baxter. He could turn so quickly. One minute he'd be laughing and tossing the kids up in the air, then one of them would splutter something silly or kick him accidentally, and his face would darken and he'd shout and smack. He hadn't smacked me for years because I was too quick and wary, but I caught him staring at me sometimes, his eyes darting this way and that as he looked me up and down. I knew he was waiting to get

70

me. I didn't want him here with no Mum around.

'Nothing, Mikey,' I said. 'OK. I'll tell Mum she can't go.'

'That's right. Where *is* she? Let me talk to her.'

'I can't, she's busy right now.'

'Busy with this boyfriend? You tell her to keep her mind on my kids, that's what she's there for.'

'I'll tell her,' I said, and then I pressed the off button on the phone. I could hear the dialling tone. I said into the mouthpiece, 'I'll tell her you're a horrible pig and I hate you and I'm not having you come and look after us. You can't even look after yourself, you drunken slob. You make me sick sick sick.'

Baxter was in the kitchen squirting Pixie with the cream, but Bliss was in the doorway. Her mouth was wide open, listening to me.

'There, goodbye now,' I said. I held the receiver over to Bliss. 'Do you want to say anything to your dad?'

Bliss backed away, shaking her head.

'OK then,' I said, and put the phone down. Bliss was staring at me like I'd slain all the dragons, drowned the wicked witches and chopped off all the ogres' heads in her fairy-tale book.

'So Dad's not coming?' she whispered, breathing out.

'Nope. We don't want him, do we?' I said.

'Nope,' said Bliss, copying me. Then she looked over her shoulder. 'Baxter wants him.'

'Oh, Baxter,' I said airily. 'I'll take care of him.'

I went into the kitchen and grabbed the cream can, clonking it on Baxter's head.

'Stop it! Look at all that cream you've wasted! Poor Pixie!'

'It's not wasted, we can lick it off her,' said Baxter, trying to grab hold of her.

'Don't be so disgusting! Pixie, I'm going to have to dunk you in the bath. Come on, you can all have a bath, and we'll play it's the seaside and we'll put all the ducks and the fish in too. Oh, by the way, Baxter, your dad sends you a big hug and says he can't come this week, he's busy up in Glasgow, but he'll come and see you soon, OK?'

Baxter halted in his tracks.

'Dad's not coming?' he said, and he suddenly looked as little as Pixie.

'Yeah, but it's OK, I'm here. I'll look after you. It's going to be ever such fun, I promise. Come on, kids, it's swimming time. Let me run that bath.'

I herded them into the bathroom, letting them select mad armfuls of stuff to take in the bath with them: a bouncy ball; a plastic doll; empty milk cartons; even a teapot. By the time all three kids were squeezed into the bath too it was literally standing room only. But that made it better. They shouted and splashed and squealed, forgetting all about Mikey. They really seemed happy to accept that I was in charge.

The bathroom got completely soaked and Baxter was so excited he threw all the towels in the water too, so I eventually had to mop them dry with old jumpers. It didn't really matter, he seemed happy enough. When I tucked him up in bed he did murmur, 'Is Dad coming tomorrow, then?'

'No, he's up in Glasgow, remember? I'll be your dad, Baxter.' I made my voice go really deep and growly. *'Now then, son, settle down or I'll give you what-for.'* I didn't sound remotely like Mikey but it made Baxter laugh and then snuggle down to sleep. Pixie went out like a light, having stayed up way past her bedtime three nights in a row. Even Bliss seemed fast asleep when I crept in later to check on her.

I was the only one wide awake. I felt like reading so I went into Mum's room so as not to waken the kids. This was a mistake. I looked around at all of Mum's things – her jewellery hanging from her mirror, old scent bottles and powder puffs and make-up scattered messily over her dressing table, a little pile of tights and pants strewn in a corner.

I held Mum's big hairbrush and carefully unpicked strands of Mum's blonde hair, then rubbed them together to make one soft little lock. I tucked it in my pyjama pocket and got into her bed to read. The sheets and pillows smelled of Mum's scent. I buried my nose in them, breathing in deeply.

I had to sit up properly and start reading quick to stop myself crying. Bliss's old fairy tales were strangely comforting. Mothers sent their children off into wild woods where there were wolves, they locked them up at the top of towers, they poisoned them with apples. No fairy-tale child would so much as raise an eyebrow at a mother going off on holiday for a week. Maybe it was no big deal at all. Maybe heaps of mothers did the same and nobody let on.

I decided I'd have to be very careful at school tomorrow. But what about Bliss and Baxter? I knew just how much it would worry Bliss. If you told her to keep a secret she'd clamp her lips together and do her very best, but if questioned she'd flush a raw red and she'd start trembling. Whereas Baxter could never keep anything quiet. If you specifically told him not to mention something he'd shout it out at the top of his voice. And what about Pixie? She'd started going to nursery now, and every morning their nice soft teacher sat them in a circle and they had special Talking Time. Little girls and boys said that it was their birthday or Daddy's car broke down or their brother's hamster had died. Pixie would be bursting to tell her news: *My mum's gone on holiday with her new boyfriend and my stepdad can't come to look after us so we're all alone.* I could just *hear* her blurting it all out.

I was ready for them the next morning. I'd fallen asleep in Mum's bed and they all came tumbling in, Pixie just in her T-shirt.

'She wet her bed,' said Baxter sternly. 'She's dirty and smelly.'

'No, I'm not. I didn't wet my cot. Bliss climbed in and did it,' said Pixie firmly.

'I didn't, I didn't!' said Bliss, appalled.

'I know. Never mind, Pixie, we'll change your sheets. Come in Mum's bed and have a cuddle just now.'

'But it's late, Lily, we're going to be late. It's half-past eight,' said Bliss. 'We have to go to school *quick*.'

'No, we don't,' I said taking her by the wrist and pulling her into bed with me. 'We don't have to go to school quick, we don't have to go to school slow, because we're not going to school at all.'

That made them stare.

'Is it a holiday?' said Baxter.

'Yes, hurray, hurray!' I said.

Bliss was frowning anxiously.

'I don't think it *is* a holiday,' she said. 'We've had half-term already.'

'It's *our* holiday. Mum's on holiday so we're on holiday too. We can do whatever we like today. No boring old school, yippee. So we can all snuggle up and have a lovely lie-in.'

'Yuck, I'm not doing sissy snuggling,' said Baxter. 'So what are we going to do, then? Can we go to Chessington World of Adventures? That's where all the boys in my class go on their holidays.'

'Yeah, well, if you've got the money, Baxter, I'll take you,' I said.

'If my dad was here he'd take us,' said Baxter. 'I want to go on that ride that goes swoop swoop and then turns you upside down.'

'Oh, *this* ride,' I said, grabbing him round the waist and tipping him up so he was dangling in mid-air.

Baxter squealed and I shook him and then dropped him carefully on the bed.

'Me now, me now!' Pixie squealed.

'Don't do me, please don't!' said Bliss.

'Yeah, but where *will* we go?' Baxter persisted, his voice muffled by the pillow.

'Well, we'll go to the adventure playground,' I said.

Baxter cheered, but Bliss looked worried.

'What about the big boys?'

The last time we'd gone there after school there were seven or eight boys hanging out there, drinking and smoking and swearing as they mucked about in the kids' den. Baxter had run up the ramp fearlessly to join them, but they'd thrown a lager can at him and pushed him over. I'd gone to rescue him and they'd thrown cans at me too, and said all sorts of horrid stuff. When I got all the kids home I'd sworn we'd never go there again – though Baxter moaned and complained, saying he *wanted* to go and play with the big boys.

'The big boys won't be there just now,' I said.

'Will they be at school?' Bliss asked.

I nodded, though I was pretty sure they weren't the sort of boys who *went* to school. Still, I knew they stayed up half the night, so they'd likely be fast asleep till lunchtime.

'And we're really really really not going to school?' said Bliss. 'Won't we get into trouble?'

'No, I told you, we're on holiday. Now all go and get dressed. Pixie, I'd better dunk you in the bath.'

I served them cereal for breakfast and I let them put extra sugar on their Frosties. While they were all happily crunching away in the kitchen I went into the living room and picked up the phone. I dialled Mum's mobile. I wasn't going to tell her about Mikey. I just wanted to tell her we were all OK – and I needed to check she was fine too. But dialling didn't get me anywhere. I just heard a recorded message: *I'm sorry, it has not been possible to connect your call.*

I tried again, just to check, and got the same message. Mum must have her mobile switched off. *Too busy with Gordon,* I thought, clenching my fists.

'Lily?' Bliss was standing at the door.

I slammed the phone down quickly.

'Were you ringing Mum?' Bliss whispered.

'She's having a lovely time on holiday and says she hopes we're having a happy holiday too,' I said quickly. 'Bliss, you've got bright purple lips.'

'Baxter poured us some Ribena.'

'You're meant to *dilute* it. Haven't you lot had *enough* sugar? Your teeth will be black by the time Mum comes back.'

'Lily, *is* Mum coming back?'

'Of course she is,' I said, and I made myself laugh. 'Honestly, Bliss, you're hopeless. You always have to get in such a state over things. You're such a baby!'

I was being horrible to her simply because she'd said aloud the thing that was starting to worry me dreadfully. It made me feel momentarily better to pour scorn on her. It was as if I was mocking my own worries and it might help make them go away. But then I saw Bliss's poor little face, her eyes watery with tears, and I felt terrible.

I flew across the room and put my arms round her.

'I'm sorry, I'm sorry, please don't cry. I don't know how I could have been so horrid. Here, Bliss, you get your own back. Say something really mean and spiteful to me.

Go on, say it.'

Bliss fidgeted. 'Come *on*, Bliss.'

'I can't think of anything,' she said. 'But don't be cross again, Lily, please.'

'It's OK. I promise I won't be cross again.'

'Ever?'

'Well. I can't really promise that.'

'All right, promise you won't be cross again this week,' said Bliss.

'I promise,' I said, and we stood quietly together, still hugging hard.

Then I heard a great swooshing sound from the kitchen. It sounded horribly like someone tipping the whole jumbo packet of Frosties onto a plate.

'I *will* get cross with Baxter though,' I said, running into the kitchen. 'Baxter, for goodness' *sake*. Tip them back in the packet.'

'I wanted to see how many bowlfuls there were,' he said. 'I'm still hungry.'

'No, you're not, you're *greedy*. Come on, help me

clear up, you lot, then we'll go to the adventure playground.'

Baxter made himself scarce at once, and I had to stop Pixie helping after she dropped a plate, but Bliss was very obliging.

'Good girl, Bliss. You can take Headless to the playground.'

Headless was Bliss's favourite cuddly teddy. She slept with him in her arms but Mum never let her take him out because he looked so awful. He used to be called Whitey because he was a polar bear, but now he was a sickly yellow-grey. He really *was* headless. Baxter had tried to tug him out of Bliss's grasp and his head had come right off. Mum had tried to sew it back on but she couldn't stitch it tight enough. His head wobbled alarmingly and fell off again when we were crossing a road – and a car ran over it. Mum wanted to put the rest of Headless in the bin but Bliss wouldn't hear of it. She loved him more than ever now he was mangled.

'I want *my* teddy,' said Pixie.

'Yes, we can take all the teddies – we can have a teddy bears' picnic!'

I wrapped all the battered animals in Pixie's old cot blanket and took the rest of the Frosties, a packet of Jammy Dodgers and a bottle of Coke from the kitchen. Pixie ran along beside me, wanting to add all sorts of weird stuff.

'Let's take a chair for all the teddies to sit on! Let's take the teapot so the mummy teddy can have tea! Let's take the washing-up bowl so we can do the washing up! Oh, let's take the washing-up squirty thing so we can make bubbles!'

Bliss and Baxter could barely talk when they were Pixie's age, they just mumbled together in their own twin language. I started to wish Pixie was a twin too – she was like a little woodpecker drilling into my brain. Still, it stopped me thinking too much. I was learning that the trick to stop feeling scared was to keep busy busy busy.

So I carted the teddies and their picnic to the door and sent the kids off to the toilet to do a wee because I didn't want to get all the way to the playground and then have to trail back almost immediately because of an urgent call of nature. I was actually pulling the front door shut behind us when I suddenly stiffened. The door key! I felt sick. The flats seemed to slip sideways, as if there was a sudden earthquake in south-west London.

Mum had gone off with her handbag – and the keys were in a little pouch inside. Had she taken them with her? I rushed back inside, leaving Baxter and Bliss playing with the fork-lift truck, while

81

Pixie started setting up a preliminary picnic on the doorstep. I looked on the coffee table, on the kitchen worktop, in all Mum's drawers in the bedroom. I couldn't find a spare key anywhere.

Mikey still had a set of keys, I knew that, and hated the way he could burst in on us any time he wanted. But he was in Glasgow now, so couldn't help out.

What were we going to do? We couldn't stay stuck inside the flat till the weekend. And what if Mum didn't come back then?

I knew you could get new keys made, but you had to have another set to copy. You could get a whole new lock with a set of new keys – folk were doing it all the time on our estate to keep people out – but that cost a lot of money. We didn't have any money, apart from a few pennies to rattle in an old piggy bank.

'Come *on*, Lily, we want to go to the playground!' Baxter shouted.

'The bears are hungry, They're growling, grrr, grrr, grrr,' said Pixie.

'I'm *coming*,' I said.

I couldn't keep them in. They'd be like wild bears themselves by lunchtime.

I put the door on the latch and pulled it closed. I looked up and down the balcony to see if anyone was watching. If any kids saw they could get in they'd steal stuff and trash the flat. I stood biting my thumbnail. Still, we didn't really *have* any stuff worth stealing. And the three kids had done a pretty good job of trashing the flat already, especially Baxter. We still had his purple crayon marks all over the walls and a great hole in the plaster where he'd bashed into it trying to skateboard. Bliss hadn't made any marks, but there were lots of discoloured patches on the pale carpet where Pixie had peed, just like a little puppy marking her territory.

I gave the door another pull and set off down the balcony.

'Come on, you lot,' I said.

I put my finger to my lips as we passed Old Kath's flat. We all went on tiptoe – but Kath's got these great bat ears that are always flap-flap-flapping. There was a tap from inside her kitchen window. I pretended not to hear and pushed everyone past, but Kath was at her front door while I was still trudging for the lift.

'Hey, you kids,' she yelled, and she caught hold of Pixie. She moved quicker than a rattlesnake for all she'd got a zimmer frame.

Pixie gave a little squeal. Old Kath kept hold of her firmly with her gnarled old fingers and made ridiculous coochy-coo noises as if Pixie was a little baby instead of a person.

'How's my little angel then?' said Old Kath.

'She's fine. The lift's here. Come on, Pixie,' I said urgently.

'Where are you going?' Old Kath asked, still with Pixie in her clutches.

'We're going to the adventure playground and I'm going to be boss of the whole den,' said Baxter. 'I'll shoot anyone who comes near,' he said, turning his arms into a machine gun and making mad ack-ack-ack noises.

'That's not very nice,' said Old Kath, because he was clearly aiming straight at her. 'Why aren't you kids in school? It *is* Monday, isn't it, girlie?' she said to Bliss.

Bliss looked agonized and said nothing.

'Yeah, it's Monday, but we've got an Inset day off school so the teachers can have a staff meeting,' I gabbled.

'Honestly! They never had that sort of thing when I was at school,' said Old Kath. She looked up the balcony towards our front door. 'Where's your mum, then?'

'Oh, she's just gone down the stairs. She doesn't like to use the lift because it's so smelly,' I lied.

'Yes, it's them wretched lads. They pee there on

purpose,' said Old Kath. She glared at Baxter. 'Don't let me catch *you* weeing in the lift, young man.'

'No, I'll wee on you instead,' said Baxter.

Old Kath gasped. I grabbed Baxter and shook him hard.

'Oh, wait till I tell your mum on you!' said Old Kath. She clutched her zimmer frame and hobbled to the edge of the balcony.

'Where is she, then?' she said, peering down.

'Oh, maybe she's gone to buy some cigarettes. We'll catch up with her. Say sorry, Baxter, and come *on*.'

I pinched his arm really hard so that he blurted out a mumble that could have been sorry. Then I picked up Pixie and made a run for the lift, Bliss leaping after me, terrified of being left behind. We were in the lift before Old Kath could stop us.

'You *hurt* me, you mean pig,' Baxter whined, examining the red mark on his arm.

'Yeah, well, I *meant* to hurt you. All of you, I *told* you to keep quiet going past Old Kath's. She'll still be squawking about telling Mum when we come back. She might even come stomping along to our flat, and *then* what are we going to do?'

'Tell her to bog off,' said Baxter.

'Stop that silly talk right this minute, Baxter,' I said, putting my face up close to his. 'If she finds out Mum's gone she'll tell someone. Maybe she'll even go

85

down the council office and send a social worker to see us.'

'Well, we'll tell *them* to bog off,' said Baxter, laughing stupidly.

'Yes, and *then* they'll lock us all up in a children's home,' I said, as we clattered out of the lift. '*Separate* ones. And you'll probably end up in a special strict one for bad boys.'

'Good, see if I care,' Baxter shouted, but he was looking scared now.

Bliss took hold of his hand and he didn't pull it away.

'Mum's coming back by Saturday,' she said.

'Yes, but the social workers will think she's an unfit mother because she left us,' I said. 'You don't get it, any of you, do you?'

They all stared up at me, eyes big, faces white – and I felt terrible for frightening them so.

'But it's all right, everything will be fine, so long as you're good and keep quiet when I say. Now, come on, we'll go to the playground.'

We had the adventure playground all to ourselves, apart from one girl who had taken her baby there. The baby was asleep in his buggy, his head lolling. The girl swung listlessly backwards and forwards, looking half asleep too.

I wondered if Mum and I had looked like that once. I suddenly wanted Mum so much. I wanted to crouch down and whimper like Pixie when she's tired, but I made myself organize the kids instead. I let Baxter stagger up the slide to the makeshift den on top. It was just a few planks of wood but it was where the

big boys hung out. Baxter whooped triumphantly
when he found a cigarette butt and a crumpled can
of beer. He squatted up at the top, cigarette in one
hand, beer in the other, yelling, 'I'm the boss of this
den!'

Pixie wanted to clamber up after him and perch
there too with her teddies and all the paraphernalia
from home, but I knew Baxter wouldn't want to
share.

'I know a *much* better place for our picnic,' I said,
and I spread out the rug on the top of the little roundabout. I hoisted Pixie up on top and helped Bliss after
her. I felt foolish getting the teddies all settled too,
glancing at the girl with the baby, but she didn't seem
the slightest bit interested. So we sat and spun slowly
round and round and round, propelled by my foot.

'More, more, roundy roundy,' Pixie yelled every
time we slowed to a halt. Then she decided she felt
sick and giddy. Headless had the same problem. Pixie
grabbed him and made him throw up.

'How can he be sick when he hasn't got a *head*?'
said Bliss.

'He can't *help* not having a head. And he's still very
very sick – listen,' said Pixie. She was making
Headless make horribly realistic noises.

'I think I feel sick too,' said Bliss, holding her
stomach.

'No you don't. No one feels sick any more,' I said firmly, 'because it's time for the picnic.'

I got the Frosties and Jammy Dodgers and started sharing them out, giving tiny portions to each teddy too. Baxter came tumbling down from his den, demanding his own share, and some for his fork-lift truck. He was still clinging to his soggy cigarette and can of beer.

'Throw them *away*, they're disgusting,' I said. 'You don't know who's had their mouths all round them.'

'Yes, I do. It was one of the big boys – Jacko or Lenny or Big Boots – I'm in their gang now,' said Baxter.

'You wish,' I said.

'I *am*. I'm the boss of this whole den,' said Baxter. 'I'm your boss, Lily Green, and you have to do exactly what I say.' He kicked at me and hurt my leg. I decided to teach him a lesson.

'OK then,' I said submissively.

'What?'

'*You're* the boss, Baxter. You can tell us all what to do and when to eat and all that stuff. You're in charge now.'

'Yeah, *I'm* the boss,' Baxter said, kicking his heels.

'Are you listening, Bliss and Pixie?' I said. 'We all have to do what Baxter says now. He's looking after us. He's going to tell us what to do.'

'You bet I am,' said Baxter, but he sounded un-
certain. He bashed his can of beer on the planks of
wood. 'You girls just do what I say, OK?'

'OK, boss,' I said, and Bliss and Pixie said it too.
We all looked at Baxter.

'Yeah,' he said again, and started picking his nose.
He looked at me as if he wanted me to tell him he was
being disgusting. I just raised my eyebrows and
whistled casually. I made a little crumb meal for all
the teddies.

'Is Headless feeling like eating now?' I asked, and
Bliss nodded yes.

We three girls helped all the teddies have their
picnic too. Then we let them slump over, sleeping it
off. We slumped too.

Baxter was watching us.

'What shall we do now?' he said.

'Well, you've got to say. You're the boss,' I said.

'Yes. Well. We'll . . .' Baxter looked all round for
inspiration. 'We can have some more food,' he said
eventually, licking his finger and dabbing up a few
biscuit crumbs.

'Good idea, boss. So where are we going to get it
from?' I said.

'We'll steal it,' said Baxter, looking fierce.

He looked over at the girl with her sleepy baby in
the buggy.

'I bet they've got biscuits,' he said.

'OK. Go and steal them then,' I said.

Baxter swallowed. He looked hard at the girl. She was twice his size and was frowning. She looked like she'd slap him one if he even dared speak to her.

'Maybe I'm not really hungry,' said Baxter. 'This is *boring*,' he said. 'You be the boss now, Lily. You tell us what we're going to do.'

I had it all figured out. It had just suddenly occurred to me. I was so excited by the idea. I had little goosebumps all the way up and down my arms.

'We'll go to the park,' I said.

'What park? Parks are boring, boring, boring,' said Baxter.

'Not *this* park. The great park we can see from the flats. The one with all the hills and trees.'

Baxter stared at me. So did Bliss.

They'd come up to the top-floor balcony with me, they'd seen the hills and trees for themselves, but it was like something they'd seen on television.

'Can we really get to *that* park?' said Bliss.

'Of course we can,' I said, though I'd never really thought about it before. Mum had never taken us – but Mum didn't wear the right shoes for parks. She either wore her high heels or flip-flop sandals in summer that let in all the grit and stones and made her swear.

'Do you know the way, Lily?' said Bliss.

'Of course I do,' I said.

Well, I thought I did. Our flats seemed almost next door to the park when you looked from the top balcony. But down on the ground I wasn't really sure how to find it. I knew the way to the bus stop to get into town, I knew how to get to the chippy and the sweet shop, I knew how to get to school – so I reckoned if I turned the *other* way we'd find ourselves in the park in no time.

Perhaps it would have been easier on my own. It was hard work herding Baxter and Bliss along, especially with all the teddies and teapots and stuff, and I didn't have Pixie's buggy so I had to carry her half the way.

'Where *is* the park then?' said Baxter, peering all round. 'This is all just houses.'

'Yes, it's right down this road, I'm sure of it,' I said, but we trailed up roads, down roads, all over, and still couldn't find it.

'Are we lost?' said Bliss anxiously.

'Of course we're not lost,' I said, but my heart started thumping hard in my chest. We hadn't found the park and now I wasn't certain how to find our way back to the flats.

'Should we ask someone?' Bliss suggested.

'No! They'll wonder why we're not in school,' I said.

They didn't look the right sort of people to ask anyway. They weren't ordinary people out here. They were all very posh people: this old lady cutting flowers in her garden in her funny padded waistcoat, and this old man getting into his shiny car, and this big woman striding along in her checked shirt and ironed jeans taking her lollopy Labrador for a walk . . .

Ah!

'We'll follow that lady,' I said.

She marched down the road, turned left, the dog straining forward eagerly. I saw iron gates right up at the end of the road.

'*There's* the park!' I said.

There was an ice-cream van parked by the gates and all three of the kids clamoured for a whippy, but I didn't have any money. Pixie started howling, kicking me hard as I held her.

'I want an ice cream!' she wailed, her mouth square with grief.

'Stop that kicking, it hurts! Look, Pixie, we're going in the park now. Isn't it lovely?'

'No, it's horrid, I don't like the park, I like *ice cream*,' Pixie yelled, still kicking – but after a minute or so she calmed down and started staring around, astonished.

'Shh now,' I said. 'See, it *is* lovely here.'

We seemed to have stepped straight from the town to the countryside. I'd never seen so much green before, all different shades of green, from the leaves, the ferns, the grass. Even the birds squawking above our heads were green, flocks of parakeets. It wasn't flat and boring like other parks. There was a big hill right in front of us with a pebbly path leading upwards.

'Come on, race you to the top,' said Baxter.

He started scrambling upwards. Of course he got there long before us because all he had to carry was his fork-lift truck. I had Pixie, who was still refusing to walk, and Bliss lugged the blanket full of teddies. The teapot fell out of the blanket halfway up and broke its spout and handle.

'Oh look!' said Bliss, panicking. 'Mum will be so cross!'

'No, she won't, she hardly ever uses it,' I said quickly.

'Can't we mend it?'

'It looks too broken,' I said. 'But never mind.' I kicked the teapot hard into the bushes. 'There! It's gone now. It's not a teapot any more. It's a little home for a hedgehog or a squirrel, OK? Don't look so worried, Bliss, Mum won't ever know.'

I dumped Pixie, gave Bliss a quick hug, then held my sisters' hands and pulled them up to the top of the hill where Baxter was waiting for us, scarlet and triumphant.

'I won, I won! You're all slowcoaches. I got here *ages* ago! And look, there are animals!'

We were standing on a grassy plain and only a little way away a large herd of red deer were staring at us, blinking their big brown eyes. There were several deer who stood tensely, their noses in the air, but most of them went on munching grass, flicking their strange little tails. They were mostly females with their young, beautiful little fawns that danced about, but there was one big stag with great antlers growing out of his head like massive branches.

'Will he hurt us?' Bliss whispered, clutching me.

'I don't think so,' I said.

'Lovely doggies,' said Pixie, and she started running towards them fearlessly.

'No, Pixie, stop,' I said, catching her by the back of her T-shirt. 'Don't – you're startling them. Don't make them run away.'

'I *want* them to run,' said Baxter. 'And I'll run after them and I'll get a long stick and spear them and kill them all dead.'

'Stop it, you monster, you can't want to kill them, they're *beautiful*,' I said.

'Yes, I do. You hunt deer, I know you do, and I'm a hunter,' said Baxter, swaggering about, miming his spear – but when the stag raised his huge head and took one step towards us, Baxter clutched my hand tightly and pressed up against me.

'He's coming to get us!' Bliss squealed.

'No, he's not, he's just looking at us to see we're OK – and we *are*,' I said. 'Let's sit down and stay quiet and watch them.'

We sat down and counted them – well, three of us did. Pixie had no idea about numbers and went 'One, two, three, twenty, a hundred.' The deer kept moving around so we all got muddled. There were about thirty altogether. Bliss and I tried to sort them into families. I rather liked the idea of having lots of mothers and children all living together with just one father.

We started choosing names for some of them. I chose Brown Eyes and Bramble and Moonbeam and Fleetfoot and Apple and Treewind and Jumper and Snufflenose and Wagtail. Baxter called the stag King and the others Soldier and Sailor and Badboy and Fighter and Kung Fu and Bighead and Gnasher and Fang, all boys' names, though I kept telling him they were girls. Bliss chose real girls' names – Judy and Shelley and Katy and Claire and Ella and Sarah and Hannah and Lizzie and Mandy. We let Pixie choose names for the smallest – Fluffy and Muffy and Duffy.

We couldn't really keep track of which was which,

apart from the stag and the small ones, but it was a good game, and we repeated our own names over and over so that we would remember them.

Then a man walked past with a dog. It was on a lead but it barked at the deer and they all ran off, King and all his ladies and children. We stood up and ran after them, but they were much faster than we were. We followed them through the trees and then onto another grassy plain where there were lots of little grey rabbits popping in and out of their burrows.

'Oh, a rabbit, *please*, Lily, can we have a rabbit?' Bliss begged.

'I'll catch you one,' said Baxter, but thank goodness he was nowhere near quick enough.

We carried on walking through more trees. Some of them were very old and gnarled, with strange knots and warty bits so they looked like faces.

'They're just like the trees in my fairy-tale book,' said Bliss. 'Can we play we're princesses, Lily?'

'Of course we can, Princess Bliss,' I said. 'We're three enchanted princesses dancing through the forest and Baxter's a handsome prince.'

'No, I'm not, I'm a big bad ogre and I'm going to stamp and stomp after all you silly princesses and bash you with my stick and bake you in a pot and eat you for my supper,' said Baxter.

'No, no, you can be an ogre, but you bang your head on the topmost branches of the tree because you're so tall and you fall down bleeding all over the place, wailing and moaning, and we princesses take pity on you. We dip our petticoats in a handy stream and wash the blood away and put special herbs on your gaping wound and bandage you up with more petticoats and you're so grateful you become our friend and protect us when we all go on our journey,' I said, and we acted it out, even Pixie.

Several times people walking their dogs came by and smiled – but one woman stopped and stood watching us. I heard my voice go all high and silly, worried that she'd think me such a baby for playing pretend fairy stories.

'That sounds a fun game,' she said. 'But why aren't you in school?'

I felt my cheeks flushing and I saw the others go red too. Baxter clenched his fists and I knew he was going to blurt out something cheeky, which would be a big mistake.

'We've had chicken pox,' I said quickly. 'We're better now, but still not well enough to go to school.'

'Oh goodness, chicken pox,' she said. She was peering at us. 'I can't see any scabs.'

'I said, we're almost better now.'

'But are you playing all alone?'

'No, no, our mum's here with us,' I said.

The woman looked around.

'Where is she?'

I wished Baxter was a real ogre and could simply kill her with his stick.

'She's over there,' I said, waving vaguely. Then inspiration struck. 'She told us not to talk to strangers so we've got to go now. Come on, you three.'

'Well, that's very sensible,' said the woman. 'Though of course, I don't mean you any harm.'

'Yes, but Mum says you can't trust anyone nowadays,' I said. 'Come on, you lot, let's run back to Mum.'

I grabbed Pixie and started running. Thank goodness Baxter and Bliss ran along beside us. I was scared the woman would run right after us, but she was quite old, and thank goodness she didn't even try.

'Keep running,' I panted, wanting to be sure, so we ran and ran down sandy paths through the trees until the woman was no longer in sight.

'I . . . can't!' Bliss puffed.

'OK, we can have a little rest now,' I said, and we all leaned against a big oak tree, gasping.

'Nosy old bat,' said Baxter at last.

'Yes, wasn't she?'

'But you told her, Lily.'

'Yes, I did, didn't I!'

'Where's Mum?' said Pixie, peering all around.

'Oh, darling, Mum's not really here, I was just pretending to that lady.'

'I *want* Mum,' said Pixie.

'I want Mum too,' Bliss whispered.

Baxter didn't say anything, but he started kicking the tree, his face screwed up.

'I know,' I said. 'I want Mum too. But she'll be back soon. She's having a lovely holiday – and so are we, aren't we? *Aren't we?*'

They all nodded solemnly at me because I was asking so fiercely.

'Let's walk on a bit, then. I'm sure that nosy old lady's gone now,' I said.

We set off again, Pixie walking, thank goodness. She kept stopping to examine stones or pick a dandelion, but at least I didn't have to lug her about. Bliss was the one who was floundering, staggering along with Headless and all his friends.

'Come here, let me carry that lot for you,' I said. 'Shall I carry you too, Bliss?'

I was joking but she looked hopeful.

'Oh dear, I can't really, you're too big now,' I said. 'Come on, let's just walk together.'

'Where are we walking *to*?' Bliss asked.

'Well, we're princesses in the enchanted forest, and we're trying to find . . .' I looked around wildly. There was an iron railing on the left, enclosing thick woods and shrubs. I saw a flash of pink far away. 'We're trying to find the magic garden,' I said.

Then further up I saw an ornate black gate.

'There we are, there's the gate! We've found it! Come on, let's see if we can get inside.'

We went through the gate. It was as if we really were in a magic garden. It seemed much quieter than the rest of the park, but the birds were singing louder. A flock of green parakeets circled over our heads, screeching at us. We held hands and walked down one of the stony paths. Suddenly we were surrounded by colour, deep red, scarlet, orange, apricot, pink and purple, flowers in long hedges, flowers in bushes, flowers in trees. They were all different flowers but I didn't know their names.

'They're magic roses,' I said. 'Aren't they beautiful? And they're blooming just for us!'

We walked slowly down the path admiring the flowers, almost on tiptoe. Even Baxter seemed awed, pressing his nose against the blossoms.

'Watch out a bee doesn't go up your nostril!' I said.

'Can we pick the flowers, Lily?' asked Pixie.

'No, absolutely not, then they won't be magic any more,' I said.

She ran ahead. A stream trickled beneath the flower hedges, with wooden footbridges. Pixie skipped onto one and then put her foot out tentatively.

'Paddle?' she said.

'No, it's a magic stream. If you paddle in it you could turn into a duck. Look, see those poor silly children – they've all been turned into ducks.'

I pointed to several mallards quacking further up the stream. Pixie put her foot back on the bridge, sharpish. We found a real duckpond further into the garden, and then another right at the end, with a huge weeping willow. We hid under its long trailing branches and pretended it was our cave. There were more people at this end of the garden, old couples walking very slowly round the pond and feeding the ducks. I knew they could still see us through the green fronds but they didn't try to talk to us.

'Isn't it lovely to see the kiddies playing here?' one old man remarked to his wife, and she agreed happily.

A group of younger women with buggies came along and spread themselves out on a sunny patch of grass, unpacking a picnic. We peeped out at them enviously as they shared sandwiches and gave their babies carrot sticks and little tubs of yoghurt.

'*I* want some,' said Pixie. 'Where's *our* picnic?'

We'd long since eaten the biscuits and the Frosties.

'I'm hungry too,' said Bliss.

'I'm *starving*,' said Baxter.

They looked at me as if they expected me to magic a picnic out of thin air.

'We're going to have magic food,' I said. 'Look, we've got a set of solid gold plates and they're full to the brim of beautiful fruits and we've got goblets of magic lemonade—'

'You're talking rubbish,' Baxter interrupted. 'I don't want silly magic stuff, I want something *real*.'

'Don't be so rude and ungrateful. I'm trying my best,' I said.

'Ask them ladies for some of their food. Go on,' said Baxter.

'Don't be silly. I can't possibly,' I said. 'Stop thinking of your stomach and play the game.'

'I don't want to play your stupid games,' said Baxter, and he hit me with his fork-lift truck.

But we got lucky. One of the toddlers was in a bad mood too. He started whingeing and fussing and tried to snatch another baby's banana. His mother tutted and took the banana away, so he threw himself down on the grass and kicked and screamed.

'That baby's hurting my head,' said Bliss, her hands over her ears.

'He's so naughty,' said Pixie smugly.

One of the little babies started wailing too. The mothers shook their heads and sighed and started gathering up their stuff and slotting the babies back in their buggies. The toddler was still screaming, arching his back and refusing to co-operate.

'You did that when you were little,' I told Baxter. 'It used to drive Mum demented.'

'Yeah, I bet I really yelled,' said Baxter proudly.

One of the mothers was gathering up the picnic. She tossed all the sandwiches, the half-eaten yoghurts, the banana skins and carrot sticks, the crumbling rusks and half-sucked oranges into one big carrier bag – and then she crammed it in the rubbish bin! We all stared. The moment they were moving, a wagon train of buggies, babies and bags, Baxter was *off*, darting to the bin and yanking out their discarded picnic.

He brought it back under our willow tree and I started reassembling it on the ground.

'But it's got all muddled up. There's yoghurt on this sandwich and biscuit crumbs everywhere,' said Bliss. 'We can't eat it like that.'

'Of course we can,' I said. 'Don't you think all your food gets muddled up in your tummy?'

'Yes, but I don't have to see it like that,' said Bliss.

I found her a totally pristine sandwich and an

untouched yogurt and she was happy. Baxter, Pixie and I were less picky and ate the rest between us.

'This is better than all that magic mucking about,' said Baxter, with his mouth full.

When we'd finished every last scrap we lay down, Pixie's head on my tummy, the twins either side. The girls fell asleep. Baxter mumbled quietly, driving his truck up and down my legs. I dozed a little myself, happy in the magic garden.

Pixie woke me up when she wanted to do a wee. I let her go behind a bush. Baxter went too, but Bliss was too bashful to do likewise. She pretended she didn't need to go, but got very pink and fidgety. Luckily when we went wandering back to the front of the garden we found a little toilet cabin, so she and I could go in comfortable privacy. We played a game of hide-and-seek amongst all the rosy bushes, Pixie and I playing against Baxter and Bliss, and then we ran races up and down the stream, charging across the little wooden bridges.

Most of the people in the garden smiled, but one old man with binoculars made shushing noises at us.

'You'll frighten all the birds away,' he said.

The birds didn't seem the slightest bit frightened, screeching above our heads.

'I love love love this garden,' I said, and the others agreed.

'Can we come here again tomorrow?' said Bliss.

'Yes, of course we can.'

'And the next day and the next?'

'You bet. And we'll carry on coming here when Mum comes home.'

'Will Mum love it too?' said Bliss.

'Well . . .'

'Never mind, you can be our mum in the park,' she said.

It was a mistake talking about Mum though. We all started missing her a lot. Pixie started grizzling, Baxter started showing off and swearing, and Bliss started biting her nails.

'Come on, we're all tired. Let's go home now,' I said. 'It's OK, I promise we'll come back tomorrow.'

We found our way to the garden gate easily enough, but we got lost going through the proper park. We were wandering for ages through the trees, up and down hills, never finding the right path. I tried to turn it into a game but I was tired too, and soon I started snapping at all three of them. I couldn't carry Pixie any more and dragged her along. I prodded Bliss and swatted Baxter.

We had to ask a middle-aged couple in matching green-and-purple sweatshirts how to get out. They pointed us in the right way, but looked at us uneasily.

'Aren't you a bit young to be playing in the park by yourselves?' the woman asked.

'We're not. We wandered off and lost our mum,' I said.

'What? For goodness' sake, she'll be frantic!'

'No, no – I phoned her on my mobile,' I said, patting my empty jeans pocket. 'She just said to come straight to the park gates and she'll meet us there.'

'Well, we'd better come with you, to make sure you get there,' said the woman.

'No, please don't. Mum will get even crosser then. It's all my fault, I was meant to be looking after them,' I said, and I screwed my face up as if I was trying not to cry.

I thought she'd feel sorry for me and let me go, but she looked more worried than ever.

'No, we absolutely insist. You might get lost again. It's a good fifteen-minute walk, maybe longer. Come along, it's this way,' she said, while we stared at her, horrified.

Pixie started crying for real and the woman looked concerned.

'Oh dear, is she hungry?' she asked.

'Yes, yes!' Pixie wailed, as if she hadn't eaten for days.

'Poor little pet. What do you want, darling?'

'Ice cream!' said Pixie.

Oh, I saw what she was up to. She'd heard the word *gate* and remembered the whippy van.

'We haven't got any ice cream, dear, but we've maybe got a nice peppermint,' said the woman. 'Arnie, you've got the Polos in your pocket, haven't you?'

Arnie didn't look as if he wanted to share his Polo mints but he got them out and offered the packet nervously in the direction of Pixie, as if she was a snappy dog and might bite. She grabbed at the packet and then turned up her nose at the smell.

'It's toothpaste!' she said, looking accusingly at Arnie as if he'd played a dirty trick on her.

'*I* like Polos,' said Baxter.

Arnie handed them round to all of us.

'Say thank you,' I hissed.

But Baxter wouldn't and Bliss was too shy and Pixie too intent on whining for ice cream. I could have shaken all of them. I didn't know what to do. Arnie's wife was trying to make conversation all along the way: what were our names, where exactly did we live, which school did we go to? I started telling her a whole load of lies to stop her tracking us down.

'I'm Rose, and this is my brother Mikey and my

108

sister Bluebell and my littlest sister Bunny,' I said, picking names I knew the kids would like so they'd go along with this charade. I said we lived on a different estate the other end of town, and I had us all going to a different school too. Then she twittered on and on about it, asking us what we liked best at school.

'I like art,' I said truthfully.

'I do too,' said Bluebell, in a tiny whispery voice.

'Is art painting? We do finger painting at nursery and I love getting in a mess,' said Bunny.

'I like fighting,' said Mikey, punching the air.

It turned out Arnie and his wife, Elizabeth, had been schoolteachers once upon a time, but they'd both retired now.

'Though we're so busy I don't know how we ever had time to work,' said Elizabeth.

Yes, they were busy busy busy poking their sharp teachers' noses into our affairs. I didn't have a clue how we were going to get rid of them. I kept wondering if I should simply yell, *Run!* and grab Bunny and yank Mikey and Bluebell into action – but I still wasn't very sure how far the gate was. Although old Arnie walked in a tottery kind of way, his wife bounced along in her trainers. Perhaps she'd been a PE teacher – I could imagine a whistle bouncing on her big chest. I didn't want her blowing the whistle on us.

I tried to think of some way we could successfully escape, nibbling at the skin on my lip as we walked.

'You're looking really worried, Rose,' said Elizabeth. 'Do you think your mother will get *very* cross?'

I didn't know what to say for the best.

'Yes, she'll get really mad and start whacking us ever so hard,' said Mikey, thinking he was helping me out.

Elizabeth looked shocked.

'Your mother *hits* you?' she asked.

'No, of course she doesn't,' I said quickly.

'Yes, she does, she goes *whack whack whack*,' said Mikey, gesturing. 'But it's OK because I go *kerpow kerpow kerpow* and I always beat her and get to be the winner because I'm the best at fighting.'

'I think you're the best at story-telling,' said Elizabeth, relaxing.

We got to the top of the hill – and then started on the downward slope, me holding Bunny by her wrist to stop her tumbling. I saw the car park and the gate. Bunny started clamouring, 'Ice cream!' until I thought my head would burst.

'Nearly there,' said Elizabeth. 'Can you see any sign of your mum?'

But then – oh glory! – some couple got out of their car, with a daft spaniel leaping up and down. They started calling and waving. 'Elizabeth! Arnie! Oh my goodness, fancy seeing you here!'

'Good Lord! Are these your grandchildren?'

'There's Mum!' I shouted, while they were distracted. 'Thank-you-very-much-goodbye!'

Then we ran for it. I started waving wildly at a woman by the gate, a fat, silly-looking woman *nothing* like our mum – and she waved back, startled, obviously feeling she knew us. Bliss and Baxter ran beside me, and I managed to clutch Pixie. We could hear Elizabeth and Arnie calling as the dog barked but we just ran faster. When we got to the gate I threw my arms round this complete stranger, practically knocking her over.

'Hello? What's all this about?' she said, laughing nervously.

'Oh! I thought – I thought you were someone I know,' I said. 'I'm sorry. I've go to go now. Come on, kids.'

We ran again, dodging up the first side street so we'd not be visible from the gate. When we were round a corner I let us slow down. We leaned against a garden wall, all of us utterly out of breath.

'Phew!' said Pixie.

It was such a strangely old-fashioned thing for

her to say that we all burst out laughing.

'Phew, phew, phew!' Pixie repeated delightedly.

We trudged on up the road, all of us phewing like anything.

'My feet hurt, right on their underneaths,' said Baxter, limping a little.

'My everything hurts,' Bliss mumbled.

'Never mind, we'll be home soon, and we'll all have a nice hot bath and a special treat for supper,' I promised. 'You'll get your ice cream, Pixie. I know Mum put some in the freezer.'

'I want whippy,' she moaned.

'Yes, well, I'll squish it around and make it whippy. And we'll put cream on the top.'

'Can I have cream too?' asked Bliss.

'We'll all have cream.'

'Am I still Bluebell?'

'If you want to be.'

'No, I think I want to be me now.'

'Then that's who you are, who we all are, Lily and Baxter and Bliss and Pixie, and we're nearly home.'

We got back to our estate safely without going all round the moon. I started worrying now about the unlocked door. Maybe we'd get back and find the whole flat ransacked, mess everywhere. I'd seen what some of the boys could do if they wanted to teach you a lesson. My chest felt tight and I could scarcely breathe as we crept along the balcony, trying to avoid alerting Old Kath. But when I peeped round the door everything was just as usual, certainly not neat and tidy, but it was only our own mess. There was a little beeping noise in the hall-way. It was a message flashing on the telephone.

I pressed the button on the phone and Mum's voice spoke into the hall.

'Mum! Mum! Mum! Mum!' We all called her name. Baxter jumped up and down. Bliss doubled over, clasping her tummy. Pixie wriggled, clutching herself. We were all making so much noise that we couldn't properly hear what she was saying.

'Shh! Shh, you lot,' I said. 'Oh, if only we'd been *home*.'

'Mum, I want to talk to Mum!' said Pixie, trying to clutch the phone.

'No, darling, it's just a message from Mum. *Listen!* Maybe she's telling us when she's coming home. Come on, shut up, all of you, it's important!' I said.

Mum said goodbye. Baxter and Bliss whispered goodbye back and Pixie started crying. I pressed the button again as soon as the tape had rewound.

'Hi, you kids. Where are you then? I figured you'd be back from school by now. I bet Mikey's taken you down McDonald's. Anyway, listen, my blooming mobile doesn't work here, don't ask me why, but I've sneaked off and I'm using a pay phone though its eating all my change. I'm just checking up and making sure you're OK. You're looking after them all right, Mikey, right? Lily, you give Pixie a cuddle from me, eh, and see she gets to bed on time – you know how ratty she is if she doesn't get enough sleep. Baxter, you be a good boy now for your dad, and Bliss, you speak up for yourself. Lily, you should see it here, you'd love it. My God, the colour of the sky, it's bright bright blue just the way you crayonned it when you were little. I'll take you here one day when I'm in the money, I'll take you all – that's a promise. Well, gotta go now, nearly out of money. I'm having a great time. Gordon's a sweetheart. You should see the way everyone looks up to him. How'd you like him for a new daddy, eh? Ha,

ha, only joking. I'll be back soon. Maybe the week-end, whenever, but I know you're in good hands with Mikey, eh? Bye then, darlings. Bye bye!'

Baxter and Bliss said goodbye all over again. Pixie shivered, her knees together.

'Ugh, look, she's wetting the carpet!' said Baxter, pointing.

'Oh, Pixie,' I said, picking her up and whipping her to the toilet.

'I want Mum,' she wept.

'Yes, darling, we all want Mum, but she's coming home soon,' I said, yanking her soggy knickers down and sitting her on the toilet.

But she still hadn't said *exactly* when she was coming home. *Maybe the weekend, whatever.* Did that mean she hadn't even booked her flight yet? I stood hanging onto the cold edge of the wash-basin, loving Mum and hating Mum all at the same time. I thought of her lying on a beach towel with 'new daddy' Gordon underneath this bright blue sky – and I wanted to kick sand in her face. How could she leave us like this? But then she thought we were with Mikey. *In good hands.* I thought of Mikey's huge fists with their self-inked tattoos and their big sovereign rings and I shuddered. At least we didn't have to put up with *him* all week.

'I want Mum!' Pixie wailed on the toilet.

116

'Look, I'll be your mum just for this week,' I said.

'You're Lily,' said Pixie.

'Yeah, I know, but I'll be your Lilymum, OK?'

'Lilymum,' Pixie repeated. Luckily she quite liked the sound of it. 'Lilymum, Lilymum, Lilymum!' She laughed as I gave her a quick wash and found her dry knickers.

'That's right, Lilymum's going to get you a lovely tea now,' I said. 'Do you want to come and help me do the cooking, eh, Pixie?'

Pixie clapped her hands. We went to find the others. Baxter was curled up on the sofa, his head on a cushion, while Bliss softly patted his back. She was crying too.

'Hey, hey, no tears now. Mum's coming back soon and meanwhile I'm Lilymum and I'm going to cook you all tea.'

'If you're Lilymum, am I Bluebell again?' Bliss asked, sniffing.

'You can be whoever you like, darling. Come on into the kitchen – you can help make the tea too.'

'What are we having?' said Baxter, his voice muffled by the cushion.

'Sausages! And then ice cream.'

I cooked the sausages under the grill because I didn't want to risk the frying pan, not with them all jumping about the kitchen with me. I got Baxter to prick them first with a fork. He pretended each one was a little pig and stuck it to death. I let Pixie sprinkle a packet of oven chips onto a tray and then popped them into the oven. I opened a can of beans and let Bliss stir them in the pan, as I knew she'd be the most careful. I took a block of ice cream out of the freezer and lined up the can of cream and some raspberry jam all ready, and poured us each a glass of lemon drink.

The kids got a bit fidgety waiting for the chips to crisp up and I didn't want them bumping into me while I turned the hot sausages so I sent them off to watch telly for ten minutes. I didn't call them back till I'd dished up. I felt so happy when they clapped their hands at their full plates.

We ate heartily. I didn't nag about table manners and let them eat their sausages and chips with their fingers, though I did make them use forks for their baked beans. Then I mashed the ice cream until it was *sort* of whippy and smothered each scoop with cream and jam, creating my very own ice-cream sundaes.

'Happy now, Pixie?' I asked.

She grinned at me. 'I love you, Lilymum,' she said, smacking her lips together.

It was the most peaceful evening. We just lolled around the living room watching television. Pixie nodded off where she was so I picked her up and carried her to bed. Bliss was nearly asleep too, snuggling up to Headless and sucking her thumb. Even Baxter was still for once, flopped full-length on the carpet like a tiger-skin rug. I gave them another half-hour and then scooped them up too.

When they were tucked up on the mattress I felt so tired I wanted to crawl in with them, but I was Lilymum now. I cleared up the kitchen, washing up the glasses and plates and putting the pans in to soak. Then I got the broom and swept under the table and wiped it down with a damp cloth. I hummed softly and smiled sweetly even if there was no one to see me. I wanted to look like all those pretty cosy mums you see in the telly adverts. I wasn't imitating *my* mum – she always left the dirty dishes till morning and rarely swept up.

'Life's too short to faff around with a mop all the time,' she'd say. 'Why should I waste it on housework?'

I found I quite *liked* getting the kitchen clean and tidy, even though I was so tired. I daydreamed about my own flat in the future. I'd clean it every single day, even though there'd be no children to make it messy. I supposed I'd let Bliss and Baxter and Pixie come on a visit, but most of the time I'd be there alone. I'd play beautiful music and loll on my gorgeous rugs and stare out of my picture windows.

My flat would be very high up – the penthouse suite!
– so maybe I'd be able to see all the hills and trees of
our special park. I wouldn't ever ever ever go off on
holiday.

I went into Mum's bedroom and breathed in her
special scent. I fiddled with some of her leftover
make-up, smearing grey on my eyelids and purply-
red on my lips. Then I opened her wardrobe and
selected one of her dresses just to see whether I
could look properly grown-up. I stuffed my feet into
some high heels and wiggled across the carpet to the
mirror, but I looked ludicrous, a small shiny clown
in a stupid dress. I tore off all the clothes, washed
my face, and then got into Mum's bed.

'Come *back*,' I said into her pillow. 'I'm not big
enough. I don't want to be the mum. Come back
right now.'

I felt it so fiercely I was almost certain that Mum
in Spain would feel it too. She'd clutch her heart and
go, 'My kids! I'm sorry, Gordon, I have to get home to
my kids.' She'd get a taxi to the airport right that
minute . . . I thought about her return ticket. What
if Gordon wouldn't pay for it? She had her dodgy
credit card, but what if that wouldn't work either?

I couldn't stop thinking about it. I started thumping my forehead to try to stop all the worries. I shut
my eyes and tried to invent an alternative world.

I wasn't Lily Green, older sister of Baxter and Bliss and Pixie. I was Rose – and Mikey and Bluebell and Bunny didn't exist. I had long fair hair down to my waist and big blue eyes and I wore wonderful designer clothes every single day. I didn't have a mother or a father. No, I had a lovely kind fabulously rich uncle just like Mr Abbott at school, and he indulged me terribly. He took me out to a West End show every night, and afterwards we had tremendously grand suppers at posh restaurants with waiters in fancy outfits and we both drank champagne. At weekends my uncle took me to art galleries and we walked round all the paintings hand in hand. At the end of each visit my uncle told me to choose my favourite painting and then he had it wrapped and sent to me.

When I woke in the middle of the night, the mum thoughts were whirling around in my head again and I couldn't pretend vividly enough to blot them out. I didn't realize I was crying until I heard someone creep into Mum's bedroom and wriggle into bed with me.

'Lily?' said Bliss, her cold little fingers patting me. 'Lily, don't cry. It will be all right.'

'No, it *won't*,' I sobbed.

'Yes it will. You'll look after us. You're great at looking after us. Better than Mum,' said Bliss.

'I'm sick of being the mum.'

Bliss was quiet for a moment. Then she put her arms round my neck. 'It's OK then, *I'll* be mum tomorrow,' she said.

'Oh, Bliss,' I said, crying more.

'I'm the mum and you're my little girl and I'm going to give you a great big cuddle and then you're going to go fast asleep,' said Bliss.

Bliss couldn't look after anyone, not even herself. But when she held me, she did feel a bit like a real mum. I fell asleep again and we didn't wake up till morning.

There was no sound coming from Baxter and Pixie so we left them sleeping. Bliss and I stayed curled up, still playing that she was the mum and I was the little girl.

'I'm hungry, Mum,' I said, in an ickle-baby voice.

'Don't worry, baby, I'll feed you,' said Bliss.

I was expecting pretend food, but she slipped out of bed and disappeared into the kitchen. She came back with a packet of crisps.

'Here you are, darling, baby rusks,' she said, shaking the packet at me.

She got back into bed and started feeding me crisps, popping several into her own mouth too.

'Oh dear, we're getting a lot of crumbs in the bed,' I said. 'Mum will murder us when she comes home.'

'No, we'll murder her for leaving us all alone,' said Bliss.

'Hey! Bliss, that's not like you!'

'I'm not me any more. We're all getting different.'

'What, you mean Baxter's very quiet and gentle and sensible?' I said.

We both giggled and dabbed our fingers round the packet for the last little crumbs of crisp.

'We won't need any breakfast now,' I said, but when the others woke up and we were all sitting at the kitchen table, Bliss and I ate a mound of toast. I was a bit worried about the bread running out, but I couldn't help it. I didn't feel exactly *hungry*, but there was an empty sick feeling inside me and food helped fill it up.

I was just buttering a third piece of toast when there was a knock on the front door. We all stared at each other.

'Mum!' said Pixie.

'No, it won't be Mum, silly. Mum's got a key.'

'Dad!' said Baxter.

'Your dad's in Scotland, it won't be him. Anyway, he's got his own key too. Listen, we won't answer it, just in case,' I whispered. 'Keep quiet, now.'

We sat still, not even munching. There was another knock – and then the letter box rattled.

'Lily! Lily Green, are you there? It's me, Sarah,' she called.

She lived on the next floor up from us, and was in Mr Abbott's class too.

'What does she want?' I decided I'd better go and see if she was going to carry on like that. I didn't want Old Kath hearing her and shuffling down the balcony to investigate.

I went to the door and opened it a crack, peering round. Yes, it was Sarah in her green checked school dress.

'Aren't you up yet?' she said, squinting at my pyjamas.

'No, I've got a bug. We've all got it. Don't come too near, Sarah.'

'OK, don't breathe your germs on me! Anyway, Mr Abbott wants to know if you're coming on the gallery trip tomorrow. He says to tell you he's saved a place on the coach.'

'Oh! But I haven't paid.'

'He says you're not to worry about that. It sounds as if he's going to pay for you.'

'Really! Oh, he's so lovely!'

Sarah wrinkled her nose. 'Mr Abbott? He's not lovely, he's weird.'

'No, he's not.'

'Well, you would say that, because you're a bit weird too,' she said.

'Will you tell him thank you?'

'Yes, OK. And I'll say you're coming?'

I hesitated. I badly wanted to go on the school trip with Mr Abbott. I imagined this gallery lined with famous paintings and Mr Abbott and me walking round it together. Mr Abbott would tell me about each painting and then ask me solemnly if I liked it, acting like he really wanted to know . . .

'I'll come if – if I'm better,' I said.

Pixie scrabbled at my back, squeezing through my legs.

'Mum?' she said.

'What?' said Sarah. 'I'm not your mum, dopey!'

'Pixie's not very well either,' I said, picking her up. 'Come on, darling, we'd better put you back in bed. Bye, Sarah.'

I shut the door on her. Pixie struggled with me.

'Not bed, not bed, don't want to go back to bed.'

'No, I was just pretending. It's OK, Pixie.' I let her run back to the kitchen. I stayed in the hall, thinking about lovely Mr Abbott. Could I risk going to school on Wednesday? Could we all go? But they'd wonder where Mum was – they'd certainly ask at the nursery – and Pixie would talk. Was there any way she could stay at home? Bliss could perhaps look after her? No, Bliss was far too little. She could maybe manage Pixie but she'd never be able to control Baxter, he walked all

125

over her. I couldn't leave them. I couldn't go to the gallery.

I stamped back to the kitchen, wishing I was an only child. Everything the kids said got on my nerves. I'd planned to take them back to the magic garden in the park but it was a grey, gloomy day, already drizzling, and by the time we'd all got dressed it was really pouring with rain.

'Well, we'll just have to stay in instead,' I said, sighing.

'*I'm* going out,' said Baxter. 'I don't mind a bit of rain. I'm going to that park.'

'No, you're not. No one goes out when it rains like this. People will notice and think it's weird.'

'No one will see me if no one goes out,' said Baxter triumphantly. 'I'm going, so there. You can't stop me.'

'Stop being such a pain, Baxter.'

'No, *you're* the pain, bossing us about. I'm nearly as big as you and I'm the boy anyway. *I* should do the bossing. So you can just shut your big mouth, right? I'm going *out.*'

'Oh, go out then, see if I care,' I snapped.

'Right! Well, I'm *going*,' said Baxter.

'OK. Go!' I said.

'Yes, watch me,' said Baxter, and he marched out. He slammed the front door behind him as hard as he could.

'Oh, great, Baxter, let Old Kath know too,' I muttered.

'Baxter's naughty,' said Pixie.

'Yes, he is,' I said.

'He won't really go to the park, will he?' said Bliss. 'He might get lost.'

'Good,' I said.

Bliss started nibbling at her fingers.

'Don't look so anxious. You're such a wuss, Bliss. Of *course* he won't be going all the way to the park. He might go as far as the den, but I doubt it. He's probably just lurking on the balcony. He wants us to worry but I'm not worried one little bit. Now, are you girls going to help me wash up?'

I fetched a chair for Pixie and she stood at the sink with Bliss, washing up the dishes. They poured so much washing-up liquid into the bowl that soap-suds came up to their armpits. When they'd done all the dishes I fetched my old Barbie dolls and they gave them a deluxe spa treatment.

I kept listening out for Baxter. Every now and then I thought I heard him and went running to the door, but there was never anyone there. I hung over the balcony, peering along to the playground, but I couldn't see him there. It was still bucketing down, so if he had any sense whatsoever he'd be huddled up in the den, out of sight.

I waited until the Barbies had had their plunge baths and massage and their hair newly styled, and I'd organized a glamour photo shoot in the studio under the kitchen table. Bliss and Pixie laughed uproariously as I made the Barbies show off their pointy chests and strut about provocatively, but Bliss's laughter sounded high-pitched and hysterical, and I knew she was near tears.

Baxter was generally pretty mean to his sister, bossing her around and giving her a thump whenever he felt like it, but she acted like she'd lost an arm and a leg whenever they were apart. Maybe it was a twin thing and she simply couldn't help it. Pixie didn't seem to be missing Baxter at all.

'Lily,' Bliss whispered, as we dressed the Barbies. 'Lily, do you think Baxter's all right?'

'No, Baxter's all wrong, we all know that,' I joked. 'OK, OK, I'll go and fetch him back. He'll be hiding in the den. You shouldn't worry so, Bliss.'

I went to get my coat and tied Mum's leopard-print scarf over my head.

'Can we come too?'

'No, you stay here, Bliss, with Pixie. There's no point all of us getting soaked. Now, be good girls, won't you, and don't answer the door to anyone.'

I went out, along the balcony, creeping past Old Kath's and down the stairs. I wondered if Baxter might simply be hiding there on the stairwell, but there was no sign of him. I sighed, and trudged across the yard towards the playground.

The rain pelted down. In a few seconds Mum's headscarf was flattened against my head and my coat was drenched.

'You idiot, Baxter,' I muttered, squinting through the solid sheet of rain.

I went stomping and splashing to the slide and hauled myself up the steps.

'Baxter, for goodness' *sake*,' I said.

I expected him to leap out at me, but nothing happened. I got to the den at the top and scrambled inside. I peered around in the dark. I even felt the sodden logs. Baxter wasn't there.

I stood up in a panic, banging my head.

'Baxter!'

I poked my head out again and looked all round the playground. There were the swings, swaying slightly as the rain beat down on them. There was the muddy little roundabout. There was the pole with the rubber tyre dangling. No Baxter. No Baxter anywhere.

I'd been so certain he'd come here. So where *had* he gone? Surely he hadn't really tried to go to the park all by himself?

I didn't know what to do. My chest was so tight I

couldn't breathe properly. How was I ever going to find him? I thought of that vast park stretching for miles. And now it would be a sea of mud. I pictured Baxter up to his knees, struggling, screaming for me.

'I'm coming, Baxter!' I said, and I started running through the estate. I tried desperately hard to remember which way to go – and if I couldn't remember, how could Baxter? And what was I going to do about Bliss and Pixie? I couldn't leave them for hours while I trailed round the whole park. Bliss would get in a panic, convincing herself I wasn't coming back.

I stood still, dithering, sucking my lips into my face to stop myself crying.

A woman from another block trudged past, shopping bags dangling from her arms as she struggled to keep her umbrella over her head.

'Nice weather for ducks, eh?' she said. 'Well, don't just stand there, you're getting soaked. Go and take shelter!'

I suddenly wondered. Where could you keep dry on the estate? On the balconies, the stairs, down in the rubbish shed . . .

I nodded at the woman and ran back to our block of flats, right round the corner. I pushed open the wooden door to the bin area – and there was Baxter, sitting on the filthy floor amid a load of rubbish, flipping through the grubby pages of someone's girlie magazine.

'*Baxter!*'

He jumped when I yelled at him and then grinned.

'Hey, come and look at this funny magazine – it shows all their rude bits!'

'Put it *down*. Come here, you bad, bad boy. Don't you *dare* go off like that again!'

'You told me to go! You said you didn't care,' said Baxter.

'Well, I was bad too. Of course I care. Oh, Baxter, I was so worried about you.'

I grabbed him and hugged his bony little body hard. For just a second he hugged me back, but when I tried to rub my cheek against his bristly head he wriggled and squirmed.

'Ew! Don't kiss me!'

'I'm *not* kissing you. No fear. Come on, let's go home. Bliss will be worrying so.'

'Bliss always worries,' said Baxter. 'Especially about me.'

'Yes, so you should be kinder to your sister. *All* your sisters,' I said.

We walked back towards the stairs.

'You don't half look funny with that headscarf on,' said Baxter.

'Thanks a bunch,' I said, whipping it off and stuffing it in my pocket.

'And what have you got your coat on for, it's summer?'

'I'm trying to keep *dry* because my mad brother went out in the pouring rain and I had to go looking for him,' I said, giving him a shove.

He shoved me back, but he was grinning. We ran up the stairs and knocked at the door. We waited. Nothing happened.

'Come on, Bliss,' I muttered, and knocked again.

The door stayed shut. I opened the letter box and peered in. I couldn't see anyone. The flat was silent.

'Maybe they went out looking for me too?' said Baxter.

'Bliss wouldn't do that,' I said, but my chest was tight again. What if she'd got so worried she'd taken Pixie and they'd run out after me? Where were they now? And how were any of us going to get back safe indoors without a front door key?

'*Bliss!*' I yelled through the letter box.

No one came – but I thought I heard whispers.

'Bliss, are you in there? Come and open the door!'

I listened. More whispering, out of sight. Then I heard Pixie squealing.

'Pixie? Pixie, *you* come and answer the door!'

Pixie came running into view, bobbing along the

hall. Bliss came rushing after her, trying to pull her back.

'For heaven's sake, will one of you silly girls answer the door, we're soaked to the skin!' I said.

Bliss crept fearfully along the hall towards me.

'That's it. Come on, *open* it!'

Pixie jumped up before Bliss and managed to wiggle the latch all by herself. She got the door open and Baxter and I shot inside.

'*Thank* you! Bliss, what are you *playing* at?'

Bliss burst into tears.

'You told me not to answer the door. You did, you did, when you went out. And then you were gone so long, and I didn't know what to do, and then you came back and knocked and I was scared because I thought you might be a robber or some-one bad so I told Pixie we mustn't mustn't mustn't open it.'

'But I called out to you!'

'Yes, and it sounded like you, but it could have been a robber *pretending* to be you, speaking in a girl voice,' Bliss sobbed.

'Bliss is being silly, isn't she?' said Pixie.

'Bliss is always silly,' said Baxter.

'Oh, Baxter, I thought you'd run away to the park without me,' said Bliss.

'I'm not daft, it's too wet,' said Baxter.

'Exactly!' I said. 'Come here, let's get a towel to dry you a bit.'

I rubbed at him fiercely while he wriggled.

'This towel smells!' he said.

He was right, all the towels were smelling a bit now. We'd badly needed clean ones even when Mum was here. We were running out of clean T-shirts and pants and socks too. We had a washing machine but it didn't work any more. Mum had been meaning to go down the Social and beg for a new one but she hated going there so she'd never quite got round to it. She went to the launderette instead, pushing great bags of washing in Pixie's buggy. I could do that, I knew exactly how to do a wash and then a dry. I'd done it heaps of times with Mum – but we didn't have any money.

'I know what we'll do this morning. We'll do all the washing at home,' I said.

I made them collect up all the piles of dirty clothes while I ran the hot tap into the kitchen sink and chucked in lots of washing powder. When the kids saw the bubbles they wanted to do the washing with me, which slowed things down considerably. Pixie insisted on getting *in* the sink and jumped up and down on the clothes.

'I'm stamping the dirt out!' she shouted.

I don't know about the stamping – she was

certainly splashing. The kitchen floor was getting a good wash as well as the clothes. They all lost interest when it came to rinsing and then wringing out the soaking clothes. I had to struggle on by myself, water running up my sleeves right to my armpits.

I didn't know what to do with the clothes when I'd finished at last. I could hang the light things up on the line in the bathroom that Mum used for her tights and undies but the big drippy towels would break it. In the end I switched on the electric fire, arranged the chairs around it, and hung the towels from their backs.

'This is very, very, very dangerous,' I said. 'You mustn't go anywhere near or you'll start a fire.'

I managed to impress this on Baxter and Pixie enough for them to play at the other end of the room. Poor Bliss hid in the bedroom, calling out to us to be careful every two minutes. I turned the towels round every now and then, baking them on each side – and in an hour they were bone-dry.

'There!' I said triumphantly, burying my face in the towels. 'They smell lovely now, all fresh and flowery.'

'Let's play bullfighters with them,' said Baxter, grabbing a towel and flapping it wildly. 'Come on, Bliss, you be the bull, and I'll shove all my sticks in you.'

'*Stop it!* Not with the fire on!' I said, switching it off quickly. 'And not with the fire off either. Stop jabbing at poor Bliss.'

'She's not Bliss, she's the bull. Bellow a bit, Bliss, and put your hands up to look like horns,' Baxter encouraged her.

'Maybe I should have left you out in the rain, Baxter,' I said.

I gave us lunch early, just for something to do – fish fingers and oven chips. I'd hoped it might stop raining by the afternoon, but it poured even harder. We watched television. Well, Bliss, Pixie and I watched television. Baxter acted out everything on the screen, pretending to be an antique expert and a quiz show host and a comedian and Tracy Beaker, repeating everything they said until we were all driven demented.

It actually stopped raining about five o'clock and all three kids clamoured to go out. I was desperate to go too, but I couldn't help wondering if Mum just might phone again. It would be terrible to miss her twice – and maybe she'd worry if we weren't around for a second time. So I said we couldn't go out and Baxter yelled at me and Pixie threw herself on the ground and kicked. Even Bliss pouted and acted fed up with me.

Mum didn't call, though I sat hunched up beside

the phone, willing it to ring. I went from longing to hear from her to hating her for not even bothering to try to talk to us again. I hated Baxter and Bliss and Pixie too, crying and moaning and complaining all the time.

I barricaded myself in Mum's bedroom with my drawing book and invented a pure white, utterly sound-proof bedroom for myself. It had white walls and white carpet so soft it was like fur. I had white satin sheets and a white silk nightie with white lace. I sat on a white velvet stool in front of the glittering Venetian glass mirror of my dressing table and brushed my hair with an ivory-backed brush, and then I lay down in my soft bed in utter silence. I lived all alone. I had no mother, no brother, no sisters.

I muttered to myself as I drew, even though I could hear Baxter bashing and Bliss begging and Pixie yelling her head off. But then Bliss started crying too, high-pitched and panicking, and I couldn't blot them out any more.

'What *is* it?' I said, stamping to the door and flinging it open.

Bliss covered her face and made frantic gulping sounds, trying to stop crying. I looked at Baxter, who was red in the face.

'What have you done to her?' I demanded.

'I haven't done anything!'

'Yes, you jolly well have!'

'I haven't even touched her,' said Baxter, widening his eyes and jutting his chin, acting innocence.

'Bliss, what did he say?' I asked.

Bliss shook her head. She'd never ever tell tales on Baxter, no matter what he did. Luckily Pixie blabbed like anything. She stopped her own howling to gasp, 'He said you'd run away!' and then carried on yelling.

'Stop that silly noise! You're giving us all a headache. What's this rubbish about, Baxter? Of course I haven't run away, silly. It was *you* who did that, not me.'

'Yeah, but I said you *could* run away and not come back, like Mum. I said you were maybe running away right that minute because we couldn't get in the bedroom door and you were ever so quiet and wouldn't answer us. I said you might have done a runner out the window.'

'Baxter, we're on the first floor! If I jumped out the window I'd fall to my death!'

'*I* know that, but I can't help it if Bliss is silly enough to believe it,' said Baxter.

'Oh, you're so horrible to poor Bliss. Come here, darling!' I cradled Bliss in my arms. Her eyes were screwed shut but tears still seeped down her cheeks and her nose was running too. 'Look at the state of you! Baxter, don't you feel sorry?'

'No, she's silly,' said Baxter.

'*I'm* not silly,' said Pixie, bouncing up, suddenly bored with crying.

They chased each other all round the flat, squealing, while I sat Bliss on the edge of Mum's bed and rocked her in my arms until she stopped gasping and heaving.

'There now! Better?'

Bliss sniffed and nodded, nuzzling against my chest.

'You mustn't let Baxter tease you so. He walks all over you,' I said gently.

'He didn't walk on me,' Bliss mumbled, taking me literally.

'I know, but he just wants to wind you up. You mustn't take him seriously. You *know* I wouldn't jump out the window!'

'Yes, but you could maybe creep out the door,' Bliss whispered.

'I'm not going to do that. I'm going to stay with you and Baxter and Pixie for ever. Well, if I *do* have to nip out for anything, I promise I'll always always always come back.'

We sat there, hugging hard, thinking about Mum.

It rained again on Wednesday and I grew desperate, trying to think of some way to amuse the kids. I wished we could go to school. I longed to see Mr Abbott so that I could go on the gallery trip. I knew *I'd* be fine. I could lie and bluff until the cows came home. But I couldn't leave the kids to their own devices all day long in the flat. Baxter would break everything and terrorize his sisters, Bliss would tremble into a jelly, and Pixie would scream her head off until Old Kath came knocking. Then she'd find out Mum had gone off and she'd tell and we'd be taken away to some dumping ground for neglected kids and never be allowed to see Mum again.

We couldn't go to school – but perhaps we could *play* school. I gave the kids a good breakfast: corn-flakes and ice cream because we'd run out of milk. Then I told the kids to stay sitting at the kitchen table, while I dressed up in Mum's navy skirt and grey top and her navy high heels.

'Me wear heels too!' said Pixie.

'And me,' said Bliss.

'No, I'm wearing them because I'm your new teacher, Miss Green. You're my pupils, all three of you. You're coming to my special school.'

'I thought you said we were on our holidays,' said Baxter. 'I don't want to go to your stupid special school.'

'Oh, you'll like *my* school, I promise you, Baxter. Sit down, all of you. I'm going to make you your own little notebooks. Baxter, you can cut the paper with the sharp scissors because you're such a careful big boy.'

I was taking a serious risk. Baxter might well have run amok with the kitchen scissors and cut off Bliss's thumb and Pixie's curls, but he rose magnifi-cently to the occasion. Under my instruction he carefully cut six sheets of my previous drawing pad into quarter strips. I gave Bliss a needle and thread and showed her how to sew the folded paper into little booklets. Pixie clamoured to help too, so I set her to sharpening pencils. She liked this job so much she sharpened them into stumps, but at least it kept her quiet and happy.

'Right. Now, lesson time!' I said, clapping my hands. 'Good morning, class. You say "Good morning, Miss Green".'

'Good morning, Miss Green,' they parroted back.

'We're going to have a spelling test first,' I said.

Baxter groaned.

'I'm not doing boring old spelling,' he said, flinging down his pencil.

'This is exciting new spelling,' I said. 'The first word is . . . knickers!'

They all giggled.

'No giggling now. Write down "knickers". Come along.'

Neither Baxter nor Bliss knew about the weirdly silent 'k' in knickers, but they did their best to spell it out. Pixie couldn't write anything yet, but she did a lot of scribble at the top of her page, joining in.

I carried on, going through as many rude and silly words as I could think of – quite a long list. Baxter was terrible at spelling but even he could make an accurate stab at some of them, mostly because he'd seen them scribbled all over walls. When we were done I pretended to mark their papers and drew them each a big star at the bottom, even Pixie.

'Now we'll have a maths lesson,' I said.

'We don't do proper maths yet,' said Bliss.

'You can do *my* maths,' I said. 'It's special counting.'

Mum had bought a bumper pack of Smarties tubes she'd hidden at the back of the cupboard. I opened them all up and tipped the brightly coloured sweets into our glasses.

'Ooh, pretty,' said Pixie, reaching for a handful.

'No, you mustn't *eat* them, Pixie. Not yet. This is a maths class. Don't worry, I'll help you. You can be teacher's pet.'

'Will you help me too?' Bliss said.

'You won't need help, Bliss, I promise. Now, look at your glass of sweets. OK! Write down in your work book how many you think there are.'

'But we don't know,' said Bliss.

'You have to make a guess,' I said. 'It doesn't matter if you get it wrong.'

Bliss guessed forty. Baxter guessed a hundred. Pixie and I guessed sixty.

'Now, here comes the good bit. Tip your glasses up and we'll count how many Smarties we've really got.'

'I can't count that many,' said Bliss.

'We'll all count together,' I said. 'We'll do yours first, Bliss. Tip them out carefully on the table.'

I helped Bliss start counting, moving her Smarties into neat little rows. We all counted out loud together. Pixie couldn't manage accurate consecutive numbers and yelled, 'One, two, three, twenty, fifty, a hundred,' which was off-putting, but we persisted, doing two counts to make absolutely sure. Bliss had fifty-eight Smarties.

'Now it's your turn, Baxter,' I said.

He tipped his Smarties out so enthusiastically that half of them spilled off the table onto the floor. Baxter's Smarties got a bit fluffy but he didn't seem to mind. He counted hurriedly and not always accurately, so we had to keep starting again. Eventually we discovered he had sixty-two Smarties.

'Hurray, hurray, I've got the most,' he said.

'Well, we don't know for certain sure. Pixie and I haven't counted ours yet,' I said. 'Come on, Pixie, tip ours out – *carefully*. That's it. Now, you move them slowly, one by one, from this side of the table to the other and we'll count them out together.'

Pixie and I had exactly sixty.

'So we guessed right, Pixie!'

'But I've got the most, so I've won!' said Baxter. 'I'm going to eat mine now.'

144

'No, no, no, wait! This is a *maths* lesson. Now, let's see. How can we work it so that we all have an equal share? How many Smarties should Baxter give to Bliss so that we've all got the same?'

'I'm not giving my Smarties to Bliss – they're all mine, from my glass!'

'Just try putting these into Bliss's pile,' I said, moving a couple of his Smarties.

Baxter roared as if I was extracting two of his teeth.

'That's not fair, now *she'll* have the most!'

'Well, let's count and see.'

So we counted all over again and of course we all had sixty. Well, Pixie must have been secretly helping herself, because we only had fifty-five now. She swore she hadn't had any, but she had little bits of Smartie shell glittering on her teeth.

I allowed Baxter and Bliss to eat five too, and then we lined all our Smarties up by colour. Then we had to count how many were in the pink line, the blue, the yellow, the orange, the red and the brown. Then we tried a complicated swapping game, so that Baxter got all the orange Smarties, Bliss all the blue, and Pixie all the red. She kept licking hers so she could make lipstick for herself. All the Smarties were getting pretty sticky by this time so I gave in altogether and let them eat their sums.

Then I announced that it was playtime because I couldn't think what to do with them next. Baxter drove his fork-lift truck all round the flat, Bliss put on Mum's necklace and high heels and played at being Princess Bluebell, and Pixie went to the beauty salon and applied multi-coloured Smartie make-up all over her face.

I got my drawing pad and designed my own kitchen. I'd have a big shiny fridge full of posh meals for one and a long wooden table with six chairs. From Monday through to Saturday I'd sit at a different chair each time, and on Sundays I'd have my meals on a tray in my own bed, careful not to spill anything on my beautiful silky sheets.

I was a bit worried about the contents of our own fridge. We'd already run out of milk and I'd had to throw away some ham way past its sell-by date because it'd gone a bit green. We didn't have any vegetables either, but that didn't matter, because nobody liked them. We had some more fish fingers and a big pizza and eggs and bacon and oven chips, plus cake and biscuits and cornflakes in the cupboard, but that was all. It was only Wednesday. We'd have to start rationing things out a little. We'd had all the Smarties just now, so perhaps we could do without lunch.

I was willing to give it a try, and I certainly

hadn't had my fair share of Smarties, but the others started clamouring, whining that they were starving. The twins were used to eating lots at lunchtime because we all had free meals at school.

I heated up the big pizza, hoping that we might be able to save half of it for tea, but I couldn't stop myself wolfing down my own share when it was there on my plate, and the others didn't even try. We watched cartoons for a bit afterwards, but then the kids started getting fidgety and bored all over again.

'I want to go *out*!' Baxter moaned.

'Look, it's *raining*. We had this stupid argument yesterday. You're not going out, especially if you're just going to hang round those horrible bin sheds.'

I tried opening up my school again, organizing an art lesson, but they weren't in the mood any more and started chucking my precious felt tips around.

'I'm bored, I'm bored, I'm bored!' Baxter yelled, right in my face.

'I'm bored too!' I shouted back. 'All right, all right, we'll all go out, even though it's pouring.'

'Can we go to the magic garden?' said Bliss.

'Yes, we'll go there, but we'll have to watch out for that couple with the dog, we don't want them asking any more questions, do we?'

I knew it was mad to go out but there was a roaring in my head and I just couldn't stand to be stuck in the flat with the kids any more. I made Baxter and Bliss put on their winter jackets. They didn't have any raincoats, though Pixie had a silly little see-through plastic coat with a matching sou'wester hat. She liked the hat, pulling it down very low so she couldn't see where she was going. She had welly boots too. They were really only baby size but she didn't mind stuffing her feet in them. We only had our Tesco trainers, but I hoped they were waterproof.

I made them all quieten down in the hall, and then we crept out, leaving the door on the latch. A headscarfed lady was walking along the balcony but she just nodded at us timidly and let us pass.

The rain hit us full pelt when we were down on the forecourt, but after the first shock it didn't seem to matter. We tilted our heads and drank the raindrops and then ran madly, waving our arms and twirling around like crazy people. Once we were out of the estate we ran pell-mell down all the streets and round the corner, knowing exactly where we were going now.

'Ice cream!' Pixie panted, hopping along in her stubby boots.

But the ice-cream man wasn't there, probably

thinking he wouldn't get many customers in the pouring rain. When we went in the park gates it seemed pretty deserted, only ten or so cars in the car park. I looked around warily all the same, ready to do a runner if Arnie and Elizabeth loomed into view – and spotted a little playground behind a wooden fence.

'Look! Let's have a little play, there's no one there.'

'It's a baby's playground, not a big boy's playground with a den,' said Baxter.

'Can't we go to that magic garden?' said Bliss.

'We'll let Pixie have a little play here first and then we'll go to the magic garden,' I said. I was starting to wonder if it was really such a great idea. Bliss and Pixie were shivering, their hair in rat's-tails, and Baxter had splashed mud up to his kneecaps. They got in a worse state jumping about in the little playground and hurtling up and down the slide. Baxter actually started rolling on the ground, but I decided it wasn't really doing any harm and at least he was using up some of his energy.

'You're like a little piglet playing in the mud, Baxter,' I said.

Baxter made revolting grunty pig noises, and the others joined in. Pixie pulled her boots off, because they were starting to hurt her now. She announced she was 'paddling'. I played 'This little piggy went to market' with her and she squealed with laughter. Bliss kicked off her trainers, wanting me to do it to her too. They were having such mad fun in the mud I felt tempted to kick my own shoes off and run around madly, just for the fun of it – but then another car drew up in the car park. There was a slamming of a door and then a lot of shouting. At us.

'What on *earth* are you children doing?' this posh woman shrieked. Her snooty-nosed elegant long-haired dog started barking enviously. It was plain she never let *him* have a lovely roll in the mud.

'They're just playing,' I said.

'For heaven's sake, it's pouring with rain!' she declared, as if we somehow hadn't noticed. 'Look at the *state* of you!'

I was pretty muddy by this time and the three kids were covered all over, as if they were chocolate-coated. Baxter even had it in his bristly crewcut, so he looked like he had a mud helmet.

'It's only mud. It'll wash off,' I said.

'Look at your *jackets*!'

Yes, I was beginning to worry about their coats.

'Whatever will your mother say? Where *is* she?'

I gestured vaguely towards the toilets at the park gate.

'Well, you go and find her then! I don't think you should be allowed back in this lovely playground. You've made all the seats and slide muddy – look! Now run along at once.'

'You can't tell us what to do,' said Baxter, his chin jutting. 'It's not your park. It's for everyone.'

'It's for people who love nature, not for little guttersnipes and vandals who want to spoil everything.' She peered out at us from her silly checked rain-cap, looking like she really hated us.

So we hated her too. When Baxter bent to scoop up a handful of mud, I didn't stop him. He straightened, took aim – and threw it at her. It landed right on top of her rain-cap, as if a flying cow had done a dollop on her. She looked so incredibly funny we all burst out laughing – we simply couldn't help it.

She turned a hideous beetroot colour. I grabbed the kids quickly.

'Run!' I said.

So we ran for it. I picked up Pixie while Baxter and Bliss legged it for themselves. I hoped she'd give up when we ran towards the gate, but she stormed after us, her delicate-looking dog lolloping along, teeth bared.

'Run *faster*!' I panted.

We got to our corner, whizzed round it, and then I darted through a gate and hid behind someone's hedge, Baxter and Bliss tumbling after me. We flung ourselves down on the muddy ground and lay still, trembling. I put my hand over Pixie's mouth just in case she cried. We heard barking, hasty footsteps, angry shouting. I was sure the dog would sniff us out, but perhaps his long nose was too refined for smelling. We heard them hurtle past us. I waited a little, my heart pounding in my chest, and then dared peep through the hedge. They were much further up the road, veering from pavement to pavement, still looking for us. We had to get moving before they came back down.

'Quick – and *quietly*!' I whispered.

We scrambled through the hedge to the gate and ran back down, along the road, and then up the next street, which I was pretty sure led to our estate. Bliss and Baxter were running in their bare feet, but they'd had the wit to grab their trainers.

'My welly boots!' Pixie mumbled mournfully, waggling her bare toes.

'We'll have to go back for them tomorrow,' I said. 'Come on, let's get home now, quick.'

We'd slowed down, trudging upwards, Bliss limping now and brushing her sodden coat anxiously, though Baxter still stamped along, happy to be a mud boy. We got to the top of the road – and found it joined up with the first road, and – oh no, oh no – there was the rain-cap woman and her dog coming panting into view.

'Run again!' I gasped.

We ran for our flats this time. There was nowhere else to go. The woman was much slower now, clutching her chest, her face still purple-red under her rain-cap, the mud still perched on top even after all that running.

'Don't let her follow us back to our flat!' I gasped. 'We have to hide.'

'I know where!' said Baxter.

He charged past the first block, ducked round the corner, and into the bin sheds. We pressed ourselves back against the huge metal container, ankle-deep in horrible smelly rubbish, clutching each other. We waited. We heard a dog barking far away in the distance – but nothing more.

'Has she gone?' Bliss whispered.

'I think so. Better wait a few minutes more though.'

'Didn't she look funny with that mud on her hat!' said Baxter, sniggering.

'Shh! It was very, very bad of you, Baxter,' I whispered, but I started giggling too.

We all shook with laughter. When we finally emerged and there was no sign of scary rain-cap lady and her dog, we whooped and shouted and high-fived each other.

'Right! Let's get *home*,' I said. 'We're all badly in need of a bath.'

'What if Mum's come back?' said Bliss. 'She'll go bonkers if she sees our clothes.'

'She won't be back, not yet,' I said. My voice wobbled. Baxter slid his hand into mine, surprising me.

'We don't need her back. It's more fun without her,' he said.

'Yes, it is,' said Bliss. 'You're our mum now, Lily.'

Pixie hadn't even been listening, but she said, 'Yes, yes, yes!'

'Shut up, you soppy lot,' I said, dangerously close to tears.

Even so, the kids ran into every room when we got back indoors, obviously looking for Mum everywhere. They all drooped when they found the flat was empty.

'Bath-time, bath-time, bath-time!' I shouted into the silence. 'You three can all have a bath together and we'll squirt washing-up liquid in so we'll have bubbles everywhere. Come on, off with those dirty clothes – and stop running about, you're getting muddy footprints everywhere.'

'You're sounding like a real mum now,' said Baxter.

I got the bath running and swirled washing-up liquid around liberally. I helped Pixie out of her clothes and then dangled her in the bath, letting her bounce in the bubbles. Baxter and Bliss came running into the bathroom naked, their bodies pink, their faces and arms and legs chocolate brown.

'You get in the bath too, Lily!' Bliss begged.

'No, there's no room. I'll have my own bath in a minute, after I've got you lot clean,' I said.

I let them play for a bit while I sorted through their clothes. I could wash their T-shirts and jeans easily enough but their jackets were going to be a problem. I tried sponging them with an old rag but it just stirred up the mud and spread the stains around. I left them in a soggy heap, deciding to wait until the morning. At least I could scrub the children clean. I set to while they squirmed and wriggled and shrieked, and soon they were pink all over.

I hoisted them out of the bath one by one and wrapped them in towels. Baxter and Bliss were old enough to dry themselves but I rubbed them down even so, cosseting them, and I swaddled Pixie, picking her up in my arms, pretending she was my baby. I found them all clean T-shirts and clean pants and then sat them down in front of the television while I went to have my bath in peace.

I had to scrub out the tub first because the bottom was all silted with mud, but when it was clean at last I ran myself a fresh bath, with lots more bubbles. I lay back with a sigh, up to my chin in bubbles, the blood throbbing in my head. It felt so good to stretch out. My arms and back were aching after lumping Pixie around all that time. I closed my eyes and played the Lily Alone game: I was lying in my beautiful jade-green marble bath strewn with rose petals, sipping a glass of champagne. When I was sufficiently relaxed I'd step out, grab the twenty snow-white towels from the cupboard and dab myself dry. I'd slip on a silky robe and saunter into my white living room. I'd lounge on my vast white velvet sofa and switch on my enormous television, taking up an entire wall. I'd watch a film in total peace, no one wriggling or kicking beside me, no squabbling over the remote, no complaints that the film was too girlie, too scary, too silly. I was Lily Alone and no one could ever disturb me, and if the doorbell rang I simply ignored it . . .

The doorbell was ringing! I sat up so swiftly the water swooshed over the side of the bath.

'It's Mum back!' Baxter yelled, and I heard him running.

'No, no, don't go to the door, Baxter!' I shouted, jumping out of the bath and running too.

Baxter got to the door before me, jumping up and opening the latch, shouting, 'Mum, Mum, Mum!'

It wasn't Mum. I heard a man's voice. No, it wasn't Mikey, thank goodness. This was a kind, gentle voice, deep – the sort of voice that could tell you all sorts of stories and you'd never get tired of listening ... It was Mr Abbott! And oh, my goodness, there I was, stark naked, dripping in the hall! I flew back to the bathroom, slammed the door and leaned against it. I gnawed on my thumbnail, trying to think what to do. I hoped against hope that Baxter would somehow get rid of him, even slam the door in his face – but I heard more talking, then footsteps. Oh my God, Mr Abbott was in our flat now!

I stood there, shivering, utterly helpless. Then I heard knocking on the door.

'Lily?' It was Bliss. 'Lily, it's your teacher, Mr Abbott, come to see you.'

'Well, I can't see him. I'm in the bath. Look, tell him I'm ill. Tell him we're *all* ill.'

'Yes, Baxter's telling him a whole load of stuff, but he says he still wants to see you. And Mum.'

What was I going to do *now*? I couldn't let Baxter

rabbit on. He'd tell Mr Abbott the whole story if I didn't shut him up.

'Tell him I'm coming,' I hissed. I didn't have time to go and look for clean clothes. I pulled on my damp T-shirt and jeans, still thick with mud, and rushed out.

Mr Abbott was sitting in the living room with Baxter, Pixie perched on the arm of his chair. She was prattling away to him, saying stuff about a funny lady with a dog, but luckily he didn't seem to be listening properly. Baxter was strutting around the room in his pants, telling Mr Abbott that he didn't know where Mum was and he didn't care because she was bad.

'Baxter!' I said sharply. 'Don't you dare say that about Mum. Of course you know where she is. She's gone to the chemist's to get us some more medicine for our bad tummies.'

'Bad, bad, bad,' Pixie echoed. I didn't know whether she meant bad tummy or bad mummy. I'm not sure she did either.

Mr Abbott was staring at me. I felt myself blushing scarlet. What must he think of me looking such a muddy mess?

'Hello, Lily,' he said gently. 'I'm sorry you and your family aren't well. You've been off school three days now. Have you seen a doctor?'

I hesitated.

'Well, Mum says she'll take us if we're not better tomorrow.'

'Yes, that's a good idea.'

'It's – it's very catching. I wouldn't stay too long. You don't want to go down with it yourself, Mr Abbott,' I said.

'Well, I'll just stay until your mother gets home,' he said.

I felt my throat go dry. I tried to swallow.

'I'll – I'll make a cup of tea,' I said desperately. 'Baxter, Bliss, stop prancing about in your under-wear. Go and put some jeans on, clean ones.'

'*You're* all dirty,' Baxter pointed out unkindly.

'Do as I say, Baxter,' I said fiercely. 'And Bliss, you find Pixie her dungarees. Pixie, leave Mr Abbott in peace and go with Bliss.'

'I *like* Mr Abbott,' said Pixie, patting his cheek.

'I like you too, Pixie,' said Mr Abbott. He smiled as she hopped across the room. Then he followed me into the kitchen. 'She's a sweet little poppet. Very friendly. She tried to climb on my knee.'

'Yes, she just wants attention,' I said, putting the kettle on.

'And Pixie's been poorly too? I must say, she seems full of beans today,' said Mr Abbott.

'Oh, she's been very poorly, we all have,' I said.

'You certainly look a bit tired and wan, Lily. Such a shame you had to miss the outing to the gallery today.'

'Yes,' I said sadly. 'It's a great shame.'

'That's partly why I've popped round. I've bought you a little souvenir,' said Mr Abbott, and he took a little white paper bag from his pocket.

'Oh, Mr Abbott!' I said, so thrilled that I knocked a teacup over.

'Don't get too excited. It's nothing much, just a few postcards.'

I had to pour the boiling water into the teacups with two hands because they were shaking so much. Mr Abbott had bought me a present! I went to the fridge to get the milk, and then remembered we didn't have any. I stood, agonized, trying to think what to do. I could hardly offer him ice cream with his cup of tea.

Mr Abbott was watching.

'I take my tea black,' he said quickly.

'Oh! Yes, so do I, it tastes much better that way,' I said gratefully. I rubbed round the saucers with a teatowel where I'd spilled a little tea. 'There! Do you take sugar?'

I knew we had a whole bag of sugar but he didn't want that either. I sat beside him, terribly conscious of my wet hair and filthy clothes.

'Here,' he said, pressing the paper bag into my hands.

I opened it up. There were six postcards inside, with pictures of paintings, all blue and pink and scarlet and gold.

'I thought if you couldn't come to the gallery I'd bring a little bit of it to you,' said Mr Abbott. 'I picked out all the angels I could find. I remember we had a very interesting conversation about wings once. These angels have wonderful multicoloured wings – and look how they vary in size. This one has tiny little flimsy things that fold up like a fan, whereas *this* one has wings far bigger than himself. If he came to visit you here he'd have to be very careful getting in the lift or he'd get them trapped.'

'Oh, Mr Abbott!' I said again, thrilled. *He* was an angel, flying here to see me and give me my special present.

I wanted us to sit together for ever, sipping tea and discussing angels, but Baxter and Pixie came running in, sniggering. They were wearing each other's clothes: Baxter was squeezed into one of Pixie's tiny T-shirts and she was wearing his jeans, shuffling because the empty ends trailed across the carpet. Bliss crept in anxiously behind them, clearly worried she would be blamed.

'Oh, ha ha, very funny,' I said, sighing. 'Watch out,

Pixie, you'll fall over. And Baxter, take that T-shirt off, you'll rip it.'

Baxter tried to pull it over his head and got stuck.

'Can't!' he said, charging up and down like a bull.

I caught him with one hand and whipped the T-shirt off with the other. Then I grabbed Pixie.

'Come on, Bliss, help me pull her jeans off.'

Mr Abbott watched me, smiling, as I sorted them out.

'You make a marvellous little mother, Lily,' he said.

I smiled back at him shyly.

Mr Abbott looked at his watch.

'When did your mum go out?' he asked.

Bliss and Baxter looked at me.

'Oh, not long ago,' I said quickly. 'She might be quite a while, especially if she decides to do a big shop. I wouldn't wait if I were you, Mr Abbott.'

'Your mum has a mobile, doesn't she? Perhaps we could phone her and tell her I'm here? I'd really like to talk to her.'

Bliss gave a little gasp of dismay. I went on looking steadily at Mr Abbott.

'I think I'd better be truthful, Mr Abbott,' I said.

The three kids stared at me.

'I think Mum might be a bit – a bit embarrassed if she knew that *you* knew she'd left us on our own,'

I said, as calmly as I could. 'She knows she's not supposed to leave us, but it's difficult, see. She's got to do the shopping and she can't cart all of us with her, especially with this bug and us needing the toilet all the time.'

'Does your mum often leave you in charge of the children, Lily?'

'Oh no, hardly ever. She gets our neighbour to look after us, doesn't she, Bliss? Old Kath along the balcony.'

Bliss nodded vigorously, doing her best to be helpful.

'And my dad Mikey comes too,' said Baxter.

'Yes, he does, but just this once they were all out, you see, so Mum took a chance. *We* don't mind. You said how good I was with the kids, Mr Abbott.'

'Yes, you are. It's just – well, you're still quite young to be in charge. Lily, don't get me wrong, I don't want to get you or your mum into trouble. I just want to see if I can help in any way. I know how hard it must be for your mum bringing you up single-handed. Maybe if we spoke to social services—'

'No! Oh please, don't. That would get Mum really upset. You won't say anything, will you? Oh please, Mr Abbott, promise?'

'Well, I don't know what to do for the best,' he said.

'The *best* would be for you to go away now, before

163

Mum gets back. Please. We'll all get into trouble if she finds out we let you in the house. We're not supposed to even answer the door. Mum will go nuts if she knows.'

'I can understand that,' said Mr Abbott uncomfortably. 'Well, I certainly don't want to get you into trouble. All right, I'll go away now, but I'll leave you my phone number. If Mum hasn't come back in an hour or so, will you give me a ring? Do you promise?'

'Oh yes, I promise,' I lied.

'And I hope to see you in school tomorrow. If not I'll come round again. Now don't look so worried, I just want to make sure you're all right.'

'Yes. Thank you. And thank you very much for my lovely angel postcards. I think they're really lovely, Mr Abbott,' I said, and then I blushed because it sounded so silly.

'I think you're really lovely too, Lily,' said Mr Abbott. I think he was just teasing me. I hoped he might have meant it just a little bit, but when I looked in Mum's mirror after he'd gone, I groaned. I looked even worse than I'd imagined, my hair all stringy, a smear of mud still on my nose, and my T-shirt and jeans looked *awful*, as if I'd been rolling around in a pigsty.

Bliss followed me into the bedroom.

'Are you going to phone Mr Abbott?'

'Of course not.'

'Are we going to school tomorrow?'

'Nope. We can't leave Pixie.'

'Then Mr Abbott will come round again and want to see Mum.'

'Yes. Just stop saying the bleeding obvious, will you, Bliss. You're doing my head in,' I snapped.

'But what are we going to *do*?'

'I don't know. Oh, for goodness' sake, don't cry. Trust me, I'll think of something, OK?'

I lay awake half the night trying to think what to do. Then I got up really early and sat on the living-room floor with my angel postcards spread all around me. I stroked their wings with the tips of my fingers. I imagined white feathers sprouting from my back, great strong wings so I could soar into the sky, right up over the park . . .

And then I knew what we had to do. It was simple. I sat up and started writing a letter in my best handwriting.

Dear Mr Abbott,

    Mum has decided to take us all on a little holiday to see if some sea air will make us better. We will be back soon. Thank you very much for my postcards.

    Love from Lily

I decorated the corners of the letter with flying angels to make it look pretty, colouring them in carefully, and I drew a lily flower beside my name.

Then I sat with my head on my knees, planning. I heard Pixie starting to mutter to herself, bouncing about in her cot. I went into our bedroom. Bliss and Baxter were still asleep, curled up together like two little dormice. Pixie smiled at me and put her arms up to be lifted out of her cot.

I hauled her out and gave her a big cuddle and then took her to the toilet. When she was sitting there I played 'This little piggy' with her toes and she giggled delightedly, as if it was a brand-new exciting game.

'There now, Pixie. Let's wash our hands and then make breakfast. What would you like for a special treat? Let's see: gravy powder, salt and pepper, cooking fat – or ice cream?'

'Ice cream!' said Pixie. 'Ice cream, ice cream!'

Baxter woke up and heard the magic word too. He hurtled after us into the kitchen.

'Hey, sleepy boy,' I said, catching hold of him and swinging him round.

He clung to me like a little monkey and rubbed his bristly head against my cheek.

'Why don't you stay cuddly like this all day long, eh?' I said. 'Come on, you get the ice cream out of the freezer.'

I bustled about, setting the table, the children helping me. Bliss hadn't yet appeared when the others were already tucking in, so I went to fetch her. She was still curled up in bed clutching Headless, but her eyes were open.

'Bliss, baby, what's up? Don't you want to come and have some ice cream for breakfast?' I said.

'Are you still cross with me?' she whispered.

'Oh, darling, I'm not the slightest bit cross. I'm sorry I was mean to you last night.'

I gave my sister a great big hug. 'I do love you, Bliss. Come and have some breakfast quick, or Baxter and Pixie will have eaten up all the ice cream.'

I let them finish up the whole carton, together with a can of peaches.

'There now! Good breakfast, eh?'

'Can we have cornflakes now?' said Baxter.

'No, greedy-guts, we're saving the cornflakes. I'm going to pack up lots of food. Go and get me Mum's big shopper.'

'Are we having a picnic?' said Bliss.

'Yes, we're going to have lots of special picnics.'

'In the magic garden?'

'We are going to have picnics all over the park. Because do you know what? We're going to camp there, just till Saturday, when Mum will come back.'

'Camp!' said Baxter, clapping his hands. 'Where's our tent?'

'We haven't got a tent, you know that. But we'll take a blanket and pillows and the plastic tablecloth to go over the top of us in case it rains,' I said, proud that I'd thought it all out.

'Will there be horrible creepy-crawlies if we camp?' said Bliss. She'd watched *I'm a Celebrity, Get Me Out of Here!*

'Absolutely not. If even the tiniest little ant dares to come anywhere near I'll swat it flat, I promise,' I said.

'What about the deer?'

'Oh, Bliss! You're the only person in the entire world who could possibly be afraid of deer. They're so sweet and shy and soft and gentle.'

'They've got those big horn things,' Bliss persisted.

'Antlers!' Baxter shouted. 'I'm a huge great daddy deer and these are my antlers.' He held his arms in an arc over his head, and started making snorty noises. 'Now I'm going to *charge*.' He lunged at Bliss, who started squealing.

'Stop it, Baxter,' I said, grabbing him.

Baxter subsided, screwing up his face.

'What? You're not *crying*, are you?'

'No!' Baxter shouted, though his eyes were watering.

'I didn't hurt you. I barely touched you,' I said, astonished as his tears spilled over. 'What *is* it?'

'I want *my* daddy,' Baxter sniffed.

'Oh, for goodness' sake,' I said. I tried to put my arms round him but he pushed me away.

'I don't want you, I want *Dad*.'

I sat on the bench, running my finger round my ice-cream bowl and licking it. I didn't know what to do. I knew Mikey's mobile-phone number. All right, he was in Scotland, but if I told him Mum had gone off and left us I thought he'd come, job or not. He loved Baxter, I knew that. He loved Bliss too, though she irritated him. He was fond of Pixie. They'd be safe with him. But I wouldn't. I hated the way he looked at me, some of the things he said. It was just about all right when Mum was around. It would be much too scary without her.

No, we'd be fine. We just had to hide in the park for two days and then it would be Saturday and Mum would be back.

I started packing Mum's big shopping bag with cornflakes and biscuits and chocolate and apples and Dairylea and crisps. I put cans of Coke and Lilt in another bag, and filled two empty squash bottles with tap water. There! We had just about enough to keep us going for a couple of days. The bags were very heavy though. I'd have to hang them on Pixie's buggy. I could stuff the buggy with our blankets and pillows too, plus the plastic table-cloth. So what else did we need? A change of clothes each, in case the kids got muddy again. It would be best to pack several pairs of knickers for Pixie, just in case.

I gathered up clothes and inspected our coats. I'd forgotten to hang them up so they were still in a dank sodden heap. Well, it wasn't cold any more. I had to hope it wouldn't rain again. I found sweat-shirts for each of us, because I knew it would be cooler at night. I didn't think we need bother with pyjamas. We could just sleep in our clothes.

The last bag was for our favourite things. I packed my angel postcards, my drawing pad and crayons, the fairy-tale book, Headless, the fork-lift truck and Pixie's pink plastic handbag.

'There!' I said at last. 'Come on, get dressed. And put your sweatshirts on.'

'It's too hot!' said Baxter.

'Yes, but we can't carry them, not when we've got all these bags. I want *you* to carry the biggest bag, Baxter. I hope it's not too heavy for you.'

'Heavy! It's ever so light. I can carry it easy-peasy,' said Baxter proudly.

'And you must carry the favourite things, Bliss. Do you think you can manage it?'

'I think so,' said Bliss. She was scrambling into her clothes, but she looked at her trainers doubtfully. They were thick with mud. 'Look!' she said, holding them at arm's length.

'It's OK, we'll just brush it off. It's easy now it's gone hard. Look, we'll put a newspaper on the floor and then you can bang them together.'

Baxter started banging his together without benefit of the newspaper, sending flakes of mud everywhere. Pixie sat on the floor wiggling her pink toes.

'No welly boots!' she said.

'Well, go and get your shoes, silly. You can put them on yourself because they've got sticky straps.'

Pixie put her shoes on and stomped about un-certainly.

'They feel funny.'

I looked. 'You've got them on the wrong feet, silly. Swap them over. Honestly!'

It seemed hours before I got them all ready. When we were going out of the door at last I had another thought. What if Mum came back early, on Friday? She'd go spare if we were missing. I used up another precious page of my drawing book scribbling her a note:

Dear Mum,
    Don't worry, we are safe and we'll be back Saturday, I promise. Hope you had a lovely holiday.

I paused, looking around the flat.

Sorry we've made a bit of a mess, don't be cross.
Lots and lots and lots of love,
Lily

Baxter and Bliss wanted to print their names at the bottom too, and Pixie did a scribble and a kiss. Then I folded the letter up and put it on Mum's pillow.

'There!' I said. 'Now, let's go.'

I left Mr Abbott's letter sticking out of the letter box. Then I stood for a good two minutes in front of

173

the door not knowing what to do. If I closed it we couldn't get back in. And yet if I left it on the latch, Mr Abbott might notice and think it odd.

'What do you think we should do about the front door?' I asked Bliss.

She blinked at me anxiously.

'Shut it?' she said. 'Or leave it open?'

'Yes, but *which*?'

'Shut it!' said Baxter, and pulled it. I think he only meant to demonstrate but he pulled too hard. The door shut with a bang.

'Now you've done it!' I said unfairly.

'Want to do a wee-wee,' said Pixie, fidgeting in her buggy.

'Well, you can't. You'll have to wait till we get to the park. OK, come along, all of you.'

I started wheeling the buggy along the balcony as quickly as I could, shushing the twins – but Old Kath already had her door open.

'Do you kids *have* to bang the door?' she said, glaring. She had a cigarette in her mouth and she kept it there when she talked so it moved weirdly up and down.

'Sorry, Kath,' I said, wheeling Pixie quickly past.

'Where are you lot going with all them bags?' Kath asked.

'We're . . . we're just going down the launderette,' I said.

'Looks like you're washing clothes for an army,'
said Kath, looking at the two bulging bags in the
buggy. 'That mum of yours! Even got the little ones
lugging stuff.'

She poked at Bliss's bag and felt the hard edges
of my drawing pad.

'What's this then? You lot started to wear cardboard knickers?' She cackled at her own stupid
joke, the cigarette end wobbling, but staying
put. Did she stick it to her lower lip with Sello-
tape?

I forced myself to smile at her.

'These are our favourite things, to keep the kids
quiet in the launderette.'

'Keep you lot quiet! That'll be the day. Your mum
couldn't keep a goldfish quiet, I'm telling you.
Where *is* she then? I want a word with her.'

'She's downstairs with another two bags of
washing,' I said.

'She's getting like the blooming Scarlet
Pimpernel, your mum. You seek her here, you seek
her there, and she's always nipped off somewhere
else, leaving you in charge. She's got a right cheek,
turning you into a nanny all the time.'

'I *like* looking after the kids,' I said.

'Yeah, well, *you're* just a kid too, or had you forgotten?'

'I need a *wee-wee*,' Pixie said, still fidgeting.

'No, you don't, darling, you've only just gone,' I lied. 'Well, we'll have to get going.' I craned my neck to one side, ear up. 'I think that was Mum calling for us.'

Old Kath narrowed her eyes.

'I didn't hear anything.'

'Well, you don't hear so well when you get older, do you?' I said.

'You cheeky little madam!'

'Come on, kids,' I said, wheeling Pixie past her door, making for the lift.

It didn't come straight away so we were stuck there, Old Kath calling along to us.

'You watch out. Next time I'm down the Social I'll be telling them a few tales on you lot. Your mum's a shocker, letting you kids run wild and cheek your elders and betters.'

Why couldn't the old bag mind her own business? When the lift came at last Baxter stuck his finger up at her – and I'm afraid I did too. We shot down in the lift, spluttering and giggling.

'You'll make her more cross now,' said Bliss.

'I know. But it was worth it, seeing her face,' I said.

'Can I do wee-wees in the corner of the lift?' asked Pixie.

'*No!* Look, wait till we get to the park. There are toilets at the entrance. You can wait till we get there.'

Pixie couldn't wait. I had to take her knickers off and hold her out over a drain on the way.

'I want to go too,' said Bliss.

'Well, you're too big to do it in the gutter,' I said.

'I can,' said Baxter – and demonstrated.

A woman stomped past in high heels, glaring.

'Dirty boy!' she said.

I saw the look on Baxter's face. I knew he was going to aim at her any second.

'Don't you *dare*,' I hissed. 'Hurry and *finish*.'

Baxter took no notice, but luckily the woman had stomped on out of firing range.

'Put it away – you *are* a dirty boy!' I said. 'Now look, Bliss is right, we'll make everyone cross with us and then they really will report us. We don't want anyone noticing us going into the park. They'll know where to look if they start searching for us.'

'They're going to start searching for us?' said Bliss.

'*If*! Now come on, let's get in the park. You can hold on till then, can't you, Bliss?'

'I hope so,' she said anxiously.

It seemed a longer trek than usual to the park because I was pushing the heavy buggy and we were all loaded up with bags. When we got to the park gates at last, *I* was busting to go to the toilet, let alone Bliss. I started dragging Baxter in with us, but he struggled violently, pulling a face.

'I'm not going in the ladies' toilets!' he said. 'I won't, I won't, you can't make me.'

'All right. But wait right outside, do you hear me? Promise you won't budge.'

'I promise.'

'Promise on Mum's life.'

'*Yes!*'

So we left him outside. I wheeled Pixie into the toilets with us because I didn't want Baxter messing about with the buggy. It was so loaded up with bags that it tipped over at a touch, especially if Pixie stood up or wriggled around. I let Bliss go to the loo first while I minded Pixie, and then I had my turn.

'I want to go too!' Pixie said.

'No, you don't. You've only just been. Right in the street where everyone could see you.'

'I want to go again,' Pixie insisted.

'Nonsense.'

'I'm nearly wetting!'

I sighed and got Bliss to hang onto the buggy handle while I hauled Pixie out into a toilet. She sat there, waving her legs and laughing.

'Come on, Pixie.'

'It won't come.'

'Well, you didn't need to go, then. Come here.' I lifted her off and pulled her knickers up – but the second she was back in her buggy she started all over again.

'Want to do a wee-wee!'

'You're just playing silly games with us. You're so naughty, Pixie. It isn't funny,' I said sternly.

Bliss was covering her mouth, making little snorty noises.

'It is a little bit funny,' she spluttered.

We both laughed then and Pixie cackled too, proud that she was such a brilliant entertainer.

'Come on, you giggly sillies,' I said, wheeling Pixie's buggy out of the toilets.

'Sorry we've been so long, Baxter,' I started saying – but Baxter wasn't there.

'Baxter? Baxter! I told you to stay here. You *promised*,' I said, raising my voice.

I thought he was hiding behind the hedge, but there was no sign of him. I wondered if he'd gone to the gents' toilets and called outside. I even ran in quickly to check, but he wasn't there either.

'Oh no, where's he *gone*?' I said.

'He's so bad,' said Bliss.

'Bad bad bad,' said Pixie in a silly voice, wanting to make us laugh again, but it wasn't funny any more.

I screwed up my eyes and squinted as far as I could see – up the big hill, along the path in front, around near the road. I couldn't see Baxter anywhere.

'He's run away,' said Bliss, starting to cry.

'Of course he hasn't. He's just being naughty, hiding.' I looked over to the car park. 'I bet he's over there, hiding behind one of those cars. Come on, we'll go and look for him.'

We crossed the road carefully and went into the car park. It was hard work pushing the buggy on the gravel. I zig-zagged round the rows of cars as best I could, while Bliss ran ahead, calling for Baxter. I kept expecting him to leap out at us, shouting, *Boo!* But nothing happened. There was still no sign of him.

A man unwound his car window.

'What's up, girlies? Has your dog run away? Tell you what, why don't you get in my car and I'll drive you around to see if you can spot him?'

He looked kind and concerned but there was something odd about his smile.

'We're not allowed to talk to strangers,' I gabbled, and I ran with the buggy, tugging Bliss along with me.

'Was that a bad man?' she panted.

'I don't know. Maybe.'

'Lily, do you think a bad man's grabbed Baxter?'

'Of course not,' I said, but the idea panicked me. Baxter thought he was so streetwise but he was just a very little kid. If some Mikey-type guy in a flash car had driven up outside the toilets and offered Baxter a lift he'd have been off like a shot. Oh God, why didn't I *make* him come into the toilets with us?

The man who had spoken to us was getting out of his car now, still looking over at us.

'Quick, we've got to get out of here,' I said. 'Let's go in that little playground.'

We ran hard, Pixie jolted up and down in the buggy. She laughed at first, thinking it a game, but then she started to get frightened.

'Slow down, slow down!' she demanded.

'We can't, Pixie. We're looking for Baxter.'

'Baxter's there,' she said.

'What? Where?' I whirled round. 'No, he's not. Pixie, this isn't a silly game! Baxter's gone *missing*.'

'Baxter, Baxter, Baxter!' said Pixie, pointing up

in the air, as if her brother were floating above her head.

I crouched down at her level and looked upwards too. I saw the top of Baxter's head bobbing up and down inside the little playground. I ran – and there he was, jumping about on top of the slide, yelling, 'I'm the boss of this den!'

I parked Pixie with Bliss and scrambled up after him.

'Get *down*!'

He thought I was playing and aimed a twig at me like a gun, pretending to fire. I slapped it out of his hand and then I slapped *him*.

'Ouch! Stop it! Don't hit me! I'll hit you back, harder,' he yelled.

'I told you to stay outside the toilets and you promised you would, you promised on Mum's life!'

'I didn't want to stay outside any smelly ladies' toilets,' he wailed, knuckling his eyes.

'We thought you were lost, you stupid little idiot,' I said, giving him a shake for emphasis.

'I'm not stupid! You are! You're a mean fat farty pig and I hate you!' Baxter said, the tears rolling down his cheeks.

'I hate you too,' I said, but already I felt the anger seeping out of me. I searched my pocket and found a little screwed-up tissue. I dabbed at Baxter's face with it.

'Get off!' he said.

I didn't get off, I pulled him closer, and when I hugged him he leaned against me, allowing himself to sob because his face was hidden.

Bliss was crying too, standing forlornly beside Pixie and the buggy.

'Come on, Baxter, let's get down,' I said gently. 'We've got to give Bliss a hug too.'

I slid down and Baxter slid after me on his tummy.

'It's OK, Bliss. Baxter's safe and sound. I'm not cross any more. It's all right now,' I said.

Bliss went on howling.

'It's – not – all – right,' she gasped between sobs. 'It's *Mum*!'

'Mum? What do you mean?'

'Baxter swore on Mum's life! So now she'll be *dead*!'

'Oh no she won't. Don't say that. Especially not in front of Pixie. No, Mum's fine. She'll be having a lovely time with this new boyfriend of hers,' I said bitterly. 'She'll be lying on the beach in a new bikini right this minute, snogging away.'

'Yuck,' said Baxter.

'Yes, double yuck,' I said. 'We won't worry about

Mum, Bliss, because she's not the slightest bit worried about us. We can manage just fine without her, *if* we're all careful. We've got to stick together. Do you hear that, Baxter? This isn't a game where we can all muck about. This is deadly serious. We've got to hide here till Saturday, which means we've got to stay out of everyone's way, not draw attention to ourselves. From now on we have to act like we're invisible. We absolutely mustn't shout back at people or be rude or cheeky or do anything at all that makes them remember us. We must just look like four children out for the day with their mum or their dad – and our grown-up just happens to have run ahead or lagged behind, whatever—'

The buggy suddenly fell over. Pixie had got bored during my long lecture and had managed to wriggle out of the straps. She'd made a bolt for freedom and tipped it up. She started yelling hard. I picked her up and held her.

'Where does it hurt, Pixie?' I said, feeling her arms and legs.

'Everywhere!' Pixie roared.

When I punched and prodded each bit, she didn't roar harder, so I decided she was more or less OK.

'Right then,' I said, stuffing her back into the buggy and reloading it with the bulging bags. 'Off we go.'

I wasn't quite sure where we were going *to*. We had to make a secret camp somewhere, but I didn't know which spot to pick. I was tired out already and it was much harder work pushing the buggy over grass, but it wouldn't make sense to make our camp near the park entrance, where so many people might spot us.

'The magic garden, the magic garden!' Bliss cried.

I knew there'd be lots of hiding places there. We'd already hidden beneath the willow tree, but that was just playing a game. The willow fronds weren't thick enough. We'd be on plain view to everyone. Anyway, there were too many people circling the pond and feeding the ducks. We'd be found in five minutes. There were hundreds of big bushes all over the magic garden. We could creep under one and crouch there but we couldn't stay crouched permanently. No, the magic garden wasn't the right place for us.

'We're not going to the magic garden straight away,' I said. 'We'll go there later, Bliss, after we've found a camp and hidden all our things.

'We could camp back in that playground,' said Baxter. 'I could be the boss guy and live at the top of the slide.'

'Baxter, a children's playground isn't the *best*

place to hide. Like, there would be other children there.'

'I'll tell them to shove off. I'll be the boss, see.'

'No, we need a really *secret* place, where no one else in the park goes. Away from the car park and the playgrounds.' I looked all around again. 'Let's go that way,' I said, pointing to a yellowy sandy path in the opposite direction to the hill. At least it would be easier to push the buggy along it.

'*Follow, follow, follow, follow, follow the yellow-sand road*,' I said, singing the song from *The Wizard of Oz*. I did a little skippy dance to the tune. 'Come on, Bliss, Baxter, you've all seen the film.'

They hopped and skipped too, and Pixie drummed her heels in the buggy. Baxter picked up a fallen branch and waved it dangerously in the air, conducting us.

'We're not off to see any real wizard, are we?' said Bliss.

'No wizards whatsoever. Just us. We're going to find a very special secret place to make our camp.'

'That's easy-peasy,' said Baxter. 'This will be a good camp!' he said, whacking a very tall tree with his stick. 'We'll camp right up in the branches, and when anyone comes near we'll see them and shoot them, *bang bang bang*.'

'So how are we all going to get up in this tree, Baxter?'

'*Climb* up, stupid,' said Baxter.

He tried to demonstrate. He clearly saw himself shinning up like a little monkey after coconuts. He looked extremely puzzled when he couldn't even get as far as the first branch. He tried again and again, while we waited patiently, and then he lost his temper and started kicking the tree, as if it was being deliberately awkward.

'Oh, Baxter, stop it! You're not hurting the tree, you're hurting yourself.'

'You shut up,' he shouted and started kicking me too.

'You're being silly. Ouch, you're hurting *me* now. Look, you've been clever and found a branch. Let's all find branches too and maybe we can stick them in the ground and put the tablecloth over them so it's like a little tent . . . ?' My voice tailed away. I'd been just like Baxter. I'd pictured us in a cosy tent in the middle of this beautiful park, but I hadn't thought exactly how it was all going to work.

I tried sticking Baxter's branch into the earth. I couldn't get it to stand upright – and anyway, the tablecloth wasn't anywhere near big enough when I held it out.

187

'That's a *stupid* idea,' said Baxter. 'That's not a tent!' He snatched his branch back and poked at the tablecloth contemptuously.

'Don't, Baxter! You'll tear our tent,' said Bliss, trying to rescue the tablecloth.

'Oh, let him tear it. It's not going to work anyway,' I said. 'I don't know how to make a proper tent.'

'Perhaps with the blankets?' said Bliss, gathering them up and flapping them.

'Yes, but *how*?' I said.

A dog came running up off his lead and started barking eagerly.

'No! Go away! Help!' Bliss shrieked. She flapped harder, which only made him more excited.

'It's OK, Bliss, just stand still, he won't hurt you, he's only little,' I said – but she was too scared to listen and ran away up the grassy bank.

'Hey, silly doggy, play with *me*, not her,' said Baxter, waving the tablecloth at the dog.

The dog darted backwards and forwards joyfully, convinced this was a wonderful new game.

A youngish woman in jeans came striding towards us, whistling.

'Hey, Sammy! Down, boy! I'm sorry, kids, he's just having fun. He won't hurt you,' she called.

'He's lovely, aren't you, Sammy?' said Baxter, holding the tablecloth towards him enticingly and then flicking it away.

Sammy leaped up, caught the edge in his teeth and rolled on the ground with it, wrapping himself inside.

'He's like a big sausage roll!' Baxter said, roaring with laughter, totally over his temper tantrum.

'He *is* a sausage, my Sammy,' said the woman. 'Oh dear, is that your picnic cloth? I'm so sorry. Your mother will be furious.'

'She won't mind. It's only an old cloth,' I said quickly.

'Out you come, Sammy,' said the woman, scrabbling for him. He jumped free, his paws bicyling in the air, and then he made a mad dash for the buggy. Pixie squealed excitedly, but he wasn't after her, he was after the food bag.

'Oi, don't you dare! You're not golloping up the picnic too, bad boy,' said the woman. She clipped the lead on his collar and then fished in her jeans pocket. She brought out three pound coins and held them out to me. 'Here, buy yourself some ice cream for after the picnic.'

'Oh, thank you!' I said.

'Ice cream, ice cream, ice cream!' said Pixie happily.

'Sammy can come and play with us any time,' said Baxter.

The woman strode off, with Sammy leaping around at her heels.

'I *like* that lady,' said Baxter. 'Give me my pound then, Lily.'

'*I'll* look after the money. Pity she didn't see Bliss too – we'll have to share three ice creams between four,' I said, looking round. 'Where is she? Bliss, it's OK, you can come back, the dog's gone now.'

I couldn't see any sign of her.

'Bliss! *Bliss!*' I ran up the grassy slope and still couldn't see her. Had she kept on running? She was only little, but she could run fast, especially if she was in a blind panic. Why hadn't I gone after her straight away?

'Oh, Bliss, please, come here, you're scaring me!' I shouted.

'Silly Bliss,' said Baxter, but he was peering around too, nibbling his lip.

'Where's she gone, Baxter? Did you see which way she went?'

He shrugged. 'Over there? Or up by those trees? I don't know! She's so *silly*,' he said. 'I'll find her.'

'No, don't you go off too. Honestly! I think I

need to strap all three of you into the buggy so I can keep you safe.'

'They'd squash me! Can we have ice cream now?' said Pixie, not the slightest bit concerned about her missing sister.

'After we've found Bliss. Look, you sit still in your buggy like a good girl and guard all the bags, OK? Baxter, you come with me.'

I took his hand and we went searching for Bliss.

'Please, Bliss! Come back! The dog's gone. *Please* come back,' I shouted, blundering through the trees, knee-deep in ferns.

'I haven't gone away!' said Bliss.

Baxter and I started, spinning round. We'd both heard her, we were sure of that – but where was she? She'd sounded as if she was right beside us, but she was nowhere to be seen.

'Bliss?'

'Hello!' she said.

I peered down in the bracken, wondering if she could be hiding there.

'No, I'm *here*, look!' she said, giggling.

It sounded like she was in the huge old tree beside us, but we still couldn't see her. Baxter jumped for the first branch, hauled himself up – and then started laughing. Bliss laughed too. I climbed up after him – and there was Bliss, standing triumphantly in the totally hollow tree.

'Wow! Make room for me!' said Baxter, and he jumped down beside her.

There was much less room for me, but I slithered down too. As long as I crouched down a little I was totally invisible to any passers-by.

'You clever girl, Bliss!' I said, kissing the top of her head. 'You've found us the perfect hiding place.'

We dragged Pixie and the buggy and the bags to the hollow tree. We could just about stuff Pixie in beside us. She found it great fun, wriggling and squealing, butting her hard little head against my tummy.

'No, no, Pixie. When we're here in the tree we have to keep *quiet*,' I said. 'And we'll have to find a hiding place for your buggy or people will get suspicious.'

I clambered out of the tree again, collapsed the buggy, and hid it as best I could in the ferns. I hid the food bag in the ferns too, but I needed the blankets and the pillows in the tree with us. I padded the floor of the hollow trunk with ferns and then arranged the blankets and pillows on top to make a cosy nest.

'Now, let's all try curling up to see if we'll be able to sleep here,' I said.

We had to curl very carefully, and I ended up with Pixie's head in my lap, Bliss's elbow in my ribs and Baxter's feet kicking my bottom, but it was just about possible. I struggled up and did my best to hang the torn tablecloth above us, hooking the plastic onto little twiggy parts of the tree. It worked wonderfully.

'We've got a roof!' said Pixie. 'Clever Lily.'

'No, clever, clever Bliss for finding our tree,' I said, hugging her.

'I didn't know I was finding it. I just climbed up a bit to get away from the scary dog and saw the big hole and jumped inside,' said Bliss.

'Now can we have ice cream?' said Pixie.

I decided to risk leaving our stuff hidden there. It was so much easier walking along without lugging all the bags too, and we didn't have to stick to the sandy path as we'd left the pushchair behind. We could ramble up and down hills and run through the bracken and dodge up and down the molehills. Pixie ran happily too, not whining to be carried.

'Ice cream, ice cream!' she sang to herself.

There seemed no point trailing all the way back to the park entrance for our ice creams. I was sure there'd be another van further on in the park. We walked on, playing a Baxter game that we were robbers on the run from the police and mustn't be caught. It was a brilliant way of making the kids cautious, hiding in the bracken whenever any dog-walkers or runners came near us. Baxter turned his branch into a gun and shot anyone he didn't like the look of.

'We're not *really* robbers, are we?' Bliss whispered to me.

'Of course not.'

'And we're not really going to get ice cream, are we?'

'Oh yes we are. *Real* ice creams. Look!' I jangled the coins in my pocket. 'That lady with the Sammy dog, she gave them to me.'

'For you and Baxter and Pixie?'

'But we'll share with you, silly.'

'Because I found the tree house?'

'Because you're our Bliss.'

Bliss gave a little skip. 'I do like it here, with you. Maybe – maybe we could always stay here, just us?'

195

'What, never ever go back?' I said, thinking she was just playing.

'Never ever.'

'What about school?'

'I absolutely hate school. They tease me.'

'They tease me too,' I said. 'But I say mean stuff back and that usually shuts them up.'

'Baxter hits them. But they still don't shut up,' said Bliss. 'I want to live here in the park and never go to school.'

'What about Mum?' I said.

Bliss fidgeted, scraping her trainer in the sand. 'Maybe she could live here too,' she said at last.

'Oh, get real! Mum couldn't walk all round the park in her huge heels – and she couldn't manage without a mirror and all her make-up and stuff. And she wouldn't give up her comfy bed. You know Mum, she's hopeless, she can't manage without most things.'

'She can manage without us,' said Bliss.

We walked on hand in hand, thinking about Mum.

'I wonder if she's having a really great time?' I said. 'She was so different those last two days, after she met this Gordon. Really happy and funny and lovely.'

'I think you're her favourite,' said Bliss.

'No I'm not,' I said, though I couldn't help being pleased.

'Yes, you are, because you're the eldest. Or Pixie's her favourite because she's the littlest. Or Baxter because he's the only boy. I'm not her favourite because I'm not anything.'

'You're Bliss and you're blissful and you're *my* favourite,' I said. 'You're so much my favourite you can have all my ice cream.'

I was beginning to wonder if the only ice-cream place was right back at the entrance of the park after all, when we saw a mum with her two little boys and they all had big whippy ice creams.

'Ice cream,' said Pixie, looking like she was going to snatch a cone right out of a little boy's hand.

The mum smiled, but her boys looked nervous. It was too late to hide so I decided to be bold.

'Excuse me, could you tell me where you got your ice creams from?' I asked.

'We got them from the Lodge right over there,' said the mum, pointing up through the trees.

'Oh, brilliant,' I said.

'Are you kids OK? You have got a grown-up with you, haven't you?'

'Oh yes, we've got our mum, but – she's – she's over there.' I nodded at some bushes.

The mum stared in that direction too.

'Oh, don't look, please. She's doing a quick wee,' I said, inspired. 'She'll be ever so embarrassed if she sees you're looking.'

'Oh dear! I understand,' said the mum, giggling. 'Don't worry, we'll go off this way. Bye bye then.'

Pixie made a sudden lunge at the smallest boy but I managed to grab her by the wrist before she could touch his ice cream. He started snivelling all the same, which encouraged the mum to hurry off.

'Pixie, you're so naughty! You frightened him,' I said.

'I wanted the ice cream!' she wailed, her own lip quivering.

'It was *his* ice cream, not yours. We'll get you your own cone in two minutes. Now come on.'

'You were dead brilliant, Lily,' said Baxter, chuckling. 'Saying that about our mum having a wee! What made you think of that?'

'It just came into my head,' I said proudly.

'Can *I* say that next time? No, can I say my dad's having a wee? No, even better, can I say my dad's having—'

'Stop it! No, we're not going to talk to anyone else if we can help it,' I said firmly.

'Ice cream for *Pixie*!' Pixie said imperiously.

We went up the hill towards a long fence enclosing an enormous garden.

'Is it the magic garden with all the rosy flowers?' said Bliss.

'I think this is a different garden,' I said. 'Look, here's the gate in.'

The grassy bank was overgrown with weeds, but when we started going up a long trail of stone steps we saw shrubs and heather planted out like a proper garden. There were white tables and chairs with people sitting at them eating meals – but no ice cream. We walked into the big café, peering in awe at all the food on display, such *different* things – hot meals bubbling in metal containers, salads and sandwiches in glass cabinets, cakes set out on plates so you could just grab a slice. I had to hold Pixie and Baxter's hands. We'd eaten out heaps of times, but just in McDonald's, where you always knew what you were getting.

'I'll have some pie and chips and that big fat sandwich and the cake, all of it, and a bottle of beer,' said Baxter.

'We're having ice creams, silly, not a proper meal,' I said. 'Come on, maybe you get ice cream outside.'

We went through the café and out the other side, raced across the neat green lawn, out of the gates – and *there* was the ice-cream hut!

'Ice cream, ice cream!' Pixie squealed, and Baxter and Bliss danced up and down.

'How much are the smallest cones, please?' I asked the ice-cream man.

'A pound each – one twenty with a chocolate flake,' he said.

'Can I have three small cones then – no chocolate,' I said regretfully, digging in my pocket for the money.

The ice-cream man was peering at us.

'Don't you mean four? Or isn't the little kiddie big enough for ice cream?'

'I'm big! I'm very big, and I want a big ice cream!' said Pixie indignantly.

'We've only got three pounds between us,' I explained, handing the coins to him.

'Oh dear, so who's going without?' said the ice-cream man.

'Her!' said Baxter and Pixie, pointing to poor Bliss.

'No, she's not! We'll all share,' I said.

'There's a nice big sister,' he said. He made one, two, three, *four* white swirly ice creams and squirted chocolate sauce all over them.

'There you are,' he said. He nodded at Pixie. 'Watch you don't make too much of a mess, very big girl.'

'But – it was *three*!'

'Yes, but I'm not very good at counting today,' he said, smiling.

'You're so lovely. Thank you very very much,' I said. 'Say thank you, all of you lot.'

'Thank you,' they said in chorus.

Pixie said, '*Thank you, thank you, thank you!*'

Then we carried our ice creams very carefully back to the grass and sat down away from every-body else. We licked and sucked and nibbled very happily indeed. When I was finished I lay down on my back. I relished the cool milky taste in my mouth as I stared up at the blue sky and felt the sun on my face. Maybe I'd get a better suntan than Mum. I felt a little surge of pride. I was coping splendidly. I'd kept all three kids safe and fed and happy, and here we were in this glorious park. Everyone was being kind to us and we had the rest of today and all of Friday to hide out in our tree-house and go exploring.

When I was grown up I'd maybe live further up the hill in the posh houses and look out at this park from my back bedroom window and remem-ber the time I hid here with my brother and sisters . . . and I felt so fond of them now. I even wondered about inviting them to live with me. I imagined Baxter grown up, strong and bold and capable,

able to fix the boiler and frighten away any burglars. Bliss would be sweet and gentle, and she'd like to keep house for us, maybe do all the cooking. Pixie would be beautiful, out every night with a different boyfriend, but she'd always come home to us, because we were her family . . .

'Lily, Lily! I need to do a wee-wee. I need to do a wee-wee right now. Oh dear, oh dear, I'm doing my wee-wee now!'

'Wake *up*, Lily, Pixie's wetting herself and it's boring here, there's no one to kill.'

'Lily, there's a big bug on my leg, get it off, it's so scary!'

No, I'd be much better off living all alone. I sat up with a sigh and flicked the tiny beetle off Bliss's skinny leg. I took Pixie by the hand and led her off towards the toilets in the café.

'You two come too,' I said to Bliss and Baxter.

'I'm not going in the ladies' toilets,' said Baxter, but I held him with my other hand and wouldn't let him go.

'You're not to be trusted, matey. You ran off last time, right across that dangerous road to the playground. I'm not risking you running off again and getting lost. You're coming with us!'

'Stop it, you're twisting my arm!' Baxter moaned.

'I'll twist your arm right off if you don't shut up,'

I said, so fiercely that he knew I meant business and stopped struggling.

I hauled all three of them into the toilets and mopped Pixie while I made Bliss and Baxter use the loo.

While they were distracted washing their hands, vying with each other to see who could make the biggest soap bubble, I dashed into a cubicle myself.

When I came out two old grannies were fussing over the kids, helping them wash their hands. Pixie dimpled at them, and Baxter chatted away, telling them he was a big boy and didn't really need anyone's help, but Bliss went rigid with fear when they tried to get her to stick her wet hands in the drying machine. She had this silly idea that it would suck her up completely.

'It's OK, Bliss, just flap your hands to dry them,' I said.

'*Bliss?* Is that the little girl's name?' said one old granny, smiling. 'What a delightful name!'

'No, no – it's – I said *Fliss*, short for Felicity,' I said quickly. 'Thank you for helping them. We have to go now. Our mum's waiting for us.'

I pushed the kids quickly out of the toilets.

'Will you quit shoving me, Lily. I'll be a mass of bruises,' Baxter grumbled.

'Yeah, like you haven't been kicking me all over and giving *me* bruises since you were Pixie's age,' I said. I grabbed hold of Pixie as she tried to run into the café.

'Hey, hey, it's this way.'

'No, I want a cake now. And a sandwich. And chippies,' she said.

'I want, I want, I want! You're such a greedy-guts. You've just had an ice cream,' I said – but I guessed it was about lunchtime, and the smell of food was making my tummy rumble.

'I want a cake too – and that pie!' said Baxter.

'We haven't got any money. You all know that, even you, Pixie. So shut up, all of you. Come on, we'll go back to our tree hidey-hole. We've got lots of food there.'

'It's not proper food though, it's just cornflakes and silly stuff like that,' said Baxter. 'You're use-less, Lily.'

I felt angry tears prickling in my eyes. I'd been trying so hard to look after them all. It was mean of Baxter to call me useless. I wondered if I could somehow have made us better food. There were eggs at home. I could have boiled some and mixed them with salad cream and made lovely egg sand-wiches . . . No, we'd run out of bread. What were we going to do if the food we had with us didn't last till Saturday? I hadn't realized we'd feel so hungry here.

It was making it worse, all of us standing staring at the food on display, our mouths watering. Pixie looked particularly wistful, reaching out her hand towards the cake.

'Ah, look at that little moppet,' said yet another granny. 'Are you hungry, darling?'

'Very hungry,' Pixie lisped, blinking her big blue eyes and looking hopeful.

But the granny just laughed at her and limped off to order some soup for herself.

'Come on, outside. We can't *beg*,' I said.

'Yes, we can. Let Pixie, she's good at it,' said Baxter.

I wavered because I was so very hungry – but I knew this would be a way of drawing attention to ourselves. One of the serving ladies was already hovering, worried we might touch the food.

'No, come on, *now*,' I hissed. The kids followed me, grumbling and moaning, back through the café to the outside terrace at the top of the stone steps.

Almost every table was occupied with lucky people eating. There was one spare table right at the end. No one had cleared it yet. It had four big plates, with quite a lot of chips left, and half a pie. Baxter spotted it and his eyes went big.

I looked around. No one seemed to be watching us, they were all too busy talking and eating their meals.

'OK,' I said softly. 'We'll sit down at that table and pretend it's our meal. 'Follow me. Act *casually*.'

Baxter over-acted, tossing his head about and trying to whistle. Bliss started to giggle helplessly, but I quelled her with a look. We sat down at the table, Baxter barging to be first so he could sit in front of the pie plate.

'No, we're going to *share* it,' I said, leaning over and cutting it into four squares. 'And we're counting out the chips, OK?'

'Is it all right to eat other people's food?' Bliss asked.

'No, it's very germy indeed – in fact I saw a fat man *sneeze* into this pie, and he licked all the chips,' said Baxter.

'Yuck,' said Bliss, pushing her plate away.

'Don't be silly, Bliss, Baxter's just tricking you so he can have your share. It *is* bad to eat other people's leftover food but we haven't any choice, have we? It's not stealing because someone else has already paid for it – and they don't want it any more. It would just get chucked in the rubbish bin so we might as well eat it, eh?'

Bliss didn't look convinced, and didn't even try one chip, but Baxter and Pixie tucked in heartily, and so did I. Our small portions were finished in three or four gulps and we were still left hungry. I looked at the people at the tables nearest to us. The two grannies from the toilet were there, eating large slices of coffee-and-walnut cake and sipping frothy coffee. The larger granny wolfed hers down, but the other one nibbled hers in a half-hearted fashion.

'I think we might be getting a bit of cake for pudding,' I murmured to the others.

We had to wait a long time because the grannies nattered to each other for ever, but eventually they heaved themselves up and tottered off in their baggy trousers and sensible sandals.

I nipped off my seat, grabbed the plate of cake, and was back at our own table in a second. I cut the cake into four and gave Bliss the biggest piece.

'No, she doesn't want any. I'll have hers,' said Baxter.

'You eat your cake, Bliss. You've seen those old ladies. You could see they weren't a bit germy, and they were very fierce about handwashing, weren't they? So you eat your cake, OK?'

She still wasn't too sure, but when she'd tried a crumb of cake and a smear of cream she decided it tasted so good she didn't care if it was crawling with germs. Baxter finished his cake in one gulp and was already rocking back on his chair, craning his neck to see if he could see anyone else likely to leave us a feast.

'Look at those girls there! I bet they never finish their chips. They're too busy giggling. I think they're going, they're picking up their bags, quick!'

He started weaving his way through the tables. He picked up a plate with a piecrust and chips, grabbed an uneaten sandwich, another half cake, a mound of salad and three cooked carrots, piling them on top of each other higgledy piggledy. He returned triumphantly with his loaded plate.

'Honestly! You couldn't be more obvious if you tried,' I said.

'You shut up. You don't have to eat it,' said Baxter, gobbling the whole of the piecrust before I could cut it fairly into quarters. I divided the rest for the girls, making them eat a carrot each because I knew it had lots of vitamins, and I ate the salad myself. It probably had lots of vitamins too, but it tasted like damp flannel.

'Now it's *your* turn to find us some food, Bliss,' said Baxter. 'I did great, didn't I?'

'I don't really like this food,' said Bliss. 'Not when it's all mixed up together.'

'It gets mixed up in your stomach, doesn't it?' said Baxter. 'You're just too scared to go and nick some.'

'It's *not* nicking, Baxter,' I said fiercely. 'I wouldn't let you do it if it was. It's just . . . clearing up the plates.'

I let him go and do some more 'clearing' because he loved doing it, and I figured the café people wouldn't be too cross with him if they caught him because he was such a little boy. We sat there a whole hour or so, with Baxter going off foraging for us every few minutes. We had such a feast at our table that little brown sparrows kept flying down for a beakful too. One of them hopped right across our table top and back, cocking his head at us cheekily.

'Oh, he's so *sweet*,' said Bliss. 'Can we keep him and tame him and have him for our own pet bird?'

'Oh yeah, and we'll have a pet rabbit too, and maybe a baby deer,' I said, but then I stopped, because Bliss's eyes were shining hopefully.

'Only joking, Bliss. They're like Baxter, you *can't* tame them,' I said, which at least made her laugh.

When we were at last so full of everyone's left-overs that *we* were leaving stuff too, we strolled off down the steps, through the gates, to sit on a fallen tree trunk in the sunshine. We kicked our legs for a while and sang silly songs, but the food and the warm sun made us all sleepy, even Baxter. We curled up in a heap in the grass, Pixie on my lap using my chest as a pillow, Bliss and Baxter either side of me, and went to sleep.

It was a long, long sleep, in spite of the hard ground and the kids squashing me, perhaps because I hadn't slept properly at night since Mum met Gordon. I dreamed I sprouted angel's wings, pink and red and gold. I floated up into the air away from everyone. I flew far away in the sunshine until the parakeets squawked so loudly that they woke me up. My wings fell off and I was left sprawling on the grass with pins and needles in my arms.

I gently slid Pixie off me and sat up, stretching. She was still asleep, but Baxter and Bliss were taking it in turns to walk along the fallen tree trunk.

'At last!' Baxter shouted. 'You've been asleep *ages.*'

'Baxter wanted to wake you but I wouldn't let him,' said Bliss. 'We're pretending to be tightrope walkers, Lily. Come and join our circus!'

I joined in the circus games, doing handstands and cartwheels. When Pixie woke up we played she was our performing monkey. Then Baxter and

Bliss were lions and I was their trainer. When they grew hoarse with roaring I became Madame Lily with my troupe of lily-white horses, and we all cantered round and round, Pixie puffing along behind us like a little Shetland pony. I was way too old to play these sorts of silly games and told myself I was just joining in to keep the kids amused.

When we were all out of breath we flopped down on the grass again and took it in turn to tell stories. I told them a story about all of us growing wings and flying off to different parts of the world. They were interested for a while, but Bliss crept nearer and held my hand and said she didn't want to fly anywhere without the three of us. She told a long convoluted story about Cinderella and Snow White and the Sleeping Beauty, who all lived in a palace together and wore a different beautiful ball gown every day.

Baxter started telling a story about a terrifying wolf man who burrowed through the bracken and attacked his victims, sinking his vicious teeth into their necks, but I shut him up, especially when he started acting it out and both little girls started squealing. Pixie was excited and yelled, 'More, more! More wolfie!' when I sat on Baxter to stop him, but Bliss was truly frightened. Pixie herself was too little to tell a proper story. She just said a whole jumble of stuff: 'Pixie did dancing, then Pixie did singing, then Pixie ate lots and lots of ice cream,' droning on and on about herself.

'Pixie did telling stories and she was *boring*,' said Baxter unkindly. He stood up, kicking through the bracken, and found an old dog-chewed ball. 'Hey, let's play catch!'

It was more a game of 'drop', playing with Bliss and Pixie, but they became two piggies-in-the-middle while Baxter and I threw the ball over their heads. Then we found a small broken-off branch that could just about serve as a bat. We invented a weird game, half cricket, half rounders, where Baxter and I bowled and batted and fielded all at the same time. Bliss lay on her back and mumbled another fairy story to herself. Pixie skipped round and round behind us like a substantial little shadow.

Baxter and I had an argument about who was winning our silly game. I eventually gave in and said he was the winner – even though he *wasn't*.

'I'm the *winner*!' he shouted, punching the air. 'Right, what do I get for a prize?'

'Here's a huge silver trophy,' I said, miming handing it to him.

'No, I want a *real* prize. Can I have another ice cream?'

'What's up with your brain? We haven't got any *money*.'

'That man gave us one ice cream for nothing. Maybe he'll give us another one. Go on, ask him.'

'No, I'm not asking! He'll think we're horribly greedy.'

'I am,' said Baxter, patting his tummy. 'Can we go back to the café then? We'll nick some more leftovers.'

'It's *not* nicking. But all right,' I said, because I was getting hungry all over again and reckoned it might almost be time for tea.

The four of us climbed up the hill to the gate – but found it was locked.

'Why did they go and lock it?' said Bliss.

'Because they're meanies,' said Baxter. '*Stupid* meanies, because we can climb over, easy-peasy.'

Baxter and I could, but we had to haul Bliss up and she went very white and wobbly halfway over and wailed that she was stuck. We had to give her a little push and that made her scream. Pixie couldn't manage it either, but she clung to me and I swung us both over.

'There we are! Come on then, let's see if we can find lots of cake,' I said. 'Stop whimpering, Bliss, you didn't really hurt yourself.'

'Yes, I did,' Bliss sniffed, but she wiped her eyes and nose and trudged along by our side.

We went up and up and up the steps until we saw the terrace – but it was empty. There were no people there at all, and all the tables had been wiped clean, and the chairs stacked. The café was clearly closed.

'Oh rats,' said Baxter, running round the tables, even peering underneath them, but there wasn't a scrap of food left.

'Never mind, it wasn't very nice food anyway,' said Bliss.

'Are you mad! It was *lovely*, especially the pie,' said Baxter.

'Yes, but not with other people's slurp all over it,' said Bliss.

'Let's have ice cream!' said Pixie.

'No, the ice-cream place must all be shut up too,' I said, but Pixie wouldn't quieten until I took her there to show her. We couldn't go through the café because it was all shut up and locked. We had to walk right round the back of the big house and then circle it. We found the ice-cream place eventually – and of course it was shut.

'*Open* it!' Pixie wailed. 'I want an ice cream!'

'I want another piece of pie with lots of chips!' said Baxter.

'Stop moaning, both of you. You're such greedy-guts.'

'It's not greedy to want tea.'

'Well, we've got lots of tea, back by the tree. Come on, we'll go back there and have a little feast,' I said.

'That's just boring home food,' said Baxter, stamping, starting to get into a real strop.

'It's all we've got – and if you don't want it, I'll give your share to Bliss and Pixie,' I said. 'Now, come *on*.'

I wasn't quite sure how far away our hiding place was. I just knew it was *too* far. We were all tired now, grubby and hungry and thirsty. Pixie started whining to be carried when we'd only been walking five minutes.

'Come on, Pixie, you're a big girl. You can walk all by yourself,' I said, trying to be bright and encouraging.

Pixie threw herself down on the ground.

'No, I can't walk, I'm *little little little*,' she declared, going stiff as a board when I tried to pick her up. I couldn't just leave her there – though I was tempted. I had to give in and carry her. It didn't feel too bad at first, in fact it felt good to have Pixie's arms right round my neck and her legs clamped round my waist, but in a little while

I felt as if I was hauling *fifty* Pixies. My neck ached, my back ached, my legs ached, and my arms felt as if they were being pulled out of their sockets.

'Shall *I* try carrying Pixie for a bit?' said Bliss.

'Oh, you're a darling, but Pixie's almost as big as you. Thank you, though, Bliss – you're a gold-star sister.' I saw that she was limping a little. 'What's the matter with your foot?'

'It's sore,' said Bliss. 'But it's OK.'

I made her take her shoe and sock off. Her sock had slipped down under her heel and her trainer had rubbed her ankle raw.

'Oh Bliss, you should have *said*. Look, take your other shoe and sock off, give your toes a treat and run around barefoot,' I suggested.

'No, it's all *dirty*.'

'It's just grass.'

'And lots of animal poo!'

'No, there isn't. Well, teeny tiny rabbit poo every now and then, but that's nothing to be scared of.'

'I *am* scared of it.'

'Well, all right, *don't* go barefoot, but pull your sock *up*. Here, wait a minute, put my sock on too, that will protect it better.'

My own trainer started rubbing after five more minutes but I just had to ignore it. We kept on trudging. Baxter was the only one of us with any energy left. He found another branch and played a mad tree-whacking game, pretending they were all enemy soldiers. At least it kept him moving forward in the right direction. If it *was* the right direction.

My heart started banging in my chest. I *thought* we were going the right way, but how could I be sure? And how on earth were we going to find our special hiding-place tree when there were hundreds, thousands, maybe even millions of trees in this vast park? Well, we'd just have to find *another* hollow tree. No, wait, what about all our food, our blankets, our special things? What about Pixie's buggy? Why hadn't I kept a careful note of where we were going? I should have left a little trail of bread or stones like the children in fairy tales.

I was getting so anxious now that I could barely breathe, and I was close to dropping Pixie altogether. The others didn't seem to notice. Bliss limped along, Baxter bashed his trees, and Pixie crooned sleepily into my chest. 'Little, little, little.'

I kept looking all around, trying to get my bearings. We were walking near a road, and I didn't think that was right at all. The road *itself* wasn't right – it was completely empty. Where had all the cars gone? The park gates must be closed, like the café. It meant we were all alone in the park.

'We're absolutely safe now. There's no one around to be nosy,' I said. 'Look, we can walk in the road, we can shout at the tops of our voices, we can strip off and wander about stark naked!'

'Yeah!' said Baxter, tearing off his T-shirt and shorts.

'I didn't mean *literally*,' I said, but I decided to let him be silly just for the fun of it.

He even took his funny little underpants off, running along totally naked apart from his trainers, taking great leaps and whooping at the top of his voice. We three girls shrieked with laughter at him. Then of course Pixie started tugging at her own clothes and had to do her own totally bare prancing. Baxter and Pixie wanted Bliss and me to strip off too, but we felt too bashful – which was just as well, because a whole bunch of serious runners suddenly thudded past. Their faces were grim with effort but they all cracked up when they saw my brother and little sister.

'Put your clothes back *on*. We'd better stay away from the road,' I commanded.

'Aren't we nearly there *yet*?' said Baxter. 'My feet hurt.'

'Mine do too,' said Bliss, who was in a far worse state.

'And mine,' said Pixie, which was monstrous, because I'd carried her most of the way.

'I'm not sure I really like it here without any cars or people,' Bliss said.

'Yes you do. It's great fun,' I said, trying to wrestle Pixie back into her clothes. '*You're* having fun, aren't you, Pixie?'

'You bet,' said Pixie, charging off with her jeans inside out and one arm still not properly in her T-shirt.

'And you're having fun too, aren't you, Baxter?' I said, as he whirled around, still naked.

'Not really, not any more,' said Baxter. He sat down and put his pants on his head.

'Oh ha ha,' I said. 'You're not really funny doing that, chum.'

Pixie found him hilarious, however, squealing with laughter and pointing at him.

'His pants, his pants!' she shouted.

Baxter smirked at her.

'I *am* funny,' he said.

'The joke's on you, Baxter, putting your smelly pants on your head.'

Baxter's smile faded.

'Then I'll put them on *your* head,' he said, trying to cram them on my hair.

'Get off, you moron,' I said, struggling with him. My fist shot out and somehow connected with his nose.

'Ow! You hit me!' Baxter yelled, punching and kicking me.

'Stop it! Put your wretched pants *on*. And the rest of your clothes.'

'I don't have to do what you say. You're not Mum,' said Baxter, rubbing his red nose.

'Yes, she is, Lily's like our mum now,' said Bliss.

'She's just a kid, like us. She doesn't know anything. She's scared because she's a stupid girl. *And* she's got us lost!' said Baxter, stepping into his underpants and jeans.

'No I haven't!' I said.

'Yes, you haven't got a clue where we are, admit it,' said Baxter.

'I do know. I'm sure we're quite near our tree. And anyway, even if we're not, it might be fun to sleep in this soft ferny part. We could make another camp here,' I said. I lay down there and then.

'Oh, it feels lovely,' I said, making little purring

noises of appreciation, as if I'd just got into a big comfy bed.

I didn't fool any of them, not even Pixie. They stood staring down at me as if I'd gone mad.

'Come and join me, Bliss,' I said.

She hopped from one foot to another.

'We're not really going to sleep there, are we?' she whispered. 'What about Headless? I can't sleep without him.'

'Well, you're maybe going to *have* to,' I snapped, sitting up. 'Because all right, I don't have a clue where our wretched tree and all our stuff is.'

They looked shocked, even Baxter.

'I want my buggy,' Pixie howled, though she always struggled to get out of it.

'I want my brand-new fork-lift truck,' Baxter snarled.

'I want Headless,' said Bliss, and she crumpled up.

'OK, OK, I was only kidding. Of course I know where the tree is,' I said, staggering to my feet and brushing myself down. 'Come on, it's this way, I think.'

We blundered on. I carried Pixie, and then for a while I got Baxter to give her a piggyback while I carried Bliss on one hip because she was limping so badly now. She kept making little gulping noises, trying hard not to cry. I felt so bad, wondering why I'd dragged the kids into this huge park instead of keeping them safe at home. I kept looking desperately for familiar landmarks, but all the park seemed strange and alien now.

'We're lost, aren't we?' said Bliss, in a tiny voice.

'No, we're not lost,' I said. 'Well, maybe just a little bit. But we'll find our way. If we get to the park gates we'll know we've gone *past* our tree and we'll simply have to turn round and go back the way we came. Now think, Bliss. You were the one who found our tree, when you ran away from that dog. Keep your eyes peeled and maybe you'll find the tree for us all over again.'

Bliss obediently opened her eyes wide and swivelled her head, looking all around.

'Maybe – maybe it's that one!' she said – but when we ran over to it, it wasn't hollow at all. We tried another and another and another, peering at every large tree we saw, without any luck at all.

'Headless will be so lonely without me,' Bliss mumbled. 'I think he's crying.'

'How can he cry if he hasn't got his eyes any more?' I said.

'He just cries inside himself, in his tummy. I can always tell when he's doing it,' said Bliss.

'You're bonkers,' said Baxter, screwing his finger

into the side of his head. 'You're all totally bonkers. I wish I didn't have bonkers sisters and a bonkers mum. I wish I had a brother and a proper dad. All you girls are useless.'

'Buggy!' said Pixie. *'Buggy!'*

'Yeah, useless, whingeing on about your stupid buggy and your stupid headless bear,' Baxter sneered.

'BUGGY!' Pixie shouted, scrambling to her feet and then charging down the hill.

'Pixie! Careful, you'll trip and fall! Watch out! Where are you *going*?' I yelled, dumping Bliss and running after her.

Then I suddenly realized. Pixie had spotted a metal handle glinting in the sunlight. She'd seen her own red buggy partially hidden in the ferns. She'd found our hiding place!

We joined hands and danced round and round our tree, celebrating. Then we sat down amongst the ferns, Pixie in her buggy like a queen on a throne, and had a feast of biscuits and Dairylea and cornflakes and Lilt and Coke. We passed the strawberry jam round too, each of us scooping out a handful. Pixie got especially sticky but I spat on a T-shirt and scrubbed her as best I could.

Then I got out our fairy-tale book and read aloud *Babes in the Wood*, *Hansel and Gretel* and *Little Red Riding Hood*, all stories we could imagine happening in the trees around us. Bliss imagined all too vividly, and hung on tight to Headless while phantom wicked stepmothers and witches and wolves crept up on her. I had to read all the way through her favourite *Cinderella* to calm her down. Baxter chuntered a little, but settled to listen, absent-mindedly spinning the wheels of his fork-lift truck. Pixie started rubbing her eyes and sucking her thumb.

I supervised a little trip behind a bush and then lifted her up into our tree, sitting her on top of a pillow, with another for her head. She looked so cute and cosy that Bliss begged to join her, and Baxter agreed happily enough when I suggested it might be his bedtime too.

I tucked them all up and then fiddled around for a while, packing up all our food (not that there was much left now) and folding the buggy back beneath the ferns. I circled the tree several times, trying to think of some way of marking it which wouldn't look too obvious to anyone else. In the end I ruined my yellow felt-tip pen by rubbing it up and down the bark. It made the tree look distinctive, but naturally so, as if lichen had started growing on it.

Then I crouched down at the bottom of the tree, perching on the roots, guarding my sisters and brother. I watched the sun slide downwards in the sky, turning it orange, scarlet, crimson. I'd seen sunsets before, of course, but never out in the open like this. I felt tears pricking my eyes as the sky faded to pinky-purple. Then I climbed up into the tree to go to sleep too.

There was really only just enough room for the three children curled round each other. I had to burrow down underneath them and they moaned at me crossly. Pixie was particularly difficult, forever thrashing about. She had the smallest arms and legs but they seemed to be everywhere.

I wondered about climbing out again and curling up at the base of the tree, but they had all the pillows and blankets inside. I stuck it out, crammed in a corner with all three kids burrowing into me – and surprisingly fell fast asleep.

I woke with a start. We all did. Something was thumping our tree hard, again and again, attacking us. Pixie started crying and I put my hand over her mouth.

'Shh, shh, don't make a sound!'

'But what *is* it?' Bliss whispered, shivering.

'I don't know!' I was shivering too.

'I'll jump out and hit it with my stick,' said Baxter bravely.

There was another whack against the tree trunk, and then strange chomping noises.

'It's an ogre, I just know it's an ogre!' Bliss whimpered.

'Don't be silly,' I said – but it sounded horribly *like* an ogre. I hung on hard to Baxter. It wasn't his job to protect us. I was the eldest. I took a deep breath and pushed the tablecloth aside so I could see out. But I couldn't see anything at all. The park was terrifyingly dark, a thick deep black everywhere, so I couldn't see a thing. But I could certainly still hear: there was that awful rustling and chomping, and then another massive thump against the tree. Was the ogre attacking us with his bare fists, or did he have a stick?

My eyes were adjusting to the darkness. I saw the shadowy shapes of *two* sticks, somehow joined onto a great head. No, not sticks, *antlers*! It was a stag, banging his antlers against the bark of our tree, and then nibbling at the leaves within its reach.

'It's OK, it's only a deer!' I said, laughing shakily.

'Let's see, let's see!' said Baxter. 'I could fight him like a bull!'

'No, he's a lovely deer, we don't want to *hurt* him,' I said.

'He's a lovely deer, but he might want to hurt *us*,' said Bliss. 'Please make him go away, Lily.'

'Well, I'll try,' I said. I stood up and poked my head

right out of the tablecloth. 'Stop now,' I said firmly.

The deer paused, obviously startled.

'That's right, off you go. Join the rest of your herd,' I said.

He had one last little chomp of leaves and then ambled away.

'He's gone!' said Bliss. 'Wow! You're like an animal trainer, Lily.'

'It's easy-peasy bossing a deer about,' said Baxter. 'You were so *stupid*, Bliss, scared of a silly old deer. I wasn't a bit scared, was I, Lily?'

'No, you were very brave. We *all* were,' I said.

'Is it time to get up now?' Pixie asked.

'No, silly, it's pitch black,' I said.

'It's too dark,' said Bliss. 'Headless doesn't like it.'

'How can Headless tell whether it's dark or light?' said Baxter.

'He *knows* things,' said Bliss. 'Doesn't he, Lily?'

'Yes, old Headless knows more than anyone,' I said. 'Stop wriggling, Pixie.'

'I think I want to do a wee,' said Pixie.

I was dreading she'd say that.

'Can't you wait till morning?' I asked.

'I don't think I can wait at all,' said Pixie.

I sighed. 'Come on, then.'

It was terrifying climbing out of the tree into

total darkness. I wondered if the deer would come back and mistake my legs for a juicy bunch of leaves. I hauled Pixie out after me. She curled up as small as she could.

'Put your feet down, Pixie.'

'No, I don't like it.'

'How can you do a wee hovering in mid-air?'

'I don't need to go now.'

'Oh yes you do. In fact I do too. I'll go first, shall I?'

'Yes, then the deer can eat your bottom and not mine,' said Pixie.

I felt my way through the ferns, Pixie stumbling beside me.

'You won't wee on my buggy, will you?' Pixie asked anxiously.

'I'll try not to wee on the cornflakes and biscuits either,' I said, squatting down beside a tree.

It was quite difficult going, and when it was Pixie's turn I had to hold her up and help her. When we found our way back to our hiding tree, Bliss and Baxter decided they needed to go too.

It took Bliss *ages*, she was so scared that some badger or stoat or rat would come scrabbling up her legs. Baxter was much easier – but he ordered me to stay close to him, disconcerted by the blackness of the night.

'I'm not one bit afraid of the dark though,' he said.

'Of course you're not,' I said. 'You're as brave as brave can be. You were all set to protect us from the deer, weren't you?'

'Yes, I'd have gone *whack whack whack*. Will you tell Mum, Lily?'

'Yes, I'll tell her.'

'And tell my dad too?'

'Well, if we see him.'

'This Gordon isn't going to be our new dad, is he?'

'No fear.'

He didn't seem real, perhaps because we'd never met him. But for that matter *Mum* didn't seem very real now. When we were at home in our flat there was a huge empty space where she had been, but here in the park we'd made a new home just for us four.

When we were all back in the tree we did our jigsaw-puzzle act, slotting arms and legs round each other, and went back to sleep. Bliss whimpered and twitched, probably dreaming of ogres, and Baxter kicked a lot, probably fighting them. Pixie slept soundly, lying heavily on top of me, making little snoring sounds. I hovered on the edge of sleep, listening out for deer. Every so often

I heard rustling around me, and the birds started singing while it was still very dark.

I started worrying about what we were going to eat for breakfast. There was very little food left. This wasn't like real camping, where you cooked sausages and bacon in a pan over a little fire. I'd heard Rosa at school talking about her camping holidays in the Lake District. She hadn't been talking to *me*. No one spoke to me very much, though I didn't get bullied any more. I'd fought one of the big boys because he used a very bad word to describe my mum. They left me alone after that, which was just fine with me. Well, I pretended it was.

I'd have liked to be friendly with some of the girls, especially Rosa, who had dark curly hair and very big brown eyes with long lashes. I'd tried to make friends with her, commenting on the fact that we both had flowery names, but she looked alarmed and then rolled her beautiful eyes at the other girls nearby. They all rolled their eyes back and several of them held their noses. They all said I smelled. I didn't *think* I did, but it made me nervous. I didn't try to make friends any more after that, but I eavesdropped on their chatter about their fancy bedrooms and their parties and their holidays. I especially hankered after Rose's camping holidays and asked Mum if *we* could go to the Lake District. I didn't think it would cost too much if we all crowded into one tent – but it was Mum's turn to roll her eyes.

'How are we going to get there, stupid, on the eighty-five bus? The Lake District's hundreds of miles away. There's nothing there anyway, just a lot of hills and water, and it always pours with rain.'

At least it wasn't raining here in the park. I wriggled up until I could peek out of the tablecloth and saw the sky fiery red again above me. I wondered if I could ever draw a sunrise with my felt tips but I knew I'd never get the colours right.

I thought about Spain. I wasn't sure if the time there was the same as our time, but they'd obviously have the same sun. I wondered if Mum was watching it too, looking forward to sunbathing on the beach all day. Or was she thinking about us four, wondering if she ought to come back home? I remembered a little rhyme we used to chant in the Infants: *Ladybird, ladybird, fly away home. Your house is on fire and your children are gone.*

I thought of mum coming back tomorrow. It seemed such a long time away. I wasn't sure how we were going to get through all of Friday. I served up the last of our food for breakfast, portioning everything out on leaf plates and making little trails of flowers beside each serving. Bliss and Pixie were enchanted when I called it a fairy breakfast, but Baxter moaned and said fairies were stupid and he wanted a *proper* breakfast.

'Well, the poor fairies have clearly wasted their time trying to please *you*,' I said huffily – though *I* wished the fairies could have magicked up a more substantial meal.

We'd just have to walk all the way to the Lodge and graze on leftover food like yesterday. This plan appealed to everyone, so we set off mid-morning, but it was a wasted effort. When we got to the Lodge at last and sat at the furthermost rickety white table, a guy in white overalls came and shooed us away immediately.

'These tables are for our café customers. You children will have to go some place else,' he said in a surly voice.

We didn't dare sit back down at the table. We hovered on the steps, pretending to be playing. We waited while old couples sipped their coffee, but after a while people walked out with trays of cakes and cookies. We watched hungrily. Baxter got ready to pounce when the first couple stood up, half a rock-cake left on each of their plates – but the overall guy was still watching us. He caught Baxter by the wrist.

'Oh no you don't!' he said. 'You kids! You're worse than the sparrows. Go on, clear off, or I'll report you.'

Baxter looked as if he might argue, but I grabbed him quickly.

'I'm sorry. He's my brother. He's a bit soft in the head. He doesn't understand,' I said quickly.

'What do you mean, I'm soft in the head?' Baxter said indignantly as I hurried him away. 'I'm *hard*, like my dad.'

'Yes, you're hard as nails, but I didn't want you to get into trouble, OK?' I said. 'Come on, all of you.'

'I want my breakfast!' said Pixie. 'I'm hungry! Let's have ice cream!'

'We *can't* go begging off that nice man again,' I said, but the other three over-ruled me. I started fantasizing about a big soft whippy cone too, so I let them drag me right round the Lodge to the front, where the ice-cream kiosk was. But it was a different man today. He didn't smile, even when Pixie started jumping up and down, going, 'Ice cream, ice cream, ice cream!'

'Come on then, make up your minds,' he said. 'Is it four small cones?'

'Well, that would be lovely,' I said, smiling at him nervously. 'The only trouble is, we haven't actually got any money.'

'So what are you doing wasting my time?' said the man. 'Come on, you're holding up the queue.'

'You couldn't give my baby sister a really tiny cone? She so wants an ice cream,' I begged.

'I'm running a business here, not a charity soup kitchen. No money, no ice cream, OK? Off you go.'

So we had to trail away, hungry and humiliated.

'I didn't like that man,' said Bliss.

'No, he was horrid. Never mind. Let's forget him. Let's – let's go and find the magic garden again, it's lovely there, with all the roses.'

'You can't eat roses,' said Baxter.

'No, but we can nibble at people's picnics, remember?' I said. 'Come on, let's set off. Find yourself another big stick, Baxter, so you can whack any nasty men who come near us. Bliss, hold Pixie's hand too and we'll jump her along for a while to cheer her up.'

I thought I knew where the magic garden was, but there was no sign of it, even when we'd been walking for half an hour. Bliss was limping again, though she didn't complain.

'I was *sure* it was over here somewhere,' I said, squinting into the sunlight. I saw a silvery gleam in the distance. I rubbed my eyes and took a few steps nearer.

'What? Can you see it, Lily?' Bliss asked hope-fully.

'I think I can see . . . water.'

'Like a pond?'

'Well, a really *big* pond. Come on, perhaps we can all go paddling!'

It wasn't just *one* enormous pond, it was two, with a sandy path between them. There was a little sand at the edge of the water too, almost like the seaside. Ducks bobbed cheerily across the rippling water, looking at us expectantly, but we didn't have any bread for ourselves, let alone them.

There was a sign that forbade swimming, but I didn't think paddling counted. We kicked off our shoes and ran into the water. Baxter went right on kicking, soaking himself and us, but it was a sunny day so I decided it didn't matter. We *all* kicked and splashed and the ducks bobbed off huffily because we'd turned their smooth pool into rapids. Pixie tried to drink the water, scooping it up in her cupped hands, until I stopped her.

'No, Pixie, it's dirty water. It'll make you sick,' I said.

'But I'm *thirsty*,' Pixie wailed.

'I know. We all are. I'll find you a proper drink as soon as I can,' I said.

I hoped the toilets would have a drinking

fountain. After we'd walked for ages in our soggy trainers and damp clothes we found a toilet, but without any drinking fountain whatsoever. I let the kids drink from the cold tap instead, though none of us liked the taste, and we were still horribly hungry.

I didn't know what to do. There were lots of people out walking their dogs or jogging along. I wondered about straightforward begging, concocting a story inside my head about some rough boys who had stolen our picnic – but I knew they'd want to know why we were in the park on our own. I went round and round things in my head, wishing I knew what to do for the best.

We were trailing along beside the high wall at the edge of the park now. If we stepped right back we could see the rooftops and windows of the big houses on the hill. I thought of the posh families inside, sitting at long tables and munching away happily. I thought of their big fridges stuffed full of food, enough to keep the four of us going for days.

I eyed the brick wall. It was much higher than my head, but if I got Baxter to give me a bunk up I might be able to scramble up and over. I loitered by each back garden, assessing them seriously. I saw one house with the French windows wide open. It was almost as if they were inviting me in.

'OK,' I said, spitting on my hands. 'Baxter, you're going to help me get over the wall, right? Bliss, you hang onto Pixie and keep her quiet.'

'Are you going to be a *burglar*?' Bliss whispered, her eyes huge.

'No! I'm not going to take any *things*. I'm just going to see if they've got any spare food. That's not really stealing,' I said. I knew it *was* – but I decided I had to do it, to feed the kids. I was the oldest and the biggest, so it was down to me.

I got Baxter to bend over, then I climbed on his back and leaped upwards. I missed the first time and scraped my hands and knees on the brick wall. I swore viciously and had another go. This time I managed to grab the top of the wall and cling on, and then dug my sore knees and feet into cracks in the crumbling mortar and hauled myself up. I wedged myself on top of the wall, holding my breath.

The garden was empty. I squinted through the French windows. I couldn't see anyone. I'd risk it. I let my legs dangle on the other side of the wall and then dropped to the ground. I landed neatly on a clump of poppies, stirring a flurry of red petals around me. I wondered how I was going to get back over the wall without Baxter to help me, but there wasn't any point wasting time worrying about it.

I ran across the green lawn, past a big plastic playhouse, an elaborate garden swing and a trampoline. Imagine being a child in this house and having this huge garden to play in!

I crept right up to the French windows, holding my breath. I could see right into the room now. It was like a playroom, crammed with brightly coloured toys. I crouched beside a big plush pull-along dog, listening. I could hear a murmur of voices: an adult voice with a funny foreign accent and some little kid burbling away. They were upstairs, maybe the bathroom, because I could hear running water.

I crept through the playroom into a huge living room with a real white carpet, just like the one in my dreams. I went on tiptoe, worried about making muddy footprints. I went out into the hall. I could hear the people more clearly now. It seemed to be just one little kid. Maybe the foreign woman was its nanny? They were definitely in the bathroom because now I could hear splashing. Brilliant! They wouldn't be able to hear me.

I darted down the hall and into an enormous kitchen. Thank goodness, it was empty. I circled the oven in the middle of the room, marvelling at all the gleaming surfaces. There was a long scrubbed table with a blue and white bowl full of apples and pears and bananas. I grabbed a big sacking shopping bag and emptied all the fruit into it, and then eased open the door of the vast fridge. It looked as if a whole supermarket had been crammed inside. I poked punnets of enormous strawberries, stroked soft downy peaches and smooth purple plums, and then snapped into action. I filled my bag with fruit, along with a big wedge of cheese, a pack of cooked chicken breasts, some sliced ham, yoghurts, a pot of cream, four chocolate eclairs, and a carton of orange juice. The bag was so full I could barely lift it, so I started decanting half into a plastic carrier. Then I realized the water noise had stopped.

'Hello?' the foreign voice called from upstairs.

Oh no, had she heard me? I grabbed both bags and ran out of the kitchen into the hall, over the snowy living-room carpet, kicked my way through the toys in the playroom and out into the garden. I stared at the trampoline, madly wondering if I could bounce up and over the wall, but I wasn't a cartoon girl. I knew it wasn't possible. I peered wildly around the garden, wondering how on earth I could leap over the wall with two bulging bags.

I heard the voice calling again. I didn't have any time to waste. I seized the playhouse, dragging it over to the wall, the bags banging on either arm. I hauled myself up onto the pink plastic roof. I slung one bag up and over, flung my leg up after it, rolled right over the top of the wall, and fell flat on the other side, the bags on top of me, knocking the breath out of my body.

'Oh, Lily! Are you all right?' Bliss asked.

'No!' I gasped. I scrabbled to my feet, thrusting one of the bags at Baxter. 'Come on, we've got to run for it!'

So we ran, all of us, even though my hands and knees were bleeding and I'd banged my elbow and twisted my ankle. We ran and ran until we were out of sight of the wall, and then I flopped down on the grass and started making hysterical choking noises. I wasn't sure whether I was laughing or crying – maybe both. Bliss and Baxter and Pixie squatted beside me, Bliss dabbing gently at my scrapes with the hem of her T-shirt.

'Poor, poor Lily, it must hurt so much,' she said.

'Yes, but never mind, who cares? Look what I've got for us!' I said, opening up the bags.

They peered in and gasped.

'Wow, it's better than birthdays! I want them strawberries – and the chocolate cakes!' said Baxter.

'They're going to be shared out equally between

us,' I said firmly. 'Let's go back to our tree and have a feast.'

We ate the fruit in awe. We had fruit at home sometimes but it was only ever apples, and perhaps little oranges at Christmas. Bliss nibbled her share of strawberries first, dipping each one delicately into the pot of cream, but Baxter golloped everything all at once: a bite of peach; half a banana; a chunk of cheese; a slice of ham; a big lick of yoghurt; a slurp of juice; and he stuck his éclair in his fingers like a giant cigar and sucked at it.

Pixie tried to eat the cream on its own, just like ice cream, but I stopped her, scared she'd be sick. I gave her a chicken breast and then some strawberries and then a banana, though I had to peel it for her. She tried to eat it with the skin on first, which made us all laugh.

I sat back, licking my sore hands clean, my heart thumping. I'd jumped right over the wall, I'd stolen sackfuls of food, and I'd fed my kids. I'd proved I could look after them, no matter what.

We were all tired out now so we stayed beside the tree. Bliss and Pixie played tea-parties with Headless while Baxter drove his truck through fern jungles. I got out my drawing book and pens and drew myself a huge kitchen with an oven in the middle and a giant fridge. When I was too tired to draw I spread my angel cards out and stroked their feathery wings.

That night, curled up with the kids in our tree, I dreamed I was flying again, with a great flock of angels this time, our wings flapping in unison as we soared over the park, keeping everyone safe.

I slept so well I missed the sunrise. I woke up to bright daylight, and Bliss and Baxter and Pixie bringing me fistfuls of fruit for my breakfast.

'Are you better now, Lily?' Bliss asked, picking up my hands and examining them.

'Much better,' I said, though they were still very sore.

'You're so brave,' said Bliss. 'I wish I could be brave like you.'

'Are you going to go and get us more food from that big house?' Baxter asked.

'Not the same one, stupid! That would be asking for trouble. Maybe I'll try one of the other houses later on today. But we've still got heaps here.'

'You were great at nicking all this stuff,' Baxter said.

'Can you nick ice cream today, Lily?' Pixie asked.

'Maybe later,' I said. 'But first we're going to find the magic garden again, OK?'

They all seemed to have lost track of time and forgotten what day it was. *Saturday*. When Mum was coming home. I kept quiet, not wanting them to get all worked up about it. After all, we didn't know she'd be back for definite. *'Maybe the weekend, whatever.'* Saturday was the start of the weekend. She might be getting on a plane in Spain right this minute. I didn't think she'd be back this morning. But maybe this afternoon . . . ?

I thought about it all the time we were in the magic garden. I'd worked out that the only safe and sure way of finding it again was to go right back to the park gates and start up the hill. It was too long a walk for Pixie and the buggy was not good for paths, so I had to give her a piggyback part of the way. Baxter and Bliss were fine though. It was funny, they'd always whined if they had to walk down to the end of the road when we were at home, but they were getting used to trudging miles in the park. Bliss's blisters had dried up and she skipped along beside me, and Baxter ran, dancing ahead and then loping back and circling us again and again.

There were more strollers and dog walkers on this route but none of them took any notice of us. There was one twinkly little lady with a tiny white poodle who smiled at us, so I dared to ask her if we were definitely going the right way to the magic garden.

244

'You mean the Plantation, with all the azaleas and the rhododendrons? Yes, it *is* a magic garden, my favourite place. Just follow the little track through the grass and you'll be there in ten minutes.'

Her poodle was just as friendly as his owner, nuzzling up against my legs. Pixie slid off my back and patted its curly little head. Baxter squatted down and patted him too – and Bliss didn't run away, though she kept her distance.

'It's all right, sweetheart, Sugarlump loves people. She doesn't ever bite. Do you want to come and pat her too?' said the old lady.

I thought Bliss would hide behind me, but she actually came forward and gave the little dog a tentative pat. She only tickled her with a fingertip, but it was still astonishing.

'There now!' said the old lady. She was still smiling, but looking past us. I knew what she was looking for.

'You're not on your own, are you?' she said to Bliss.

'We're here with our sister,' she whispered.

The old lady looked at me doubtfully.

'Our *big* sister,' said Baxter, nodding his head at some non-existent figure in the far distance.

'She's here with her boyfriend – we're just

tagging after her,' I said smoothly. 'We'd better catch her up now.'

We said goodbye, stroked Sugarlump farewell and then skipped off.

'You're brilliant, Baxter, coming out with that sister stuff – almost as good as me,' I said.

'I said sister too,' said Bliss.

'Yes, and you were very brave with Sugarlump.'

'She was quite a sweet little doggie. Lily, can *we* have a little doggie like that?' Bliss asked.

'Of course we can,' I said. Maybe it really *was* down to me now. I was Lilymum and these were my kids. Baxter had calmed down a bit and Bliss wasn't so timid and Pixie had stopped being a baby and become a real little girl. I was looking after them, finding them food, organizing their games, telling them stories, taking them for lovely long walks, finding the magic garden for them . . . Yes, I could see the trees now, the iron railings, the special gate with the swirly pattern.

'Here's the magic garden,' I said, leading them inside.

We played that we were princes and princesses and this was our very own magic garden. The other people wandering around were our servants, allowed to take the air in our royal residence because we were so kind and generous.

We eyed up two very fat ladies waddling down the path.

'They're our cooks,' I whispered. 'That's why we have to get our own food today. We've given them a day off.'

A nice old man in corduroy trousers looking at the flowers was our gardener, another man in a stripy jacket was our chauffeur. I let Baxter choose all our royal cars. Two posh ladies in dresses were in charge of our royal wardrobe. Bliss and I had a very long discussion about our ceremonial clothes. I appointed a smiley man our special royal ice-cream maker and let Pixie choose all the different flavours on offer. Her choices were a bit unusual: toffee ice cream, peppermint ice cream, cornflake ice cream, even chicken ice cream, but I told her they all sounded delicious.

An old lady was feeding the ducks on the pond with her little grandson, about Pixie's age.

'She's our special royal zoo-keeper,' I whispered. 'We don't just have ducks, you know. We have all sorts of birds – swans and geese and pelicans and flamingos – and in those other big deep ponds, the ones where we paddled, we have our very own dolphins.'

The toddler grandson was rubbish at feeding the ducks. He couldn't get the hang of throwing the bread at all. He just let go and each piece fell down onto his feet.

'No, dear, you have to *throw* it,' said his grandma. 'Use your arm a bit.'

She showed him and he tried to copy her, but he hurled his whole body forward and toppled into the water before she could catch hold of him.

'Oh, Benjie!' she shrieked, trying to reach him.

'I'll haul him out. You'll spoil your trousers,' I said, wading in and scooping him up. He was perfectly all right, just soaking wet up to his armpits, but he was howling his head off.

'Oh dear, oh dear, we'd better get you home, you silly sausage,' said his grandma. She handed the packet of sliced bread over to me. 'Perhaps you'd like to feed the ducks, dear?'

I didn't feed the ducks, I fed the four of us. The bread wasn't even stale and there were two proper slices each, and an end crust to divide into four. We were very thirsty then so we went to the toilets at the other end of the garden and drank cold water from the tap. Pixie found this fun but difficult and got her T-shirt soaked, but it definitely needed a bit of a wash.

'Will you go and nick us more stuff for lunch, Lily?' Baxter said.

'We've still got some fruit left back at our tree.

248

Maybe I'll get something for supper. Or *maybe . . .'*
I didn't finish my sentence out loud. *Maybe we'll be back home with Mum,* I thought.

I tried to think it through for hours. I was worried about us all trailing home to see if Mum was there. It would unsettle Pixie for a start, when she'd calmed down at last and didn't even mention Mum any more. It would be much better if I nipped home quickly, to check whether Mum was back or not, and then rushed right back to the park. I imagined Mum and me together, hugging each other, and then Mum telling me all about her holiday.

I was really hoping it hadn't worked out at all. With a bit of luck she'd be well over this Gordon by now. I wanted her to tell me all about him. We'd maybe have a laugh or even a cry together. Then Mum would come with me and we'd collect the kids and then go off and have fish and chips for supper back home. I'd put the kids to bed and then I'd have a cup of tea with Mum and she'd tell me I'd done a grand job looking after them.

'I'd trust you with the kids any time, Lily,' she'd say. 'But don't worry, I'm never ever ever going away without you again.' And we'd give each other a kiss and it would all end happily ever after, just like a fairy story.

It would be so disappointing if Mum *wasn't* back at the flat. I could take it, but the others couldn't. So I waited till late afternoon, when we were all playing back at our tree.

'Now listen, you lot. I want you all to get into our tree, just like you're going to bed. I need to know you're all hidden away safe, out of trouble. I'm going to go off and – and see about supper,' I said.

'I'm coming with you, Lily!' said Baxter. 'You *need* me to get over the wall.'

'No, I need you to stay here and look after Bliss and Pixie. You're in charge, Baxter, OK?'

He fidgeted, wondering whether he wanted to argue or not.

'The girls can't manage without you,' I said.

Baxter nodded at me solemnly.

'OK then, Lily. Don't worry. I'm in charge.'

'You will be all right, Lily?' Bliss asked.

'Of course,' I said. I bent near her, as if I was giving her a kiss, and whispered in her ear. 'You're in charge *really*, Bliss. Look after Pixie for me.'

I helped them all scramble into the tree and then I set off, running. It seemed so strange to be on my own. I felt so little and light without the others tagging on. I was so used to looking out for them, telling them what to do, thinking up games for them. I reached the park gates in no time. It felt even stranger running out of the park, feeling hard pavement under my feet instead of grass and sandy path. I had to lean on a gatepost to get my breath, rubbing the stitch in my side.

Please be back home, Mum, I said inside my head. *Please, please, please.*

I walked on down the road, round the corner, up the hill, my heart thumping. I went in the entrance to the estate and then started running again all the way to our block. Up the stairs, panting now, then waiting in the stairwell to catch my breath, tiptoeing past Old Kath's, along the balcony to our yellow door. I stood in front of it, fists clenched, and then I timidly rattled the letter box. I waited. I tried again, louder now. Perhaps she still hadn't heard me. I bent down and called through the letter box.

'Mum? Mum, are you there?'

I heard someone moving behind me. I whipped round – but it was just Old Kath in her scuffed slippers.

'What are you calling your mum for? She ain't in there, is she?' she said.

'I – I don't know.'

'Yes, you know all right. She's done a runner, hasn't she? We've had all sorts round here, knocking at your door – teachers, social workers, even the police.'

I felt sick. I leaned against our door, my hand over my mouth.

'Yes, they've all been on the lookout for you. Where've you been hiding? They came and told me all about it, acting like *I'd* got you, asking this, asking that, peering all round my flat. Where are the others, Lily? Bliss and Baxter and Pixie. Such bally silly names! Where does your mother get them from, that's what I'd like to know. Who does she think she is?' She chuntered on, her little eyes beady with excitement, lipstick smeared sideways on her mouth.

'You shut up about my mum, you ugly old witch,' I said.

'What? Don't you stand there mouthing off at me! Oh, you're in so much trouble, you and your brother and sisters.' She pounced on me, grabbing my arm. 'You're coming back to my flat while I call the police!'

'Are you mad? Get *off* me!' I thumped her hard in her horrible old-lady chest and ran for it.

I scurried down the dark stairwell and made for the dustbin sheds. I hid inside that horrible smelly shed and cried. I'd let myself believe Mum really would be back and yet she was obviously still in Spain, not giving a toss about us. And Mr Abbott had clearly got suspicious and told tales, and now everyone was after us. We'd get taken into care and Mum would be put in prison.

Our only hope was to stay hidden in the park until Mum came back at last, and then pretend we were all away with her. Old Kath would poke her nose in and say she'd seen me, but who would believe a mad old lady like her? Yes, that's what I had to do: stay hidden in the park till tomorrow, or next week, or whenever. Meanwhile I had to find something for the kids to eat.

I wondered about scrambling up into the rubbish bins and foraging there, but they all smelled so bad. I was sure any food would be rotten. I couldn't risk poisoning the kids.

I wiped my eyes and nose with my T-shirt and then crept out. I scurried away from the estate, sure everyone was looking at me, worried that they all knew about Mum. I went up to the little parade of shops. I wondered if I dared try to nick some chocolate from Mr Patel's, but he didn't let kids into his shop on their own.

The smell from the chippy was making my mouth water. I stood outside, breathing in the wonderful warm salty smell. Joe, the chippy man, saw me lurking and waved.

'Hey there, Lily. Come for five fish suppers?'

I hesitated. I liked Joe and he'd always seemed to like me, giving me extra chips or adding the odd little bit of batter to my portion. There was no one else in the shop. I stepped in, swallowing, trying to get up the nerve.

'What's up with you then, chickie?' he said.

Maybe I had tear-stains on my cheeks, or perhaps I just looked worried sick.

'Joe, I need four fish suppers, or maybe three. I could share with Pixie.'

'Coming right up.'

'Yes, but – I haven't got any money,' I said.

'Well, go and ask your mum, darling.'

'I . . . can't.'

He looked at me. I waited for the questions. Maybe he'd laugh at me or get angry for wasting his time. But he started turning fish in the fat and shovelling chips.

'Pay me when you can,' he said simply.

'Oh, Joe! Thank you so much!' I started crying again like a fool.

Joe served each fish supper up carefully in its cardboard box, sprinkling the chips with salt and adding a slice of lemon to the fish. He put all four boxes in a carrier and handed them over.

'There you are, love.'

'You're an angel, Joe,' I said, and took them quick before he changed his mind.

It seemed much further trudging back to the park and the fish suppers started to feel surprisingly heavy. I kept swapping hands, the carrier banging uncomfortably against my legs. I still felt horribly conspicuous, sure that people were staring at me, pointing, whispering to each other. Every time I saw someone use a mobile phone I was worried that they were calling the police. I kept peering round anxiously whenever I heard a car, sure it was them.

I got inside the park gates and started running down the sandy path. I knew where I was going. The route was familiar now and I'd marked the tree, but it seemed to be taking longer to find it than I'd thought. What if I couldn't find my way back? What if the children were stuck in the tree, waiting and waiting until it got dark? I started running again, desperate to get to them, sure they'd be worried sick by now. Poor Bliss would be beside herself, Pixie in tears, Baxter red in the face, trying not to cry . . .

I was so sure they'd be in a state that it was almost annoying to come across Bliss and Baxter swinging on one of the lowest branches of the tree, waving their legs, while Pixie capered about, grunting. They were all laughing their heads off.

'What are you all doing? I told you to stay *in* the tree!'

'It got too *squashed* in the tree, and Pixie had to get out anyway to do a wee,' said Baxter.

'We were playing such a funny game called monkeys, Lily,' said Bliss. '*I* made it up and the others liked it a lot. I was trying to look after us like you do. Don't be cross.'

'You lot aren't taking this *seriously*. People could be out looking for us, ready to grab us and take us into care. We've got to *hide*,' I said.

'But there's no one here, silly,' said Baxter. 'What's that you've got in the carrier bag? It smells good.' He tried to grab it.

'Leave off! I'll give it to you when you're all sitting down nicely. We'll go in the ferns and duck down out of sight if anyone comes.'

'What have you got for us, Lily?'

'It's fish and chips,' I said proudly. 'Enough for all of us.'

'Hurray, hurray, fish and chips!'

'*Shh!* We've got to be *quiet*. Come on, in the ferns.'

They did as they were told now, eyes bright, smacking their lips. I handed out the packets of fish and chips. They were only lukewarm now, of course, but they still tasted wonderful. It was only when we were picking out the last little crumbs of chip and batter that Bliss wriggled closer to me.

'Did you go home, Lily?' she whispered.

I nodded.

'So Mum hasn't come back yet?'

Pixie looked up, and started mouthing, 'Mum, Mum, Mum.'

'I think she could be coming back tomorrow,' I said.

'So she's not there now. She's a mean old bag,' said Baxter. 'She's bad to go away and leave us.'

'Stop it. You mustn't ever tell on her because then they won't let us live with her. They'll give you away to a new foster mum and dad.'

'I don't care. I don't need a dad, I've *got* one.'

'And we've got a mum, when she comes back.'

'Tomorrow?' Bliss said.

'Yes, I hope so. *When* she comes back we'll all go back home and pretend she never went away, and if anyone asks us, police or social workers, we'll swear we were away on holiday with her, OK?'

'But Mr Abbott came round and saw us,' Bliss said.

'Shut up! I don't want to talk about him,' I said fiercely.

I couldn't bear to think that it was Mr Abbott who had told on us. Mr Abbott, my special friend. He'd made it all so complicated now. Maybe we could *never* go back. We'd have to live in the park for ever.

When I went to sleep that night I imagined us in five years' time, still living here. I'd be sixteen then, practically grown up, so I'd be able to build a proper treehouse for us. I could plan it all out

258

in my drawing book, get Baxter to gather wood, and we'd build a house way up in the branches where we'd be safe for ever. We wouldn't just eat other people's leftovers. Bliss and I would learn about wild herbs and berries, and gather nuts and cook wonderful stews over a little fire. I thought about meat. There were hundreds of rabbits in the park, not to mention the deer. Baxter might be up to hunting, but I couldn't stand the thought of killing all those beautiful creatures. We could maybe go fishing in the ponds at night, but the rest of the time we'd have to be vegetarian.

I could teach Bliss and Baxter and Pixie all their schoolwork. We could maybe get books from one of the posh houses, pretending they were our library and we were just borrowing them. We'd need to nick more clothes though, but we could manage with just one or two outfits each year, perhaps old clothes people left outside charity shops. Maybe one day someone would leave their old banger in the car park and we'd fix it up. Baxter would be brilliant at that. Then we'd drive all round the park in our car at night . . .

I went to sleep believing we could really live here for ever, but when I woke in the night I felt small and scared again. I wondered how on earth I was going to manage. I was so cramped up underneath the others in the tree I couldn't move. I disentangled myself as best I could, climbed out, and stretched out in the ferns. I had more room now but it felt so lonely and cold, and I was scared the deer might come along and trample me. I rolled over onto my back and stared up at the moon and stars.

Please let us be safe, I wished. *Make me able to look after the kids.*

Perhaps I didn't want to live all alone in my white house when I was grown up. Perhaps I wanted Bliss and Baxter and Pixie living with me too, the four of us for ever.

I lay awake for ages, the stars spinning above me. I didn't get to sleep until the darkness faded to an eerie silvery-grey, and I knew it was nearly dawn. I fell deeply asleep until I was vaguely aware of the kids chatting to each other. I heard several little thuds so I guessed they were out of the tree. Pixie started wailing and I tried to open my eyes but she quietened after a minute or two.

When I next stirred I heard her choking with laughter. They were *all* laughing, playing happily together. I burrowed deeper into my ferny bed, wishing I could stay there for ever. I didn't want to get up and face the day. I'd have to try to find us something to eat and I was fast running out of ways to do it. I'd also have to decide whether I dared risk creeping back to the flat to look for Mum all over again. I didn't want to be the eldest any more, looking after everyone. I seemed to do that even when Mum *was* around. I wanted someone to look after *me*.

The kids were still laughing but Bliss was squealing, frightened about something. I forced myself to sit up in the ferns and looked for the children. I rubbed my eyes. Where on earth *were* they? They sounded so near but I couldn't see them at all.

'Bliss? Baxter? Pixie? I called.

Pixie giggled and then pounced on me from behind.

'You've woke up, Lily! We're playing monkeys again. I can't get up the tree but Baxter can – and Bliss.'

'Up?'

I looked up – and just about died. Baxter and Bliss were right up at the top of the tree, swinging precariously from a branch.

'Oh, you idiots! Come down! Come down this minute!' I called.

'We're monkeys. We don't come down, do we,

Bliss. We go up and up and up,' said Baxter, making silly grunty monkey noises to punctuate his sentence.

'You wait till I catch you! And how *dare* you get Bliss to do it too. Come *down* or I'll come up and *slap* you down,' I yelled.

Baxter saw I meant business. He hung there for a good thirty seconds, just to show me, and then he started edging his way back along the branch to the trunk of the tree.

'That's right. Good boy. Now you, Bliss,' I shouted.

'I'm up really, really high,' Bliss squealed.

'Yes, you are. Come down now!'

Bliss clung to the branch, wrapping her arms and legs round it.

'Come on, Bliss, edge along like Baxter. Gently now, a little bit at a time,' I called. 'Don't look down!'

Bliss did look down, and started crying.

'I said *don't* look down.'

'I'm too high up!' Bliss wailed.

'Yes, I know you are.'

'I wanted to be brave like Baxter.'

'Well, you *are*, Bliss, but that doesn't mean you go scampering up to the top of trees like a demented squirrel.' I tried to sound calm, telling her silly jokes so she'd relax a bit. 'Come along, you need to come down now, there's a good girl.'

'I . . . can't,' said Bliss.

'Yes, you can. Show her how, Baxter.'

'It's easy-peasy,' said Baxter, swinging himself onto the branch again.

Bliss screamed as he made it sway.

'Baxter, stop it. *Gently!*'

'I'm just *showing* her. Look, Bliss, like this.' He demonstrated, crawling along the branch towards her.

'That's it, Baxter. See, Bliss? Copy Baxter. Let go with one hand and move slowly along.'

'I don't know how! I can't let go, I'll fall,' said Bliss.

'*Look*, Bliss,' Baxter bellowed.

Bliss couldn't look. She was sobbing helplessly, unable to move.

'Could you jump down and I'll catch you?' I said. 'No, wait, don't, it's too far. You scramble down, Baxter. Then I'll come up and help you, Bliss, baby. It's all right, you're quite safe. Don't cry. We'll get you down in no time,' I gabbled.

'I'll fall, I know I'll fall,' Bliss said.

'No, you won't. I promise you won't fall. Just hang on a few seconds more and then I'll come and—'

But as I was saying the words, the branch started creaking.

'It's moving! Help me!' Bliss screamed.

I clawed my way up the tree, but the whole branch suddenly snapped right off. Bliss clung to it instead of trying to jump free. She landed with a crash on the bumpy earth by the tree roots.

'Oh my God! Bliss, Bliss, are you all right?' I yelled, scrambling back down the tree.

Baxter reached her before I did. He knelt down beside her and burst into tears.

'Shh, Baxter! Bliss, talk to me,' I said, running over to them.

'She can't talk. She's *dead*,' Baxter wailed.

'Dead, dead, dead,' echoed Pixie, like a little chiming bell.

'She's not dead,' I said, kneeling down beside Bliss.

She was lying crookedly, her head thrown back, her arms out, one leg all twisted. Blood trickled down her forehead. Her eyes were closed. She *looked* dead.

'Bliss, please, wake up. You can't be dead, I won't let you be dead. Bliss, please, *please* open your eyes!'

I saw her eyelids flicker – and then very slowly, as if her lids were very heavy, she opened her eyes.

'Oh thank you, thank you,' I said, putting my arms round her head.

I felt her shudder right through her body and then start crying.

'It's all right, Bliss. I've got you. We'll make you better, don't worry,' I said.

I straightened up and tried to tend her poor body. The cut on her head looked deep and scary. I needed something clean to staunch the wound but all our clothes were really dirty now. I broke off a big fern and tried to mop at it with that, Bliss wincing underneath me. I dabbed at the scratches on her arms, and then looked at her legs. One had a bloody knee but it didn't seem too bad. It was her left leg that was terrifying. It was bent the wrong way – and when I tried very, very gently to straighten it, Bliss screamed.

'I'm sorry, I'm sorry, darling. I didn't mean to hurt you,' I said. 'I don't know what to do. Your poor leg . . .'

Bliss was grey-white, tears seeping down her face. Baxter sat down beside her, very careful not to jog her in any way, and held her hand.

'Lily, her leg,' he mumbled.

'Yes, I know.'

'It looks as if it's going to fall off,' said Baxter.

Bliss gave a little gasp and tried to raise her head.

'No, you keep still, darling. Don't take any notice of Baxter, you know what he's like,' I said – though her leg really was dangling just like a doll's.

'*Is* Bliss dead?' Pixie asked.

'No, of course not. How can she be dead, she's got her eyes open!' I said.

'But she's very, very hurt,' Pixie said solemnly.

I swallowed. 'Yes, she's very hurt, but she's going to get better,' I said, stroking Bliss's bloody forehead. 'Don't worry, Bliss. I know it must hurt horribly, but if you just rest for a while then I'm sure you'll start to feel better soon . . .' My voice tailed away. I couldn't bear to hear the rubbish I was speaking. I couldn't pretend any more. It was obvious to all of us that Bliss had broken her leg, and very badly too. She also had a long seeping cut on her forehead that needed stitching.

'I – I think, just to make sure, we'd better take you to a hospital, Bliss,' I whispered.

'No! No! I can't go!' Bliss said.

'She's frightened of hospitals,' Baxter sniffed.

'No – well, I *am*, but I *can't* go, because we have to stay hidden,' Bliss gasped.

'I know, but you need to go to hospital now, Bliss,' I said, shivering.

'I'll be all right. I'll rest, like you said, Lily.'

'But your leg – it must be hurting terribly.' I could hardly bear to look at it.

'It doesn't hurt too badly,' Bliss lied.

'Bliss! You can't *move*.'

'Well, I'll keep still.'

'Stop being so *brave*, Bliss,' Baxter shouted. 'Why did you have to climb so high up?'

'Because you told me to!'

'Yes, but you don't have to do what I say. Look what's happened. You have to get better or it's all my fault,' said Baxter, still hanging onto her hands.

'It's *my* fault, I should have stopped you all playing stupid monkeys,' I said, stroking Bliss's hair.

'It's *my* fault, I said let's play,' Pixie whispered.

'It's *my* fault, I fell,' said Bliss. 'But it's OK, I'm starting to feel a lot better now.'

She was still grey and her head was still bleeding and her leg was smashed. I knew we didn't have any choice. We had to get her to hospital straight away. I got Pixie's buggy, thinking we could somehow squash Bliss into it and push her out of the park, but when Baxter and I tried to lift her, she screamed again, and then I think she fainted. Her eyes didn't close properly. We could see an eerie slit of white beneath her eyelid.

'She really does look dead now,' Baxter sobbed.

'We'll have to get an ambulance to come for her. They'll know how to lift her properly. We're going to break her more if we haul her about. You two stay here with her.'

I ran through the ferns, up the slope, towards the road. I stood by the side and started waving my arms frantically. The very first car stopped and a lady wound down her window.

'What's the matter? You know, I'm not supposed to stop here. This isn't a silly game, is it?'

'No, I swear it's not. It's my little sister. She's broken her leg and she's bleeding. Do you have a mobile? Oh please, could you call for an ambulance to come and take her to hospital?'

She phoned straight away, and then she parked her car by the side of the road with her hazard lights flashing. She ran down the slope with me, her shoulder bag bumping against her side.

'Oh my goodness, you poor little thing!' she said, when she saw Bliss. 'What happened?'

'She was playing in the tree and she fell,' I said.

'You were playing by yourselves?' said the lady. 'What about your mum?'

I was so distraught I couldn't think of a single thing to say. I just shook my head and cried. The lady knelt down beside Bliss.

'Don't worry, dear. An ambulance is coming and

we'll get you to hospital very shortly,' she said.

Bliss moaned, her eyelids fluttering.

'Make her stop looking so funny,' said Pixie, and started crying.

'Don't cry, don't cry,' I said, over and over, one arm round Pixie, one arm round Baxter.

We all stared at Bliss, shaking, for what seemed an age – and then at last we heard the ambulance coming. The woman scrambled back towards her car to show the ambulance people the way.

'What's going to happen to us, Lily?' Baxter asked.

'I don't know. But we have to save Bliss, don't we?'

'They won't take her away?' said Baxter.

'I won't let them. We're all going to stick together, the four of us,' I said.

Then the ambulance people came running, a man and a woman, and they knelt beside Bliss and asked her questions, but she still couldn't open her eyes properly so I answered for her. Then they lifted Bliss very, very carefully onto a stretcher. I gathered up Headless and my crayons and sketch-book and angel cards and Baxter's fork-lift truck and Pixie's handbag and our fairy-tale book. I left the blankets and pillows and Pixie's buggy because there wasn't time to collect them, and they didn't seem important now.

269

'We can come too, with our sister?' I said, running after the ambulance lady.

'Of course you can. You all look a bit groggy. We need to check all of you,' she said. 'Have you been camping in the park?'

'Well – sort of.'

'And what about Mum or Dad?'

I took a deep breath.

'We ran away,' I said.

'Why was that, love?'

'We just wanted an adventure, like in story books,' I said.

'Oh dear. Well, you've had an adventure all right – especially this poor little mite,' said the ambulance lady, shaking her head at Bliss.

'Is she going to be all right?' I tugged her arm and whispered, 'She's not going to die, is she?'

'I'm sure she'll be right as rain in no time, though she'll be hobbling around with that leg in plaster for a while.'

'She'll have one of those big heavy plasters?' said Baxter. 'I've always wanted one of them!'

'Wait for *me*!' Pixie called. 'I'm coming in the amb-lance!'

The lady from the car had picked her up and carried her, but now she was struggling.

'I'll take her now,' I said, grabbing Pixie. 'Thank

you very, very, very much for helping us.'

The ambulance man took her name and address. They wanted our names and address too, when we were all strapped into the ambulance and on our way to hospital.

'I'm Mikey, and this is Bluebell, and those two are Rose and Bunny,' said Baxter, thinking fast.

'And we live at number twelve South Block,' said Pixie, gabbling our full address, proud that she could remember it.

'She's just making that up,' I said quickly. 'Shut up, Bunny.'

'I think you're making things up too, sweetheart – and I understand why,' said the ambulance lady. 'But this isn't a game, kids. We need to know who you really are, especially your sister here. We'll need to check her hospital records, see.'

'She's Bliss,' I said. 'And that's Baxter and Pixie and I'm Lily.'

The ambulance lady frowned at me as if she thought I was still making it up.

'They're our real names, honest. Mum wanted them to be unusual.'

'And what about Mum? What's her name?'

'Kate Green.'

'And does she know you were in the park?'

'No! No, we ran away,' I said. 'It's all my fault.

It'll be all my fault if Bliss doesn't get better.'

'Now, now. I told you, I'm sure she's going to be fine,' said the ambulance lady. 'Come here.' She stayed by Bliss's side but she held her arm out. I edged nearer and she put her arm round me as if I was one of the little ones.

I let myself cry a bit then, but I had to choke all the tears away and be strong when we got to the hospital. They carried Bliss out on her stretcher and we followed, Baxter and Pixie clinging to me tightly. I thought we'd have a long wait in A & E. I'd sat there several times when Baxter had head-butted the door or stuck an acorn up his nose or cut his fingers playing with Mikey's knife – but we were taken straight through the waiting room to a little cubicle. They laid Bliss down on the bed. Her head jerked and her eyes opened properly.

'Lily?'

'It's all right, Bliss, they're going to make you better,' I said.

'We went for a ride in a real ambulance. It was a shame you were asleep,' said Baxter.

'It really went *nee-na nee-na nee-na*,' said Pixie.

Bliss put her hand up and felt her head. Her hand came back all bloody and she started crying.

'Hey, hey, don't poke around in that cut, sweet-heart,' said a nurse.

'There's a hole in my head,' Bliss whispered.

'It's just a nasty cut. We'll stitch it up for you.'

'Will it hurt?'

'Just a little bit.'

'I've had stitches,' said Baxter. 'I yelled.'

'Will you stitch her leg up too?' Pixie said.

'No, we'll put Bliss to sleep and then we'll stretch it out and put plaster on.'

'Oh, I've never had a plaster,' said Baxter.

'I don't want a plaster,' said Bliss.

'You can choose the colour, darling. You tell me and I'll tell the doctors. Would you like a lovely bright pink plaster? Or maybe purple or blue?'

'She'd like blue, wouldn't you, Bliss?' I said.

'Yes, blue,' Bliss mumbled, closing her eyes again. She reached out her hand. 'Will you stay with me, Lily?'

'Of course,' I said. I found Headless, and tucked him in beside her. 'Look, here's Headless. He'll stay with you.'

'Oh dear, he's been in the wars too!' said the nurse, chuckling.

'You stay with us too, Lily. I don't like hospitals,' said Baxter, leaning on me.

'Stay with *me*,' said Pixie, clutching me.

'I'm staying with all of you,' I said, though I didn't know how I was going to manage it.

I knew they wouldn't let me go into the operating theatre with Bliss, especially not with the other kids tagging along too. The nurse examined each of us and said we seemed fine.

'No, I've got a bad leg,' said Pixie, sticking it out. 'Can I have pink plaster?'

'You need a lovely hot bath and then you can have a pink leg,' said the nurse. 'Now, let's get your sister mopped up first, eh?'

She dabbed at Bliss's bloody head very gently.

'Are you stitching?' said Bliss, and she started screaming.

'Hey, hey, what are you doing to my kid?' said someone, rushing through the curtains.

It was *Mum*! Oh glory, it was our mum back at last, and now everything was going to be all right!

It was so wonderful to see her, brown all over, her hair really blonde, looking lovely in a new bright pink T-shirt and white jeans.

'Mum!' we all shouted. She hugged Pixie and Baxter and me and then put her head down beside Bliss.

'My poor baby,' she said, cradling her. 'Don't you worry, Mum's here.'

'How did you know where we were, Mum?' I whispered.

'The police came knocking at my door. I was

panicking anyway, wondering where you kids had got to, and then they said you'd all been taken off to hospital. My God, the shock! What were you playing at, eh?'

'Don't be cross, Mum,' said Baxter.

'I'm not cross, baby. I just want you all safe and sound back home – especially my poor little Bliss.'

I felt so weak with relief I had to lean against the wall. Mum was back and now no one need know she'd ever gone away. Bliss would get better and we'd all go back to normal, Mum and us kids at home.

I could tell it like that. I'm good at making things up. I could pretend it until it seemed as if it really happened that way.

I don't want to write the truth. There were two policeman poking their heads into our crammed-full cubicle. There was an older one with a red face and grey curly hair and a younger one with fair hair and kind brown eyes.

'Come on, Kate, you've seen your kids. You need to come with us now,' said the older one.

'Are you completely bleeding heartless? I can't leave them now! Look at my little Bliss. Please, I'm begging you, let me stay with her while she gets her head and leg sorted. You don't have to stay here. I swear I'm not going to do a runner. Please, this is killing me,' Mum said, tears pouring down her cheeks.

'You can turn on the waterworks for all you're worth, Kate, but I've been in this job too long to be affected,' said the older one.

'Haven't you got kids? I need to stay here for *their* sake. Oh please, please.'

'I'll stay with her,' said the younger one, looking at his watch. 'I'm off duty at two anyway. I'll bring her in myself, no worries.'

'Oh, you're an angel,' said Mum.

'No, you're a sentimental fool. OK, you deal with her – *and* sort out all the social worker stuff. I'm off for my grub.'

So the young policeman waited while they took Bliss away to fix her leg. He took a chair and sat just outside the curtain to give us a bit of privacy. Mum sat on the bed with Pixie and Baxter on her lap. I squashed up beside them, rubbing my head against Mum's soft shiny hair and brown neck, breathing in her warm powdery smell.

'My babies,' Mum said, holding us close. She gave us all butterfly kisses, stroking our hair. 'I love you so. You know that, don't you?'

'We love you too, Mum,' I whispered. 'I'm so sorry I didn't look after Bliss better.'

'You did just fine, lovey. You were a bit mental

going off to that park like that, but it doesn't matter now,' Mum said wearily.

'I can't believe you're really here, Mum.'

'I said I'd be back at the weekend, silly. I got the first flight back this morning.'

'Did Gordon come too?'

'No, he's staying over there. It's where his job is, I told you. And I don't blame him, it's like a little bit of heaven – and the sun! Oh my God, look at the colour of me. I've never been so tanned in my life.'

'Do you still love him, Mum?'

'Well, yes, of course I do, I'm crazy about him. Those first few days, well, it was just fantastic – but then he found a photo of you kids. I had it in the back of my purse and he asked who you were and so I thought, blow it, let's tell him. He might be thrilled to have a ready-made family, and you're lovely-looking kids, especially Pixie – but it freaked him out and then he went all holier-than-thou. He pretended he didn't mind the fact that I had kids and was a bit older than he thought. He said he couldn't stand it that I'd lied to him. Honestly, he really got on my nerves then so I said stuff too. I walked out last night – actually, stormed off, you know what I'm like – but then I felt a right idiot because I didn't have enough cash for the flight home.'

Mum lowered her voice, nodding towards the policeman's legs showing beneath the curtain. 'There's been a bit of a problem with my credit card. I think they've blocked it now,' she mouthed. 'Anyway, Gordon came looking for me and acted like Lord Muck, doling me out some dosh, making me feel like dirt. Still, he did come out with me to the airport and he said he'd keep in touch – but I think he was the one lying then.'

'I'm sorry, Mum.'

'Oh well. I'm just not lucky in love, am I? *Especially* not with that piece of rubbish, Mikey. Did he just walk out on you kids? Where *is* he?'

'He's in Scotland on a job, Mum. He never came.'

'*What*? Well, we'll tell that to that policeman lurking there. They want to pin all sorts of rubbish on me – child neglect, abandonment, whatever. I kept telling them till I was blue in the face that I'd never walk out on you kids. If I was that sort of mother, would I be frantic about my poor little Bliss? She's been gone *ages* – what do you think they're *doing* to her?'

Bliss came back at last, lying very still with her eyes closed, Headless tucked under her chin. Her leg was plastered bright blue, just as they'd promised.

'Bliss?' said Mum. 'Oh, Bliss, baby, are you all right? Open your eyes and talk to Mummy, come on.'

279

'She'll be very groggy for a few hours yet,' said the nurse.

'I haven't *got* a few hours,' said Mum. 'I'm going to be whipped off down the nick. Come on, Bliss, wakey wakey, I need to know you're OK.'

She tickled Bliss's tiny neck. Bliss twitched and mumbled, 'I'm OK, Mum,' without even opening her eyes.

'There! Well, you be a good girl while you're in hospital, darling. And Baxter and Pixie, you be good too and do what Lily tells you. You're in charge, darling,' Mum said to me.

'But, Mum—'

'Don't worry, babe. It'll all get sorted out soon, I swear it will. Just look after the kids and make sure you all stick together,' said Mum.

'Oh, Mum, don't! Don't go!' I said.

'I don't *want* to go!' said Mum, hugging me.

The policeman put his head through the curtain.

'I'm afraid I've got to take your mum away to answer a few questions – but don't worry, someone's coming to look after you. Come on, Kate. I've kept my word, you've seen the little one's safe and sound, all neatly stitched and plastered. We have to leave the moment the social worker finally arrives.'

'No! Not *yet*. Look, give me a break. You've got it

all wrong. It's their dad you want to be nicking, not me. Isn't that right, Lily?' Mum said desperately, clinging to Baxter and Pixie.

'Yes, it's all his fault, he wouldn't look after us,' I gabbled. 'Listen, you can't take our mum away. She's the best mum in the world. She didn't leave us, I swear she didn't.'

He nodded at me and said he understood how I felt, and he gave Baxter and Pixie some chocolate to stop them crying – but he wouldn't seem to take me seriously. Then a social worker came, breathless and in a rush, smelling all sweaty. She tried to prise Baxter and Pixie away from Mum. They started screaming and Mum did too.

'No, don't! Mum didn't mean to leave us! Why won't you *listen* to me? She thought we were with Mikey. You *can't* take her away now. We need her, Bliss needs her,' I shouted, over and over, but it was useless.

Mum got dragged out of the hospital and we were left on our own.

'It's mad! They're arresting Mum for leaving us – and yet they're forcing her to leave us now!'

'Come on, Lily, calm down. You're frightening the others,' said the social worker. She had a funny accent and moles on her face like little mushrooms and I hated her. 'It isn't just because your mum went off to Spain. They're making enquiries about credit card fraud.'

It was like a slap in the face, but she still couldn't shut me up.

'They can't pin something like that on my mum. It's all her friend's fault, she gave it to her. My mum hasn't done anything!'

'The police are just making enquiries, you know how it works. They'll get everything sorted out with your mum. And meanwhile I'm going to take you three off and give you something to eat and then see about finding you somewhere to stay tonight, if Mum's not back.'

'We're staying here! We can't leave Bliss!'

'You can't all camp at the hospital, there isn't room. The nurses will look after your little sister.'

'I can't leave her! She gets so frightened. She needs me. She needs all of us,' I said. 'We've got to stick together, Mum said.'

'I'm afraid you've got to do what *I* say now. Kiss your sister goodbye and come along.'

I let Baxter say goodbye to Bliss first.

'You tell those nurses I'll come and bash them up if they hurt you, my Bliss,' he whispered, patting the top of her head. 'I love you.'

I lifted Pixie up onto the bed.

'Love you, Bliss,' she said, and gave her a big kiss on the cheek.

'And I love you too, my Bluebell Bliss. Don't you worry, I'll make sure we're together as soon as you come out of hospital. You're such a brave girl, braver than all of us put together. We'll see you very soon.'

Bliss reached out her hand and I twined my fingers in hers – but then I had to let her go. We were led away, Baxter, Pixie and me. The social worker took us to the hospital canteen and said we could choose anything we liked to eat. We were still so stunned she had to choose for us – fish and chips and peas. We couldn't eat properly, not even Baxter. We just chewed a few chips.

'Eat up, possums,' said the social worker brightly, sipping her own coffee.

She got out her mobile phone and went and sat at a table by herself to make her calls.

'Possums!' said Baxter. 'She's stupid.'

'Is she our mum now?' said Pixie.

'No, of course not. We've got *our* mum, silly,' I said fiercely.

'I want her back,' said Baxter.

'I know. We'll get her back, you'll see.'

'That lady's not looking. Shall we try to do a runner?' said Baxter.

'Yeah, but I don't know where we could run *to*. Shh, Baxter, I want to hear what she's saying.'

I couldn't hear much. *Three kids, a fourth in hospital – emergency foster care – perhaps we'll have to split them up.*

I stood up and went over to her. I grabbed her wrist.

'You can't split us up,' I said. 'We have to stay together. Put us anywhere, but we have to be the three of us, four when Bliss is better.'

'I'm doing my best, Lily,' she said.

'Can't we just go *home*? I can look after the kids. I've been doing it all week, it's what I always do. *Please.*'

She looked me straight in the eye.

'I can't let you, Lily. I know you can look after the others, but it's not allowed. I'm sorry. I'm doing my best to find you a suitable place. It might be just for tonight, until we know what's happening about your mum. Don't look at me like that. I'm on your side.'

She did try – but she couldn't find anywhere that would take all of us. She found a place for Pixie first, a lady who took in babies. She didn't usually take anyone over five, but the social worker persuaded her to take Baxter as well.

'Couldn't she take me too?' I begged. 'I promise I

284

won't be any trouble and I'll help look after the kids. They'll need me so. Pixie's only little, she still likes me to carry her – and Baxter can't bear to be without Bliss and he'll start acting up if he's not handled right.'

They wouldn't listen. I had to hug the kids and then leave them with this woman in a funny little house the other side of town. The baby lady picked them both up when they started crying, even though Baxter weighed a ton. She looked as if she'd be kind to them – but she was a *stranger*.

'How can you think that lady can look after the kids better than me?' I wept, back in the car with the social worker.

'I know you're wonderful looking after the children, Lily, but it's not your job. You're only eleven, you're just a child yourself. Now, let's try and get you sorted.'

No one seemed to want me. She phoned three different families and they all made excuses. I ended up in a children's home.

'It's only temporary, Lily. Just until we know what's happening with your mum,' the social worker repeated. 'Don't look at me like that. I know this is very hard but I'm trying to do my best for you.'

So this was her best shot, a lousy children's

home, very run-down and teeming with strange kids, all yelling and swearing and fighting.

'It's a bit of a madhouse here,' said Stevie, smiling at me. She was in charge, a big woman in a silly animal sweatshirt, with a very bad haircut.

There were eight or nine boys, all with bristly hair and wearing football strip. I couldn't tell them apart even if I wanted to. There was just one girl, a little kid about Bliss's age, but there was something wrong with her. She wouldn't talk to me properly and when I just patted her on the shoulder she screamed, jerking away from me.

'It takes Sharon a while to make friends, Lily,' said Stevie. 'She'll get used to you. It'll be nice for her to have you around, just like a big sister.'

I didn't want her to get used to me. I didn't want her for my sister, I had two of my own. I couldn't stand to stay in the shabby living room with the cartoon channel blaring. I went and sat in my own room. It wasn't much more than a cupboard, but at least I didn't have to share with any of the boys.

I lay down on the bed with its horrible Spider-Man duvet and tried to make a plan. I'd watched all the road names from the baby-lady house to here, trying to memorize them – but we'd gone round the one-way system and I'd got muddled.

Still, I could try to make a stab at finding my way back to Baxter and Pixie, and somehow rescue them. Then we'd have to go to the hospital for Bliss. She wouldn't be able to walk yet. Maybe we could go to the park and find Pixie's buggy? Then the four of us could go to the police station and tell them Mum never deliberately left us, and that someone else gave her the credit card – it wasn't Mum's fault, she hadn't done anything wrong.

We'd walk out of the station hand in hand, all five of us, and then we'd go back to our flat and we'd have a celebration meal. We'd lie on the sofa, Mum in the middle of us, and I'd hold them all tight and never let them go. I never wanted to be Lily Alone ever again.

I stayed there in the tiny room, hanging onto the sides of the bed as if it was a raft. Stevie put her head round the door and suggested I join the other kids, but I shook my head and she didn't make me. Then one of the boys came barging in, plonking himself down on the end of the bed.

'I'm Ian,' he said, bouncing.

'Do you mind? Don't sit on my bed.'

'Ooh, Shirty Gertie. It's not *your* bed, it's actually *my* bed. I'm having to share with Duncan because you're here.'

'Well, I'm not here long, so you'll get your poxy bed back, don't worry.'

'What you here for then? What you done?'

'I haven't done anything.'

'Oh yeah? Come on, what did you do? Me and my brother Duncan, we kept setting light to the dustbins in our flats. It was wicked! Then one time we sprinkled a little too much petrol and *kerpow* – *nee-na, nee-na, nee-na*, four fire engines, and all these cops running around. Better than fireworks night, it was.' He rubbed his hands together as if he was warming them at his stupid fire.

'Pathetic,' I said. 'Pathetic and pointless.'

'No it wasn't, mate, it was awesome. If you didn't do nothing, you must be here because of your mum or dad.'

'I haven't even *got* a dad.'

'Stepdad then. Did yours beat you up?'

'I'd beat *him* up if he laid a finger on me.'

'What about your mum then? What did she do, wash her hands of you?'

'*No, she didn't!*' I said, sitting up. 'Clear off! Get out my room!'

'OK, OK. I just came to tell you supper's nearly ready.'

'I don't want any.'

'It's pizza!'

'I don't care what it is.'

'You're mad, you. Can I have yours then?'

'Be my guest.'

Stevie made me come down to supper, and she told me I had to eat my own pizza, but she couldn't *make* me.

'Am I going to have to feed you like Sharon?' she said, prodding my mouth with a forkful, joking around.

I heaved, so she stopped that trick pretty sharpish and let me be. The kids played a stupid indoor football game up and down the stairs after supper. Ian threw the ball at me, wanting me to join in, but I sloped off by myself and sat slumped against the front door. I wasn't sure if it was locked. I sat there, waiting for my chance.

'Hey, Lily,' said Stevie, walking down the hall and hovering beside me. 'I hope you're not planning to do a runner?'

'I need to go to see Bliss. She'll be so scared, in hospital all by herself. Please let me go and see her,' I begged.

'I can't let you go off by yourself, love, and I can't take you, not when I've got all the other kids to look after. It'll be after visiting hours at the hospital anyway, so they wouldn't let you see her.'

I put my head on my knees.

'Look, tell you what. Why don't we phone up?'

I went into her office and she phoned the hospital. It took a long time to get through to the right ward – and then they wouldn't let me speak to Bliss, but a nurse said she was doing well and was tucked up fast asleep now.

'There! Happier now?' said Stevie.

'Well, I don't *know* that's right. The nurse could just have been saying that,' I said. 'And I'm still dead worried about my *other* sister, Pixie, and Baxter too, at this Mrs Robinson's.'

'Oh, I know her. She's a lovely lady, wonderful with little kiddies.'

'Yes, but Baxter's *not* little, he'll absolutely hate being treated like a baby. Can we phone them up too, Stevie? Please? Just to say goodnight and show them I haven't forgotten them?'

'Mrs Robinson will be in the middle of getting them all bathed and ready for bed right now. Maybe we'll phone later.'

'But they'll be *in* bed then and she'll say they're fast asleep,' I said. I was in tears now. 'Please, Stevie. Please, please, please.'

So she phoned Mrs Robinson for me. Mr Robinson answered and said his wife *was* bathing the little ones. After a lot of begging he shouted out for Baxter and put him on the phone.

'Hello, Baxter!'

'Who's this?'

'Lily, you silly!'

'Hey, that rhymes!'

'Oh, Baxter, are you all right?'

'Course I am. Uncle Ted and me are watching football on the telly.'

'Who? You haven't *got* an Uncle Ted. He's just a temporary foster parent. You'll be home with me as soon as I can fix it. OK? What about Pixie? How's she doing?'

'She's in the bath with them babies,' said Baxter. 'She can't come, she's all wet.'

'Well, will you tell her I called and that I love her and we'll all be together soon, I promise.'

'OK, OK. Got to go now. They've just scored a goal and I missed it.'

'Oh, Baxter. Look, I love you too.'

'Yeah, yeah.' He paused. 'Lily, do you think Bliss is all right?'

'Yes, I phoned the hospital and they said she was fine.'

'Honest?'

'Yes, honestly.'

'Good. Well, bye, Lily.'

'There!' said Stevie, who'd been listening. 'He sounded perfectly fine, sweetheart, didn't he?'

He sounded a little *too* fine. I was astonished he was already calling a complete stranger uncle, and annoyed he wasn't sticking close to Pixie.

I needed to be with them, with Bliss, with Mum. I was trying not to think about Mum because it was too terrifying. I saw her locked in a cell, screaming, with policemen shouting at her, slapping her around, making her confess. Couldn't they see she wasn't a bad mum? She loved us to bits, she always had. She was just so young and pretty she needed to go out sometimes. She hadn't meant to leave us all alone. She thought she'd fixed it with Mikey. She was simply leaving us with a dad like millions of other mums. It was *my* fault I didn't explain things to Mikey when he phoned. It was *my* fault Mum met Gordon in the first place. I *had* tried to stop Mum using the dodgy credit card – but that hadn't been all her fault. *She* hadn't stolen it. She'd been given it by that friend.

I'd tried to tell the nice young policeman with the brown eyes, but he hadn't written it all down in his notebook.

'Stevie, can I make another phone call?'

'What? Oh, come on, Lily, you're taking the mick now.'

'I need to phone the police. I have to explain

292

about Mum. Better still, I need to go down there, make a proper statement, *show* them my mum's the best mum ever, and this is all a stupid awful mistake. I just have to *tell* them!' I was shouting now, pounding Stevie with my fists.

'Hey, hey!' She grabbed my hands. 'Calm down now. You're getting in a silly state for nothing. You can't go barging into the police station, telling them what's what, not at this stage. I'm sure you'll have your chance later. Your social worker will be having a long chat at some point.'

'I need to sort it out *now*,' I sobbed.

'No, *now* you need to eat properly and catch up on sleep. Look at your little white face and those dark panda rings under your eyes! You need to stop worrying so. You're safe, and Bliss is fine in hospital, and the other two sound perfectly happy – so you can take it easy now, sweetheart. You don't have to try to look after them any more. *You* need looking after now.'

Stevie was kind, but she didn't have a clue. I didn't have any of my own stuff with me. She gave me a toothbrush and a silly flannel – it was a tiny scrunched-up square until she put it in water and it grew. Stevie expected me to be enchanted, as if I was Pixie's age. I didn't have any nightclothes so I had to go to bed in someone's Batman pyjamas.

Stupid superheroes fought around me all night while I lay awake, sending frantic thought messages to Bliss and Baxter and Pixie.

I got up very early, wondering if I could creep out now before anyone was around, but Stevie had taken my T-shirt and jeans – she'd even taken my trainers.

I went stomping downstairs in my embarrassing boy pyjamas. I found her in the kitchen with one of her sidekicks, both of them dressed in T-shirts and trackie bottoms.

'Hi, sweetie,' said Stevie. 'Sleep OK?'

'No. And someone's stolen all my stuff!'

'Your utterly filthy jeans and T-shirt stuff?' said Stevie, pointing to a whole load of clothes airing on a huge rack. 'And did they steal your trainers too?' She pointed to my trainers, toe-to-toe on a sheet of newspaper, scrubbed free of mud and whitened so they looked brand new.

'Oh,' I said. I struggled. 'Thank you.'

I didn't *want* to be grateful to her. I wanted her to be horrible and then I could blame her for everything, even though I knew this was ridiculous.

'If you're going to be here a little while we'll have to get your clothes from home, or sort you out with some new stuff,' said Stevie. 'I'm afraid we haven't got any girls' skirts for school, so you'll have to go in your jeans today. I bet all the other kids will envy you like crazy.'

'What?' I stared at her. 'I'm not going to *school*!'

It seemed a totally ludicrous idea, but Stevie stood firm.

'You go to Oakleaf Primary, don't you? It's not too far away. Most of our boys go to Wilton Road, but we can drop you off afterwards.'

'Stevie, you're mad,' I said rudely. 'My mum might have been sent straight to prison, my sister's seriously ill in hospital, my brother and baby sister are stuck with a complete stranger, and you tell me I've got to go to *school*, like it's an ordinary day.'

'I'm not mad, sweetie. I know just how you feel but I think it would be best to do something ordinary, like going to school.'

'You don't have a clue how I feel. And stop calling me sweetie, it sounds stupid. I bet you're just saying it because you've forgotten my name.'

'You're Lily – and you're quite unforgettable,' said Stevie.

I thought if I argued long enough she'd give in, or lose her temper, and then we could have a stand-up fight, but she just kept telling me calmly I was going to school and that was that. It was weird having a proper breakfast sitting down at a long table with all the unruly boys and surly little Sharon. I ate a few cornflakes and half a slice of toast and sipped at a cup of tea.

I felt a bit sick in the mini-van, being driven off to school with all the boys. When we got to Oakleaf Stevie insisted on coming right into the play-ground with me, to the headteacher's office. I can't stick Mrs Symes, our head, and she's never thought much of me either.

'Oh dear, what have you been up to now, Lily Green?' she said, when she saw me standing beside Stevie.

'She hasn't done anything, Mrs Symes. I just need to have a little chat with you. Lily, perhaps you could wait outside, love?' said Stevie.

I put my head against the door and tried to listen, of course, but Stevie kept her voice down. Mrs Symes was easier to hear because she's got one of those booming voices that reach right to the back of the school hall. I heard 'that mother' and 'problem family' and 'doesn't surprise me in the least'.

I hated her, I hated her, I hated her. The bell went off for morning school, clanging right through my head. I made a bolt down the hall, but Mrs Symes opened her door and spotted me.

'Lily Green! Where do you think you're going?'

'To my classroom, Mrs Symes, because the bell went,' I said.

'Oh. Well, walk, don't run,' said Mrs Symes.

'Bye, Lily. I'll come and meet you this afternoon,' Stevie called.

She was acting like my jailer, determined to stop me going off to see the kids.

I stomped down the corridor, children staring at my jeans and starry T-shirt.

'What are you wearing them for?' someone asked.

'Because I want to, that's why,' I said.

It seemed so strange going into my own classroom. It felt as if I'd been away for years. The class fell silent at the sight of me. Mr Abbott stood up. His Adam's apple wobbled as he swallowed.

'Hello, Lily,' he said softly.

I stared him straight in the eyes. I saw them flicker. It was enough. He was the one who'd betrayed us. I stalked straight past him to my desk and sat down. Mr Abbott watched me, but didn't make me speak to him. He told everyone to get out their books for a maths lesson. I got out my book too but I didn't attempt any of the sums. I drew in the margin – four small stick people and one bigger one.

Then it was Literacy and we had to do work on

The Secret Garden. This was a book I loved, although most of our class hated it because it was written in a hard way, especially the Yorkshire bits. Mr Abbott kept asking questions, glancing at me now and then, because he knew I'd have an answer – but I didn't put my hand up once.

The bell rang for playtime and everyone started shoving their books away.

'All right, off you go. Have a good run around and wake yourselves up.' He paused. 'Lily, could I have a word?'

The other kids nudged each other, eyes gleaming, because it looked as if I was for it. I strolled to the front of the class, humming, acting like I couldn't care less.

'Just a minute, Lily,' said Mr Abbott, waiting until the last child was out of the room. Then he turned to me. 'How *are* you?'

I stared at him.

'How do you *think* I am?' I hissed. I didn't care that he was my teacher and I might get into trouble for talking like that. He was my favourite teacher in all the world and that made it worse.

'What happened, Lily? Tell me.'

'We've been taken into care, me and my brother and sisters, and my mum might go to prison, and it's all your fault,' I said.

Mr Abbott's head jerked as if I'd slapped him.

'You came round again, didn't you?'

'Yes I did. I was very worried about you. And then I saw your letter—'

'Which said we were all going on holiday.'

'Yes, but did you really expect me to believe that? Come on, Lily. I was pretty sure you children were on your own. I had to tell someone. Anything could have happened to you. Where did you go? How did you manage? I've been worried sick about you.'

'If you hadn't come round poking your nose in we'd have been *fine*, absolutely fine. We had to run away after you'd come round. We went to the park and my sister Bliss got hurt, and she's in hospital now, and I can't bear her being there all alone without us. Mum came back, I knew she would, but now the police have got her and I'm stuck in this children's home and it's awful, awful, awful—' I was sobbing, unable to stop.

'Oh, Lily. Don't cry. I feel so dreadful. I want to give you a great big hug but teachers aren't allowed to do that.'

'I want to give you a great big *punch* but children aren't allowed to do that,' I cried.

'I want to punch me too for upsetting you. I wish I *hadn't* interferred – but I felt it was my duty. That sounds so pompous, I'm so sorry. How is Bliss? Is she badly hurt?'

'She fell out of a tree and hurt her head and I think her leg's all broken. I'm so worried about her.'

'Well, tell you what, I'll talk to whoever runs this children's home and see if I can get permission to take you to the hospital to visit her.'

'And my other sister and brother? They've been fostered. Will you take me to see them too?'

'Yes, of course I will, if they'll let me. Lily, I'm so, so sorry.' He looked as if he really meant it. His eyes were watery, almost as if he was going to cry. He was acting like he really cared for me.

'I know you didn't mean it to work out like this, Mr Abbott,' I said. 'And I was ever so pleased you bought me the angel postcards. I've still got them safe.'

'Maybe I can take you to see the real paintings one day.'

'I pretended we did that,' I said shyly. 'I really, really wanted to see those paintings.'

'You're such a special girl, Lily.'

I stiffened. 'You mean like special needs?'

'No! I mean you're a girl with special, remarkable qualities.'

'No, I'm not. I'm not clever. I'm rubbish at maths and that. And I'm from a problem family.'

'Who said that?'

'Mrs Symes.'

'What? To you?'

'No, to this careworker, Stevie, but I heard it.'

'Oh dear. Well, I think Mrs Symes is mistaken, though don't quote me on that. You seem a lovely family, you and your sisters and brother. You were all getting along splendidly when I came round to your house. You're so good with the children, Lily. You're going to be a lovely mother one day.'

'My mum's a lovely mother, Mr Abbott.'

He nodded but he didn't look convinced.

'I was lying that night, saying she'd gone to the shops.'

'Yes, but I understand why you were telling fibs.'

'She did go off, but I swear she didn't mean us to be stuck on our own. Mr Abbott, what will happen to my mum?'

Mr Abbott hesitated. 'I'm not sure, Lily.'

'Will she go to prison?'

'I don't really know. I wouldn't *think* so.'

'So will we be able to go back to our flat, all of us together?'

'I hope so. I'm going to try hard to make that happen.'

'Mr Abbott, I really miss my mum.'

'I know you do. I'm sure you'll be able to see

301

her soon, Lily,' he said, and he gently patted my shoulder.

He was right. I was having spaghetti for tea with all the boys and Sharon when there was a ring on the doorbell. Stevie went to see who it was and came back smiling.

'Someone for you, Lily,' she said.

I went flying to the door and there was Mum, looking wonderful in her new silky dress, her hair loose and lovely on her shoulders, honey brown all over.

'Hello, gorgeous,' she said, holding out her arms.

I flung myself at her.

'Hey, gently! I'm wearing my daft heels – you'll have me over, you silly sausage. Pleased to see your old mum, eh?'

'Oh, Mum, have you come to take me home?'

'Well, not just yet. I've packed you up a little carrier of your clothes here – your school uniform and your jacket and that. What were you *doing* in it – it looked like you were all mud wrestling!'

Duncan and Ian came out into the hall and stared at us.

'Is that your mum?' Duncan said.

'Yes. See! I *told* you she'd come,' I said.

'She's pretty,' said Ian.

'Yeah, that's me, very pretty. And I must say,

you're a handsome little chap,' said Mum, tossing her hair and smiling at him – even though Ian was seven, and had knock knees and a runny nose.

'Do you think I'm handsome too?' Duncan said.

'Yes, you're positively gorgeous. Lily, any chance you and me could go off for a little stroll and have a proper chat?'

'No chance, I'm afraid,' said Stevie, coming into the hall too. 'But you could go up to Lily's room if you like. I'll make sure the other kids leave you in peace. And then you and I must have a little chat too, Ms Green. I'm sure you know you're supposed to have a proper supervised visit at an arranged time. Still, I know how much this means to both of you so I'll turn a blind eye this time.'

'Oh, thank you ever so much,' said Mum, with exaggerated politeness. She raised her eyebrows at me as we went upstairs. 'My God, I have to get permission and jump through all sorts of hoops just to see my own daughter! What an old bossy-boots. And what does she *look* like?'

'Stevie's OK, Mum.'

'Stevie!' Mum snorted. She sniffed at my room too. 'It's like a little rabbit hutch – and where did they get that awful duvet from, a pound shop? Honestly, they think this rubbish place is better than your own room at home?'

I didn't have my own room at home, I didn't even have a proper bed – I shared a mattress with the twins – but I wasn't going to point this out. I sat down on Spider-Man and Mum sat down beside me, her arm round me.

'Don't you worry, pet. I'll get you out of here. You trust your old mum. We'll be back home quick as a wink.'

'With Bliss and Baxter and Pixie?'

'Of course, all of us.'

'Oh, Mum, I'm so worried about Bliss. She'll be so scared all by herself in hospital.'

'She's fine, lovey, truly, sitting up and playing, though obviously she can't move about much because of her leg. This lady was helping her make a new head for Headless, stuffing an old sock. It looked a bit of a fright, but Bliss seemed happy enough. And look, she made you this.' Mum fumbled in her bag and brought out a Get Well card carefully coloured in, with a big *LILY* printed at the top in purple crayon, and a wobbly row of kisses.

'But I'm not the one who needs to get well, it's Bliss.'

'Yes, she got the wrong end of the stick, bless her, but I didn't like to point it out. She said to tell you she's sorry she fell out the tree.'

'Oh, poor Bliss. I so want to see her. Mr Abbott said he might take me to see her.'

'That interfering old git? *I'll* take you. We'll fix it up with Bossy-Boots with the bad haircut. Maybe I'll get Simon to run us up to the hospital – you have to wait ages for the bus.'

'Simon?'

'That policeman with the fair hair, you know, he came to the hospital yesterday.'

'You have to have a police escort?'

'No, you noodle. He'll take me as a friend. He was so sweet to me yesterday. I cried all over him and he was lovely about it.'

'So they've let you go?'

'Well, they've charged me, on two counts. Simon reckons I won't be able to talk myself out of the credit card fraud, especially as I've got previous, but it was only a few hundred, after all. If I'm lucky the magistrates will just give me community service, probably eighty hours, so that's a bit of a laugh – though God help me if I have to wear them orange overalls. It's going to be a bit of a long-haul struggle with the child neglect charge. All these know-it-alls will be making reports and filling up their registers and acting like bleeding school teachers – when it was a simple *mistake*, Mikey was coming, it was all fixed, sort of.'

'I'll tell them it was all my fault, Mum,' I said.

'No, it wasn't your fault, darling. You've been wonderful by all accounts, a proper little mother to the kids.'

'No I wasn't. I couldn't look after them properly. Bliss fell out the tree – that was my fault, I wasn't watching them.'

'For heaven's sake, you can't keep your eye on kids all the time. And she's doing fine. She'll have a little scar on her forehead but she can always grow a fringe – and her leg's setting nicely. She'll be out of hospital in no time. They won't let her home with me just yet, but there's talk of her going to that foster home with Baxter and my little Pixie, so they can all be together.'

'They wouldn't let me stay there.'

'Yes, but you're a grown-up girl, babe. You have to be brave and hang out here on your ownio, just for a little while, and then we'll all be back together.'

'You really promise?'

'Well, Simon says – that sounds funny, doesn't it, like that party game! Anyway, Simon says it's a ninety-nine-per-cent certainty, and you can't get better than that, can you?'

'I'd sooner it was a hundred per cent. This Simon – you're not getting off with him, are you?'

'Don't be so daft! Imagine having a copper for a boyfriend! Still, he is quite sweet – and I think he said something about his marriage breaking up. He earns a good wage – and he'd be a very good influence on Baxter. Your face, Lily! I'm just kidding. He was just helping me out because he felt sorry for me. Now, I've got to struggle round with another bag of clothes for Baxter and Pixie so I'd better get a move on or it'll be their bedtime, and I need to see my little man and my baby. Oh, Lily, I miss you kids so much. I'm never ever going to leave you again, not even for a night. Now, give us a kiss goodbye, there's a good girl. I'll come back as soon as I can, I promise.'

I stayed in my room after Mum went. I tried to stop myself crying by playing my Lily Alone game – but it was pointless. I didn't want to live all alone in my big white dream house any more. I tore all the used pages out of my drawing book. Then I started on a new drawing of our living room at home. I drew Mum on the sofa, with me next to her, Pixie on my lap. Baxter was curled up next to Mum and Bliss was cuddled up to me, her poorly leg propped up.

We're all going to be together very, very soon, I wrote underneath.

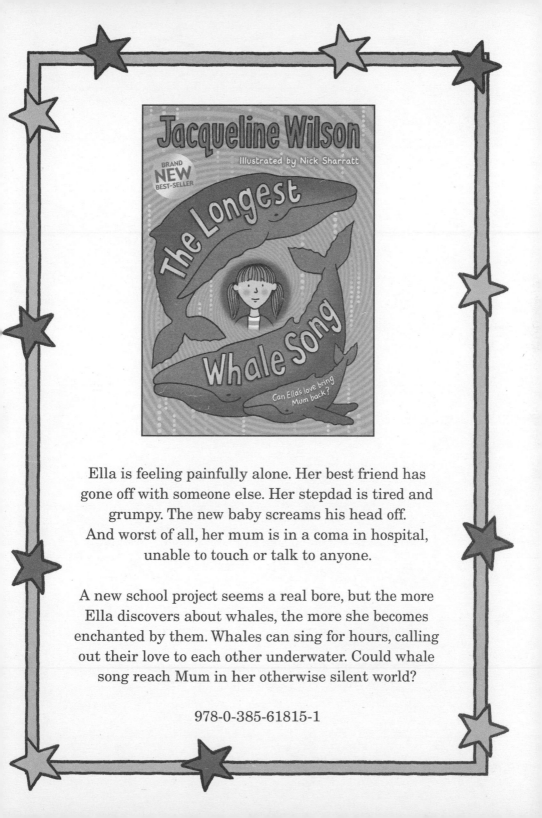

Ella is feeling painfully alone. Her best friend has
gone off with someone else. Her stepdad is tired and
grumpy. The new baby screams his head off.
And worst of all, her mum is in a coma in hospital,
unable to touch or talk to anyone.

A new school project seems a real bore, but the more
Ella discovers about whales, the more she becomes
enchanted by them. Whales can sing for hours, calling
out their love to each other underwater. Could whale
song reach Mum in her otherwise silent world?

978-0-385-61815-1

Sunset lives a glamorous celebrity lifestyle with her
rock-star dad and model mum – but yearns for
some peace and a real friend.

Destiny is the same age as Sunset but her life couldn't
be more different. She and her mum live on the edge of
a rundown estate, worrying about money and illness.

When the two girls paths cross, a surprising truth is
revealed and a very special connection is formed . . .

An amazing story from a prize-winning author,
one of Britain's most popular writers.

978-0-440-86834-7

London, 1876

Hetty Feather is just a tiny baby when her desperate mother leaves
her at the Foundling Hospital. The hospital cares for many such
children – but Hetty must first live with a foster family until she is
big enough to go to school. Hetty is poor but happy living in the
countryside with her 'brothers' Jem and Gideon. She helps in the
fields and plays vivid imaginary games. The children sneak off to
visit the travelling circus and Hetty is mesmerized by the show,
especially Madame Adeline and her performing horses.

But Hetty's happiness is threatened once more when she is
returned to the Foundling Hospital. The new ultra-strict regime is
a struggle for her. But on the day of Queen Victoria's Jubilee,
Hetty gets the chance to see Madame Adeline again – and
maybe find her real mother . . .

978-0-440-86835-4

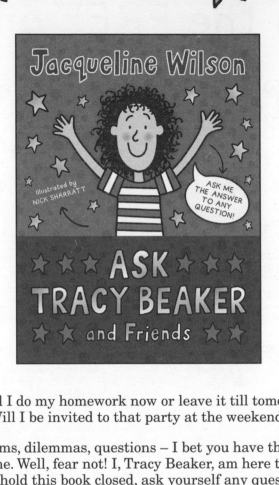

Should I do my homework now or leave it till tomorrow?
Will I be invited to that party at the weekend?

Problems, dilemmas, questions – I bet you have them all
the time. Well, fear not! I, Tracy Beaker, am here to help.
Just hold this book closed, ask yourself any question,
open at random and read the helpful answer on the
right-hand page from me or one of your other
favourite characters!

 xxxxxxxx

A wonderful new dip-in book of answers,
combined with a journal!

987-0-385-61880-9

Join the FREE online

Jacqueline Wilson
FAN CLUB

You can learn all about Jacqueline from her monthly diary, her fan-mail replies and her tour blogs.

There's also loads to discuss on the message boards, you can customise your page, have your own online diary, put your picture into your favourite Jacqueline book cover and don't forget the competitions with incredible prizes!

Sign up today at
www.jacquelinewilson.co.uk

There are oodles of incredible Jacqueline Wilson books to enjoy! Tick off the ones you have read, so you know which ones to look for next!

- ☐ THE DINOSAUR'S PACKED LUNCH
- ☐ THE MONSTER STORY-TELLER

- ☐ THE CAT MUMMY
- ☐ LIZZIE ZIPMOUTH
- ☐ SLEEPOVERS

- ☐ BAD GIRLS
- ☐ THE BED AND BREAKFAST STAR
- ☐ BEST FRIENDS
- ☐ BURIED ALIVE!
- ☐ CANDYFLOSS
- ☐ CLEAN BREAK
- ☐ CLIFFHANGER
- ☐ COOKIE
- ☐ THE DARE GAME
- ☐ THE DIAMOND GIRLS
- ☐ DOUBLE ACT
- ☐ GLUBBSLYME
- ☐ HETTY FEATHER
- ☐ THE ILLUSTRATED MUM
- ☐ JACKY DAYDREAM

- ☐ LITTLE DARLINGS
- ☐ LOLA ROSE
- ☐ THE LONGEST WHALE SONG
- ☐ THE LOTTIE PROJECT
- ☐ MIDNIGHT
- ☐ THE MUM-MINDER
- ☐ SECRETS
- ☐ STARRING TRACY BEAKER
- ☐ THE STORY OF TRACY BEAKER
- ☐ THE SUITCASE KID
- ☐ VICKY ANGEL
- ☐ THE WORRY WEBSITE

FOR OLDER READERS:

- ☐ DUSTBIN BABY
- ☐ GIRLS IN LOVE
- ☐ GIRLS IN TEARS
- ☐ GIRLS OUT LATE
- ☐ GIRLS UNDER PRESSURE
- ☐ KISS
- ☐ LOVE LESSONS
- ☐ MY SECRET DIARY
- ☐ MY SISTER JODIE